A
Nice
Steady
Job

. . . .

A
Nice
Steady
Job

. . . .

GREGORY
DOWLING

ST. MARTIN'S PRESS
NEW YORK

Design by Basha Zapatka

Library of Congress Cataloging-in-Publication Data

Dowling, Gregory.
    A Nice Steady Job / Gregory Dowling.
        p.   cm.
    "A Thomas Dunne Book."
    ISBN 0-312-11035-9
    1. Esposito, January (Fictitious character)—Fiction. 2. Private investigators—Italy—Fiction. 3. English teachers—Italy—Fiction. I. Title.
    PR6054.O862N53   1994
    823'.914—dc20   94-7149
                                                                CIP

First Edition: August 1994

10 9 8 7 6 5 4 3 2 1

ACKNOWLEDGEMENTS

· · · · · · · · · · · · · · · · · ·

All my thanks to Rosalind Ramage, Holly Snapp, and Tim Parks, who advised me on what to cut and what to keep. If I have succeeded in giving this story a reasonable shape, much of the credit is theirs. If I have not, the fault is, of course, mine alone.

A
Nice
Steady
Job

. . . .

O N E

. . .

"I HAVEN'T BEEN WORKING LONG," I said to the class. "Repeat."

"I avanta been workeen longa," they said, more or less together. And then the businessman who always sat in the front row and greeted every new grammatical rule as if it had been sent by the *Guardia di Finanza* frowned and said, "Why you use the present perfect continuous—'not been workeen'?"

"Why not?" I said. It sometimes worked.

"It's a negative, no? You no use the present perfect continuous in the negative."

"Not usually," I said slowly, sneaking a look at my watch and hoping I'd be able to say there wasn't time to go into it today. But it was only four and the lesson finished at half past. I went on, "I mean you could say, 'I haven't worked for a long time,' but that would be different."

"Why different?"

"Um, well, it would mean you haven't got a job."

"So when you say, 'I avanta been workeen longa,' it is affirmative? You 'ave the job?"

"Er, well, no. It's negative, but not—not quite so negative."

Now the whole class was frowning. The schoolgirl who usually spent the lesson reading *Grazia* said, "You 'ave the part-time job per'aps?"

The businessman shook his head. "Simon, 'e say us you

never say, 'It asna been raineen dis week,' and *you*,"—and he pointed an accusing finger at me—"you say dis."

"No, I didn't. I haven't mentioned the weather." A pity I couldn't make people stand in the corner.

There was a knock at the door and I looked round hopefully. Simon himself—the director of the school—came in.

"Phone for you," he said.

"Oh, right, thanks." It had to be my guardian angel on the line. "Have a look at the exercise on page forty-seven," I told the class, and followed him out.

"I told whoever it was that you were teaching," Simon said. So he hadn't been listening in.

"But he insisted that it was extremely urgent." His tone made it clear that it had better be death or at least serious disease to justify the interruption.

We went into his little office and he pointed a peevish finger at the desk. I had to grope amidst the volumes of literary theory for the receiver. Simon was working on a thesis on the nineteenth-century Italian novel; I'd never seen him reading a novel—just structuralist criticism. It was no wonder he was permanently peevish.

"*Pronto*," I said.

"Mr. Esposito?" A whispering voice, speaking in English.

"Yes."

"I want to see you. Five-thirty at the bar Rossi in Piazza Erbe."

"You what?"

"Five-thirty at the bar Rossi in Piazza Erbe." It wasn't a question, and hardly an order. You can't be all that peremptory in a whisper. Just suggestive—sibilantly, sinisterly suggestive.

"Sorry, who is this?" I said in the let's-have-no-more-nonsense voice I used when teaching bambini.

"Never mind. Five-thirty."

It never worked with the bambini either. "Look, I don't know that—"

"It's in your interests."

"But—"

"Your interests. Good-bye." The phone was put down.

"Well?" Simon's expression said clearly that it hardly seemed worth breaking the continuity of a didactic unit for *that*.

"Sorry," I said. "Some nut."

"Who?"

"I don't know. He wouldn't say."

"Well, really."

"Look," I said, "I'm as irritated as you."

"Well, it had better not become a regular occurrence." He nodded dismissively at me. He had his semiotics to get back to.

"I'll make a real effort not to get phoned anymore."

"Just don't encourage it. Remember you are only on your trial period here."

"I'll remember." I wasn't likely to be allowed to do otherwise. I was reminded of the fact at the end of every lesson, as he hovered around my students to catch the first complaining word. The other thing I was continually reminded of was that "there are hundreds of other people who'd jump at your job." I kept promising myself that one day I was going to stun him by saying, "Well, let them have it," and then storm magnificently out.

On my way back to the classroom I puzzled over the phone call. Who would want to whisper at me? All I'd been able to tell was that it was a male and almost certainly an English whisperer—but an Englishman who knew enough to stress the second syllable in my surname, rather than the third (EsPOSito rather than EsposITo). So, an Englishman *au fait* with Neapolitan surnames who'd got a sore throat—or who was phoning from a library—or who didn't want his wife to overhear—or who just wanted to get up my nose.

Well, if it was the last, he'd succeeded. So, I could show him where he got off by not going to the bar.

Except I wanted to know who this whispering wally was.

Oh hell . . . I opened the classroom door. Sixteen faces swivelled and the businessman said, "And if you say, 'I avanta been workeen for two years,' 'ave you the job?"

"Not necessarily," I said, trying not to wince.

Five-twenty-seven and I walked towards Piazza Erbe. I'd fin-ished the lesson at five o'clock, the students having had to make do with the explanation, "Because that's what we say," and I'd gone and had a drink and then started walking—casu-ally, no hurrying—in the direction of the square, telling myself that I quite probably would have come this way in any case.

I enjoyed the walk. Verona was still new to me. I'd turned up in the town just two weeks previously, having been advised by someone that there were quite a few language schools there. At that time I'd been earning my living by making cardboard ducks on strings and selling them on the beach at Rimini. As a job it had its plusses: I got a nice tan, picked up some German, and saw some interesting sights in and out of swimming cos-tumes, but the level of profits could be gauged by the fact that a language-school teacher's salary had sounded to me like a Jackie Collins dream. Anyway, I had found a job at the second school I walked into in Verona, which had seemed like a real stroke of luck at the time. I hadn't yet got to know Semiotic Simon properly, nor yet plumbed the depths of my own igno-rance of English grammatical rules. A week or two later I knew better—knew my unsuitedness to the job, that is, not the gram-matical rules. And knew how catching peevishness could be.

So now I made the most of the sheer pleasure of being out-side the school but inside Verona walls—muggy, druggy but ever-lovely Verona. I was now walking down Via Mazzini, Verona's main shopping street, and the parade ground for its preening citizens. Colour seemed to be the thing this Septem-ber—bright, shiny oranges and reds and yellows, which set off everyone's summer tans nicely; dark, shining arms and legs flashed from bright, shining skirts and shirts and trousers. It was no wonder so many people were wearing sunglasses, even at this hour. I was out of place and out of fashion as ever, being dressed in faded jeans and T-shirt, but at least I had a tan to rival anybody's, and my blond hair caught an eye or two. If I walked with enough nonchalance, I might even be able to per-suade observers that the jeans were designer-faded.

I reached Piazza Erbe. It's the old heart of the city, once the

Roman forum, and there's still a Roman statue in the middle, which has been rather unconvincingly turned into a Madonna by the addition of a crown, worn at a rakish angle. Around her there's the bustle of the market; a few vegetables and flowers are still on sale, but mostly the bustle is of German and English tourists choosing kitsch postcards of Romeo and Juliet and "I ♥ Verona" T-shirts.

I crossed the square to the bar the whisperer had mentioned, but before approaching it I hovered by a souvenir stall and observed the people sitting at the tables outside the bar. Well, there was no one I recognised, and there was no one obviously furtive and no one with a scarf around a sore throat. Just a few German tourists, three Italian youths, the brightness of whose clothes was matched by that of their drinks, and a waiter making a not very good attempt to disguise the fact that he was studying the legs of one of the German girls. The Italian youths managed this much better, since they were all wearing dark glasses.

I made my way through the tables and entered the bar itself. Inside there was just one old man sitting at a table, who didn't look as if he'd have had the energy to get up from his table to lift the phone, let alone whisper into it. I ordered a glass of white wine and sipped it, standing at the bar. After a few seconds, the barman said, *"Scusi, signore."*

"Yes?"

"Are you here to meet someone?"

"Yes, why are you—"

"Well, sir, a gentleman said if an Englishman with very blond hair came along, to give him this note and tell him to wait. He'd be back. In fact, he left his bag at that table there." He gave me an envelope and pointed to a table outside, on which lay a leather briefcase.

"Thanks," I said. I opened the envelope. It contained a single sheet of notepaper, and this contained the single word, "Wait."

I was beginning to get the hang of this bloke's style. Minimalism, I think Simon would call it.

"Who was it?" I asked the barman.

5 . . . .

"An Englishman. Spoke good Italian."

"Do you know him?"

"No, sir. If you'll excuse me. . . ." He moved away to pour out more rosso for the old man, who'd ordered it by lifting his head. I stayed staring at the table outside. The first logical thing was to go and sit at it. And the next logical thing would be to open that bag and root through it.

And doubtless it would at once release a powerful poison gas—or just blow up in my face. And my minimalist friend would whisper "Gotcha" from the other side of the square.

This was silly. Why should anyone be out to get me? I had no enemies that I could think of. My English lessons weren't that bad. And those ducks had been made of the strongest cardboard. I walked out and sat nonchalantly at the table, forcing my eyes away from the case. They came to land on the German girl's legs—and I could see why the waiter had left his there as well. Her eyes flickered at mine. I jerked them away—and they came back to the bag.

Well, there could be no harm in studying its outside. A simple leather briefcase, fairly new, with a brass clasp. No name, no initials, nothing.

No lock.

I forced my eyes away again. This time I let them rove over the square. For some reason, I couldn't get rid of the idea that I was being set up. Maybe no poison gas or bomb—just a posse of policemen poised to pounce perhaps.

This was paranoia.

Another paranoid thought struck me. Maybe the point wasn't to get me to open the bag, but just to sit at this particular table. And my eyes suddenly shot up to the windows in the houses around the square. A tiny movement caught my attention at one of them—the slightest of movements, a mere flutter of a net curtain. A minimalist movement.

It was a third-floor window, diagonally opposite my table; I didn't let my eyes rest on it, but continued to roll them round the square, as if admiring the faded frescoes on the house fronts. Then I looked around the tables again, the three Italian youths, their bright long drinks, the German girl, her bright long legs . . . My eyes flickered up to that window again for a quarter of a second. It was undisturbed, empty. The window was in a fairly deep recess of a building; clearly there would be no wide view of the square from it. In fact, I thought as I looked round again, I probably wouldn't be able to see the window from any of the other tables. Nor the window see me at any of the other tables.

And now I was thinking of *The Day of the Jackal* and fighting an urge to hurl myself to the ground. I remembered that melon exploding. I'd always liked melons.

I got up and strolled back into the bar. My chair didn't shatter as I left it, but its back was visibly damp where I'd leaned against it.

I paid for my drink and told the barman that I'd be back if my envelope-leaver returned. He shrugged and said the bar wasn't the post office. There was no answer to that, so I left and crossed the square. The window couldn't be seen from any other point in the square, I realised. This of course proved me right in my paranoia.

A year ago I suppose such thoughts would never have struck me. But in April I'd had a hectic few days in and around Naples, and these had limbered me up both physically and mentally, making me ready to leap to the most melodramatic conclusion at the drop of a hat, the slam of a door—or the twitch of a net curtain. I don't mean by this that I was an electrified bundle of nerves like Simon, who did aerobionic leaps if you tapped him on the shoulder; it was just that I was more expectant of the unexpected than most people are.

So as I crossed the square, I was fairly sure of my little intuition about the window. Not, of course, sure enough to want to call the SAS in. But sure enough to want to have a further look myself.

The window seemed to belong to a hotel. It wasn't the kind of hotel you could slip into unnoticed amidst the glitter of jewels and flash of credit cards. The entrance hall contained a desk, an umbrella stand, and a receptionist reading a pink sports paper. I went up to him and said, *"Buonasera."*

"Completo," he said, hardly looking up from his paper.

"No, it's about one of the guests. He left a bag in the bar on the other side of the square."

He looked at me. I was carrying no bag. "Where is it?"

"The barman just asked me to pass the message on because I speak English. He's keeping the bag. He says it's an Englishman. He got talking to him and the Englishman pointed out his room. You know, where the building goes in. There's a little kind of balcony."

I wondered if I was explaining too much, but he didn't seem to notice or care. "Room thirty-two," he said.

"So do you want to call him or shall I go up?"

He sighed and reached out for the phone. I said, "What's the name of the guy?"

He opened the register and said, "Ainsley." It meant nothing to me. He pressed 32 on the phone's dial and then handed me the receiver. A few seconds later, an English voice said, "Hello?"

"Hello," I said. "Mr. Ainsley?"

"Yes. Who is this?" A rather nervous voice. Middle-aged, if not older, and middle class if not upper.

"The barman says he's going to call the bomb disposal squad if you don't collect your case."

"If I don't what?"

"You heard. What's the game?"

"I— I . . ." There was a moment's fumbling and crackling down the line and suddenly a new voice spoke. "Come on up, Jan. Have a drink."

"Oh, my God," I said.

"Nah, just Luigi." My half-brother has a simple sense of humour.

"You stupid bastard, Gigi, what the—"

"Save it for the drink. Room thirty-two." The phone was put down.

I turned to the receptionist. "They've invited me up for a drink," I said, and tried to make it sound like the obvious outcome to the conversation.

He didn't give a damn. "Third floor," he said. "Lift's over there."

As the pre-war lift wheezed its way up I didn't bother racking my brains trying to work out what Gigi (a diminutive which he hated) might be up to; I knew I'd never get within a hundred miles of it. I just trusted that my suspicions about exploding briefcases or marksmen's rifles had been wrong at least. Last time we'd met he had, after all, saved my life.

But only because he'd first put it at risk.

I tapped at the door of Number 32 and Gigi opened it. Well, his sartorial style hadn't changed: orange shirt with top buttons undone (top five or six) revealing gold chains and medallions, bright blue trousers, green-and-white shoes.

"Good to see you, Jan," he said, and ushered me in.

"And you. Well, easy to see you." It was a drably decorated room with a single bed by one wall and faded furniture. The only thing that gave the place any character at all was an ancient-looking beam that bisected the ceiling. Gigi stood out rather in these surroundings, like a Marvel comic in a law library. The other person in the room, however, could have been part of the furnishings. He was small, with grey hair, a grey suit, and a grey expression. He was more than middle-aged, in fact, getting on for seventy perhaps. He was holding a glass with both hands as if afraid I'd snatch it. As I looked at him he smiled, a formal drab smile to go with his suit.

I didn't acknowledge it. I said to Gigi, "When are you going to start calling on me in a normal manner? You know, 'Hello, Jan, it's your brother here. . . .' "

"I'll explain it all," he said, waving a hand dismissively. "Meet Sir Alfred." He obviously enjoyed saying this.

Sir Alfred freed one hand from the drink and gave it to me quickly. It was cold and wet from the glass, to which it returned at once. He murmured something along the lines of, "Delighted, delighted, most, most . . ." and then looked back at Gigi.

Gigi said, "What'll you have?" and waved his hand again, this time in a gesture of largesse. He was showing me the drinks table: a bottle of Dry Martini, a bottle of Martini Rosso, and a tray of ice.

"Dry," I said. "So come on, what's all this about?"

"You're looking well, Jan. Doing all right then, are you?" He poured the drink out and dropped some ice in.

"Getting by," I said. "And you? Your arm okay?" When I'd left him in April, he was on his way to a doctor with a bullet wound.

"My arm? Oh that. Just a scratch. Been telling Sir Alfred about that business—discreetly mind, don't worry. We had a pretty good time togevver then, didn't we, Jan?"

"Was that what it was?"

"Come on, Jan. You enjoyed it. And we came out of it pretty well, like you did now."

"What do you mean?"

"Sir Alfred was impressed, weren't you?"

"Yes, er, most, most impressive, I must say." He nodded several times and looked back into his drink.

"Impressed by what?" I said to Sir Alfred, thinking a direct question to him might produce quicker results.

He was a bit disconcerted by this, as if it might be the lead-in to a grab at his drink. He gripped it harder and answered in short staccato bursts. "Your, em, initiative. Quick thinking. Impressive, most."

I looked back to Gigi. "What the hell's going on here? Tell me before I throttle you with that medallion."

"We just wanted to test your nous, your savvy like. You know, see if you're still on the ball."

"And I did okay, did I? Right, well, glad you liked it." I decided it wouldn't be convincing to pretend to flounce out, so I just stood and waited for further enlightenment.

"Now don't get sulky. We'll tell you what it's all about. First though, how'd you work out where we were?"

"The curtain moving."

"The curtain," Gigi said, and looked at Sir Alfred. "Pretty good, eh?"

"Yes, yes, most . . ."

"And you didn't even look in the bag? See we'd left anuvver message on a bit of paper stuck in the lining, which if you'd checked it out you'd have seen had the phone number of this hotel—though rubbed out. You'd have had to look real careful like." ·

"Sorry to have spoilt that part of the game." I picked up my drink again. No point in wasting it.

"No game, Jan. This is serious stuff. Sir Alfred wanted to be sure you're the right type to let in on this business, and I said I'd prove it to him. Show him you've got your eyes open. And you did me proud, like I knew you would."

"What business?" I said as patiently as possible.

"Sit down and I'll tell you all about it."

We all sat down, Gigi in the only armchair, Sir Alfred on a chair by the bed, which he first inspected carefully for scorpions or dust, and me on a chair by the door so I could at least pretend to myself that I was ready to walk out on them.

Gigi said, "You see, I'm doing a bit of private detective work."

"You?"

He looked hurt. "Yeah, me. And I'm getting a bit of a name round London too. This is one of me bigger fings—international complications and all that—so I suggested to Sir Alfred that I might call me bruvver in to help out. Seeing as you speak Italian and all that."

"You're really brothers?" Sir Alfred said.

"Half-brothers," I said. His doubt was understandable, since Gigi looks entirely Neapolitan in complexion and lineaments, and I'm blond and blue-eyed after my father's second wife, who was English. Nonetheless I speak better Neapolitan than he does, since my mother died when I was very small and I was brought up by my grandmother, who came from Naples to help my father out and who didn't speak a single word of English. Gigi is more of a Londoner as well, since we moved out of town when I was only eight and he was already fourteen: old enough to resent the exhaust-free air and exaggerated greenery.

"I see," he said. "And your name is January, Luigi tells me."

"Yes. English for Gennaro. At least my father thought it

was." San Gennaro is the patron saint of Naples—which is no sinecure. "But what's it all about?"

"Sir Alfred's son," said Gigi. "He's gone missing and Sir Alfred wants us to find him."

"Gone missing in Verona?"

"Near here. In the hills. So I fought wiv you working here already, it'd be a great opportunity for us to team up again."

"To team up. How jolly." Gigi's memories of the events of April seemed to be rather different from mine.

"Yeah. You see Sir Alfred's son went out to this village in the hills. And then just didn't come back."

"Hang on, hang on," I said. "I'd like to hear this from Sir Alfred. First of all, why did you go to Gigi—Luigi?"

"Ah, er, well, his name was mentioned to me as someone who carried out inquiries—em, discreet inquiries, in particular with reference to Italy."

"And why have these inquiries got to be discreet?"

"Ah, well, that is the—the crux of the matter." He was now turning his glass round and round in his hands, as if looking for a crack. "You see, I'm rather afraid that Piers—my son—might be mixed up in something, em, rather distasteful." He said this with a kind of fastidious reluctance, as if hoping I would have the good manners to change the subject.

I said, "Like what?"

"Well, Piers has always been a little, em, high-spirited. Wild, you might even say. I rather fear that he might have fallen in with some bad company."

"What sort?" I insisted. "Terrorists? Drug dealers? Bank robbers? Football hooligans? Tax evaders?"

"Sir Alfred's already given me the details, Jan. I can fill you in."

"But you haven't given me one good reason why I should want to know all this. I'm a teacher, not a vigilante."

"Come off it, Jan. You're a teacher now, but remember I've seen you in action."

"You're making me sound like James Bond," I said, with feigned contempt for these words, which in fact surprised and even chuffed me. It was worrying that I should need such cheapo chuffing.

"If you would rather not," Sir Alfred said, "then please don't feel under any constraint."

"Thanks, I don't. I'd just like to know a bit more about it all before I commit myself."

"There's a hundred quid a day plus expenses and an extra four thousand when you find him," Gigi said.

I was ready to sign on the first dotted line that came by. I said in a musing voice, "Ye-es, that seems very reasonable."

"Tax free," Gigi said.

I was already planning the words of my resignation to Simon. "So tell me when and how he disappeared," I said.

"Good on you," Gigi said. He looked to Sir Alfred. "You're happy with him, aren't you? I mean, I've done right bringing him in on the job?"

"Yes, yes, I'm perfectly convinced of his competence," Sir Alfred said. Despite his jeans, he didn't quite add. "Most impressive, as I said. You did understand my, em, my initial wariness. As I say, I came to you because of the importance of discretion."

"Yeah, well, Jan's as close-moufed as they come, aren't you?"

"For a hundred pounds a day, my lips'll be welded."

"Right then," Gigi said, turning to Sir Alfred. "Shall I fill him in or do you want to?"

"He need only hear the bare outline from me surely. He can hear the details from Rita."

"Who's Rita?" I said.

"Pier's girlfriend," said Gigi. "From Liverpool."

"She can give you a full account," said Sir Alfred. There was a note of distaste again in his voice. For her account or just her accent?

"Yes, okay," I said. "But let's have this bare outline."

"Yeah, well," said Gigi, "it looks like Piers might be involved in this little murder, you see."

"Oh." I started thinking of the advantages of teaching. "A little one, eh?"

Sir Alfred interrupted. "We merely know that someone Piers had been talking to was killed, and that afterwards Piers disappeared. These are the facts."

"Who and how?"

"Shot through the neck," Sir Alfred said, again with distaste.

"You see," Gigi came in, "Piers and Rita were staying in Sir Alfred's villa down in Tuscany and then they decided to come up norf for a bit of sightseeing and they came up to Verona and went visiting this little village here, San Giorgio Veronese."

"San Giorgio Veronese," I repeated, just to show that my photographic memory was taking it all in.

"And Piers got talking to this bloke there, Zeno Menegallo, and Rita got bored since she dun't speak Italian, and so she went off and Piers never came back and next day she sees the paper and it says this Zeno bloke got it in the neck. I mean literally."

"Okay," I said. "That's the outline, right?"

"Yeah. Like I said, you can ask Rita for the details."

"Well, yes, I might have one or two questions to put to her."

"Fine," said Sir Alfred. He seemed to think that wrapped it up for him, and now I'd have the good taste to clear off.

"Who is this Zeno for a start?"

Gigi took a newspaper from the floor by his armchair and tossed it towards me. I picked it up. It was open at the provincial pages; there was an identity-card photo of Zeno Menegallo on one side—a wide sullen face with thick lips—and a picture of policemen standing over a sprawled and fortunately blurred body on the other side. The heading read: "Another killing in the countryside," and the article went on to recount how the body of Zeno Menegallo, twenty-eight years old, a convicted drug-pusher, had been found in the woods near the village where he lived with his family. The police were treating it as another settling of scores among the various drug-peddling gangs of the area. The article reminded its readers that San Giorgio Veronese had already been the scene of violence a few weeks back, with a petrol-bomb attack on an immigrant hostel. The journalist concluded with the dark comment that the Veronese hinterland was daily becoming more and more like certain areas of the south in its crime record.

"This was the article Rita saw then?"

"Quite," Sir Alfred said. "And then she decided to get in touch with me. I came out straight away."

"Though first getting in touch with Luigi."

"Er, yes. I had heard of the services he offered through an acquaintance of mine."

"I see." I never had. "Are the police looking for Piers?"

"Not so far as we know," said Sir Alfred. "His name hasn't been mentioned at all. According to Rita there were no witnesses to their meeting in San Giorgio. That is why I think it would be best for all concerned if we could settle the matter, em, discreetly."

"Yes. But what were Piers's connections with this bloke?"

"Rita tells us that he met him for the first time there in San Giorgio. As I said, you can obtain all this information far more fully from her."

"And Piers speaks Italian?"

"With a slight Tuscan accent," said Sir Alfred, and it was clear that Tuscan was one-up on Liverpudlian. "I have been coming regularly to my villa here with the family since the fifties, so Piers has known it all his life."

"So he has quite a few Italian friends then."

"In Tuscany certainly. But we have never visited this area of Italy before."

"So how did he get to meet this Zeno?"

"You will have to ask Rita."

"But can I just ask you as his father first? Do you think he looked this Zeno up just for social purposes?"

"I really cannot imagine."

"What I mean is, did he take stuff himself?"

"Stuff?"

"Drugs."

"Certainly not."

"Are you sure?"

"Piers is not really bad. I think it is more a case of, well, teenage rebellion."

"Sorry, how old is he?"

"Twenty-two. Yes, well, perhaps a rather young twenty-two."

"Twenty-two?" I repeated in some surprise.

"I married late in life." He was obviously used to having to explain this and went on immediately: "I think it is merely that Piers has an—an unfortunate but perhaps comprehensible taste for the forbidden."

"Exactly. And drugs are forbidden."

Sir Alfred said, "But he has a basis of good common sense. It is simply that he has always been one for going his own way, and this has sometimes led him into some, em, unfortunate choices of companions. More out of a taste for adventure than anything else, I think."

"I see. So you want us to find him and bundle him out of the country."

"Exactly."

"Even if it turns out he knows something about this affair?"

"Yes." There was a pause and he went on. "There's good stuff in Piers and this business might even serve as a salutary shock to get him back on the, em, straight and narrow. So I want him to go back to England and take up his studies again, and just—just turn his back on all this. I'm quite sure that Piers's testimony in this sordid business can be of no real relevance. The victim was clearly the sort of person destined to end up so—so—"

"Distastefully," I suggested.

"Quite. Piers's involvement can only be accidental."

"Right. So where do we start?"

"I can fill you in on all that, Jan," said Gigi. "I reckon we don't need to bovver Sir Alfred anymore. I mean, the important fing is you've met and got to know each uvver, right?"

"Yes, of course," Sir Alfred said. "It's been, em, a pleasure."

"Do we sign anything?" I said.

"Don't worry," said Gigi. "Me and Sir Alfred have done all that. You know you can trust me."

I didn't know anything of the sort, but I thought it better not to argue the point in front of Sir Alfred. "All right," I said. "Just one little matter."

"Yes?"

My mouth went unexpectedly dry. I realised that the question I was about to ask was a brutal one—but it had to be asked. I took another sip at my drink and then went on: "Suppose we do find that—that by some unlucky chance Piers did pull—or help pull—that trigger?"

He looked straight at me for the first time and said, "Your job is to find him and report to me." He looked back at his glass. "Then it's my decision."

"Okay." I was perfectly happy to shuffle off responsibility. Maybe I should apply for a job in the civil service too.

This exchange seemed to have reminded him of the fact that he was the one who was paying, and he made his first positive move: he stood up, bringing the little chat to an end. Gigi and I took our cue and stood up too and shook his proffered hand. It had dried out a little.

"So I will await news, then," he said. "And when you do find Piers, don't, em, don't tell him you've come from me. At least not in so many words."

"So what do we say?" I said. "Rita sent us?"

He managed not to wince at this and said, "Just keep an eye on him, I suppose would be best. And let me know where he is."

"Discreetly," I said.

"Well, yes."

Gigi and I said good-bye and walked out, and Sir Alfred no doubt breathed a sigh of relief to be left alone in the anonymous room. I expect he just faded away into a cloud of discreet grey dust.

TWO

. . . .

WHILE WE WAITED FOR THE LIFT, Gigi said, "Your mouf's got a bit bigger, hasn't it?"

"What do you mean?"

"Well, you nearly lost yourself this job, I reckoned, wiv some of the fings you was saying. When you going to learn a bit of tact?"

"You can stand there in an orange shirt and say that?"

"It's all a question of blending in, innit. You seen what people are wearing round here. Anyway, you gonna say fanks?"

"Yes, sure, but first I've still got one or two things to say about when we last met. In Naples."

"Oh come off it, Jan. Forgive and forget and all that."

"Well, that's easy enough for you to—"

"Look, why do you fink I've got you in on this business? It's my way of making up for fings, innit?"

"Is this an apology?"

"Yeah, well, fings turned out a bit different from what I hoped down there, so yeah, I'm sorry about it. And now I've come to make amends, haven't I? You know, help you out a bit. You could do wiv the cash, I'll bet."

"Well, yes, but—"

The lift arrived and we stepped inside. He said, "Let's forget all about Naples, right? Water under the bridge and all that."

"And a drop or two of blood."

"Yeah, ficker than water though, innit?"

I was getting a bit lost in this conversation. I said, "You guarantee this new leaf, do you?"

"Look, I know I made some mistakes and I'm ready to learn from 'em."

"Okay, if you really mean it. Shake on it?" We did so as the lift came to a halt. We walked out of the hotel and the receptionist grunted as we passed him to show he was awake.

"I'd better go and get that bag," Gigi said, making across the square.

"Yes, was all that stuff really necessary?"

"Tell you the troof, it was his idea. I mean, I just mentioned to him that I fought it might be a good idea to get your help on this whole business and he came up wiv this little 'initiative test' he called it. Said he wanted to make sure you were the 'right metal.' Pure gold, I told him."

"Maybe it's part of the recruitment procedure at the Civil Service."

"I mean, I cracked you up for all I was worf, you know, but he said he wanted to be sure."

"Yes, well, thanks for all you said about me." It really had been quite a surprise to hear some of those comments come from Gigi's lips. I'm six years younger than him, and he'd run away from home when I was eleven, so I'd never really been much more than a mewling kid to him. Until Naples, of course.

"Yeah, well, I had to lay it on a bit to convince him, you know." After a pause he added, "I mean, you *were* pretty smart, mind you, wiv that bag. And down in Naples you turned out quite a surprise, like I told you. Cor, look at those legs, mate." We were back at the bar and the German girl was still there. He went over to the table where the bag lay and picked it up, shouting a *"Grazie"* into the bar. I couldn't see, but from the sudden frozen expression on the German girl's face, it seemed he must have greeted her in some way too. I suppose that kind of thing comes natural in an orange shirt. He said, "Right, let's go and see Rita then."

"Hang on, hang on," I said, as I followed him out of the square. "I've still got some questions I'd like to ask you."

"Like what?"

"Well, who is Piers for a start?"

"Sir Alfred's son, innee, what do you mean?"

"I mean how likely is he to have shot this other bloke?"

"Ask Rita. All I can tell you is he's Sir Alfred's only son, bit of a spoilt Hooray Henry, and his old man's the sort that pays on the nail to keep fings quiet, what else do you need to know?"

"Well . . ."

"Look, you're not being asked to pull the trigger on anyone yourself, just to tidy fings up a bit, right?"

"Okay."

"Oh, before I forget, here's a couple of photos of the bloke." He pulled them from a side pocket. "Got to hand it to Sir Alfred, he's got his head screwed on. I mean, he fought of bringing these along wiv him wivout being asked."

I looked at them. One was a full-face photo of a dark-haired young man with smiling good looks above an open-neck shirt; it could have been an actor's publicity shot. The other showed the same young man in full evening dress looking bored against a shimmering backdrop of brimming Pimms and slimming debs. "This is so we don't get the social setup wrong, I suppose," I said.

Gigi shrugged. "They're just two photos, in they. You can ask Rita about his lifestyle. I told her we'd see her in a bar down by the river."

"You want me to ask the questions then?"

"Well, it's your case now, innit?"

I said, "Oh, yes, sure," in as nonchalantly professional a voice as possible. "But you haven't yet told me why you want me to do it. And come to that, how long have you been doing this sort of stuff?"

"Been doing it for ages," he said. He was now leading the way down the Corso Sant'Anastasia. "Unofficial like. My name's known around the place. You know, anyone wanting discreet enquiries. I mean, I'm not linked up to CIA computers or anyfing, but I got contax, and that's what counts."

"So why do you need me now?"

"Ah, yeah, well. Sir Alfred heard about me fru this mate of his what got caught wiv his pants down—literally." He laughed. "Him and half the crew of a ship from Naples. Blackmail case. And so he got onto me 'cause he'd heard I'm discreet."

"Yes, so I see."

"Come on, Jan, you're family. So anyway I took it on. I mean, it was good money. But of course I didn't let on to him that Naples is really my scene. Or the souf, anyway. I mean, I've never had much to do wiv the norf of Italy. Can you see me going and asking questions in Neapolitan to a bunch of Veneto peasants? I can't even understand what *they* say."

"I get your point." I'd had the chance to learn proper Italian at school, whereas Gigi had never learnt anything other than dialect.

"I mean, the Liga Veneta'd probably string me up as soon as I opened me mouf. But I'd heard from Zia Rosina that you were here in Verona so it seemed the perfect opportunity like. I mean, I bet you can even do a Verona accent."

"Well, not to a Veronese perhaps." But he'd got a point. Although my usual accent in Italian is markedly Neapolitan, one of my few undisputed gifts is the ability to imitate other Italian accents. For some reason I'm no good at the same trick in English.

"Anyway, you could get fru to 'em a lot better than me."

He led me round behind Sant'Anastasia to the Ponte Pietra, the Roman bridge over the Adige. He'd probably only been in the city a day, but already seemed familiar with its backstreets. We didn't cross the bridge but made towards a bar nearby. Before entering it he said, "Tell you what, mate. Whatever kind of berk this Piers is, he could choose his women."

"Ah. She's okay, is she, this Rita?"

"Phwaaawh."

I gathered she was.

And when we entered the bar, I appreciated Gigi's point. There was no missing her. One only had to follow the direction of most of the surreptitious male eyes. She was sitting at a table on her own, with a glass of mineral water in front of her, and a cigarette between her brightly painted lips. She was wearing a denim shirt which wasn't open quite so revealingly as Gigi's, but offered rather more attractive revelations. Her cut-off denim shorts were no more discreet, and she had one leg crossed high over the other, so that a good deal of suntanned thigh and shin was on display above the tabletop. I had an idea that she wasn't unaware of the effect she was having on the place—but then I'm a suspicious swine.

"Okay, Rita," Gigi said, and he clearly enjoyed walking up so familiarly to her, "this is Jan, me bruvver."

"Him?"

I was used to surprise at this announcement, but not such outright disappointment. "Me," I said. I sat down opposite her.

"You're the feller's going to look for Piers?" There was just the slightest Liverpool intonation.

"If you'll have me," I said.

"Alfie's taken you on, hasn't he?"

I wondered if that was how she actually addressed him—and thought it might even be, if only to get that much further up his nose. "He seems to approve," I said. "So, do you?"

Gigi said, "Get you a drink," and made towards the bar. He was presumably making it clear to me that the interrogation was up to me now.

She said, "I just want Piers got out of this bloody mess."

"So what do you think this mess is?"

She didn't answer. She went on looking at me disbelievingly. Then she said, "How old are you?"

"Well, older than Keats ever was."

"I don't want a bloody 'Ode to Autumn.'"

"No, you want your boyfriend found. So right, I'm going to try. I speak fluent Italian, can understand Veronese dialect, am reasonably fit, and pretty good at crossword puzzles."

She blew a cloud at me. "You done this sort of thing before then?"

"Sort of. I'm supposed to be asking the questions."

"Go on then. But you're sure your brother can't take it on?"

Gigi came back with another martini for me and some bright green slime for himself. I said to him, "The lady's doubting my competence."

"He's the best," he said.

"Jesus," she said simply. "Go on then. Ask me your questions."

"Well, first I'd just like to hear the story from your lips." It was difficult to avoid this cliché. In that dun-colored bar, they were as noticeable as Gigi's shirt.

"Where from?"

"Well, let's start with when you went to this village."

"Last Sunday. But Piers had already been there."

"When?"

"Day before."

"And why?"

"That's what I don't know. I mean, it had been my idea to get away from the villa in Tuscany."

"Why?"

"Spend four weeks with nothing but lizards and olive trees for miles? Come on."

"Who chose Verona?"

"We both did."

"Sure of that?"

"Look, I might have come to stay in his daddy's villa with him, but I don't live in his pocket."

"Had you ever been here before?"

"No. Neither of us had. He's been coming to Italy every year all his life, but he's only ever been to Tuscany. And once to Rome. I told him he'd got to show a bit of initiative."

"But he would have been happy to stay in the villa otherwise?"

"Yeah. He's a bit of a lazy sod unless you push him." She didn't say this with any recognisable intonation—neither fond indulgence nor contempt nor disapproval. It was just a fact.

"And then what happened here?"

"So after a day or two—two days, to be exact—he said he'd like a day on his own."

"Did that surprise you?"

"No. I mean, everyone needs his own space now and again, right? Otherwise things start getting too heavy."

"I suppose so. So did you ask him what he was going to do? Or would that have been too heavy a question?"

She gave a half-smile. "If he didn't want to say, I didn't push. He liked playing things a bit mysterious-like now and then so I let him."

"And you didn't have any idea where he went then?"

"No. I spent the day shopping. Piers isn't really in to that. So it seemed like a good idea to have a break from each other."

"And then when he came back, what did he say?"

"Just that he'd been out to this little village and it seemed really nice and we should go and stay there."

"And did *that* surprise you?"

"No."

"You're a pretty unsurprisable sort of person, aren't you?"

"Blasé," put in Gigi, and we both turned and looked at him. He said, "That's what you call it, innit—blasé."

I said to Rita, "So, are you blasé?"

"Look, after you've lived with Piers for six months or so, you learn not to get too surprised."

"Unpredictable," put in Gigi now, having apparently decided his function was that of vocabulary consultant.

"Yeah," she said. "I mean, you never know what he's going to get up to next. Nor what mood he'll be in."

"I see," I said.

"Mind you," she said after drawing thoughtfully on her cigarette again, "I think he likes the *idea* of being unpredictable as much as anything. You know, always doing things on the spur of the moment. Sometimes he's a bit—a bit—"

"Predictably unpredictable."

"Yes." Again there was that completely objective tone, as if she were talking about some distant acquaintance. "So when he said we should leave Verona after just a couple of days, it was fairly standard behaviour."

"But I thought you said he was a lazy sod—would have just sat around with the lizards if you hadn't pushed him."

"Yes. He would have done. Then the moment I push him, he won't stop moving. That's the way he is."

"And you went along with it?"

She shrugged. "I'd seen Verona by then, so why not?"

"Ah. You didn't ask why or anything?"

"He was obviously out to play Mr. Mystery Man, so I knew there was no point pestering him with questions. He'd just clam up even more."

"And this never bothered you?"

"Look, are you investigating me or him?"

"Yeah," said Gigi. "Stick to the point, Jan."

"If I want to make some kind of guess as to what he might be up to, I've got to have a clear picture of who he is. And part of that picture is what terms he was on with you."

"Well, I'm his girlfriend, aren't I? We go to bed together. You want me to tell you what positions we use?"

"No, not quite that," I said, despite the encouraging (and none too surreptitious) dig in the ribs from Gigi. "But did you have any idea at all what he might be up to?"

"I just thought he was playing up the impulsive bit. You know—look at me, the man of sudden whims. And yeah, it does rile me at times, but I've learnt to live with it. He can be a lot of fun other times. That satisfy you?"

"Yes, sure." I wondered how much the villa in Tuscany counted for her tolerance—then felt a bit of a worm for thinking it. There was something essentially genuine about her. Maybe it *was* the "positions" used in bed that really counted after all. "So when did you meet this Zeno?"

"After we'd arrived and gone to the hotel, Piers said we should go up and see this castle. Must have been about two o'clock. So we went up there, and there he was. Piers must have met him the day before, because he was obviously waiting for us."

"What was he like?"

"One of those creeps that rape you with their eyes."

"Ah." I made a mental note not to let my eyes wander to her legs again. "And was he friendly with Piers?"

"Yeah, but dead creepy along with it. Shifty. Though I think that was probably the way he always acted. You know, talking out of the corner of his mouth. Chewing gum the whole time. And his eyes wandering all over. All over me too."

Mine stayed rigidly fixed on her nose. "And could you follow any of the conversation?"

"No. I mean, I didn't try too much at first."

"You just sat there being blasé."

"Just sat there being pissed off, if you really want to know. Except we weren't sitting. We were wandering all around this bloody castle."

"And why do you think they chose to meet there?"

"I don't know. Except that there was nobody else around. But this Zeno was pointing things out occasionally. I heard the word 'cappella' a couple of times, and he pointed away up the hill."

" 'Cappella?' Chapel?"

"Yeah."

"So they could have been talking about local history."

"Except that Zeno didn't look like he'd know a chapel from a discotheque."

"Right. So what *do* you think they were talking about?"

"I don't know."

"You can't even make a guess?"

"Look, like I told your brother, I don't speak Italian. I couldn't understand a single bloody word."

"What did Piers tell you?"

She looked at me deliberately and said, "He told me it was just a bit of business and he'd be through with it in a moment."

"And not to worry your pretty little head."

"Right." She ground her cigarette stub out with a hard screwing motion; I wondered whose face she was seeing in the ashtray.

"But I imagine you must have been making some kind of guess," I said. "This Zeno was apparently a drug-pusher. So does Piers use any stuff? I mean, his father says not, but he's not necessarily going to know."

"No, he doesn't—Piers doesn't, I mean. He gets pissed quite a lot, but on wine or whisky. Well, anything alcoholic. But nothing else. I mean, we've been places where there's been stuff circulating and he's never taken anything. Not even hash. And anyway, why would he have to go out to this little place in the sticks for it? Verona's crawling with the stuff. Get high sniffing the air."

"And he wouldn't be interested in it just financially? I mean, a little courier job or something like that?"

She considered. "Yeah, well, I can't say 'certainly not' "— and she caught the tones of Sir Alfred so suddenly and so well that I almost looked round for him—"because he might do something like that, just for the hell of it. I mean, he can be right stupid sometimes."

"So then what happened?"

"I got really pissed off and told Piers I was going back to the hotel and he said okay, he'd be back later. And I waited and waited, and at seven o'clock I went and took the last bus back to Verona."

"And you still weren't making any kind of guess as to what he was up to?"

"I wasn't thinking. I was just too bloody angry."

Suddenly I realised that behind the self-assured pose she was very upset. Then it struck me that it didn't say much for my investigatorial skills that I'd only just sussed that one out. Still, I guessed she wasn't the sort to want a there-there tone and an arm round the shoulders, so I went on as briskly as ever. "Then when did you see the paper?"

"Yesterday, Tuesday. I went back to that same hotel in Verona thinking that if he started feeling—feeling—"

"Sorry?"

"Well, yes. If he did, that would be where he'd look for me. And yesterday morning I was having breakfast in a bar and I saw a photo of Zeno staring up at me from the fridge top, and then I saw the name of the village, so I start trying to read the article, and all I can make out is that he's been killed."

"So you rang Sir Alfred. How come?"

"He's got money. Speaks Italian. And he's—well, he's got Piers out of messes before."

"What sort?"

"The usual thing. Him and some Hooray Henry friends smashed up a restaurant in Kensington once."

"Oh, *that* usual thing."

"Usual for spoilt rich kids," she said. "Which is all that's wrong with Piers. And if you want to know what's right with him, it's that he knows it. Most of the time."

"Spoilt by his father," I said.

"Yeah. And his mother. But what do you expect—only kid of rich parents, and they were both over forty when they had him."

"How did you meet him?"

"You mean, how does his nibs come to be slumming it with a bird from Liverpool?"

"If you like."

She looked hard at me for a few seconds and then smiled. It was the first real smile she'd given me, and it displayed her slightly crooked teeth. Somehow this imperfection made it the more genuine. "You're a cheeky sod. Anyway we're both at the same drama school in London."

"Ah." I remembered that publicity-style photo of Piers—presumably his key to fame and fortune, or at least his first coffee ad. "How did Sir Alfred react?"

"What, to me being Piers's girlfriend, or my phoning him?"

"Well, both." I could sense Gigi chafing a bit at these sociological questions. What did he think I should be doing—frisking her?

"Well, let's say that Sir Alfred and Lady don't actually wince when I open me mouth, but they don't invite me to their dinner parties either. Probably think I live on chip butties and eccles cakes. And when I rang Alfie the other day, he just said, 'I see,' and told me to wait at the hotel. I mean, he was efficient, like taking the number of the hotel, the name of the village, the newspaper details and all that. All like it was some civil service matter. Then he said, 'I'll be with you tomorrow,' and he sounded all kind of confident and official and I thought, well, I've done *one* thing right." She paused and took out another cigarette. "Then you turned up."

"What did you expect?" I said. "MI6?"

"I don't know. Maybe I was wrong to expect too much. Kind of ironic, really. I'm always getting at Piers about his running to Daddy, and now look at me."

"Running to Daddy-in-law."

"You know he really does call him Daddy?" Then she looked straight at me and said, "Don't get me wrong. I'm—well, I love Piers and I'm bloody scared for him. You'd better know what you're up to."

"He knows," Gigi said, and I was glad he'd answered. I'd have found it difficult to say anything convincing to that direct appeal—or admonition, whichever it was.

"Well, let's hope you're more together than you look." She stood up, and all the heads in the bar swivelled. I know mine would have done if I hadn't already been looking that way.

"Er, um, yes," I said. And I hoped it carried conviction.

THREE

. . . . . .

JUST HALF AN HOUR LATER I was sitting next to Gigi in his hired
car, with all my worldly belongings—a rucksack of mixed
clothes (dirty, clean and middling), a hold-all of science fiction
books and cassettes, and a Walkman—on the backseat. We
were travelling eastwards out of Verona, and I was trying to
pretend that the haze over the *strada provinciale* was romantic
and not just carbon monoxide. I was feeling good, simply because I was on the move again. I'm one of those shallow people
who get a kick out of going to places for the first time.

I'd flustered for a minute or two when he'd suggested hitting
the road, but on being pressed couldn't think of anything else I
really had to do. He'd paid my bill at the pensione with a gesture of largesse which I had done nothing to contest; it all came
out of the advance that Sir Alfred had given, he told me.

Once we got clear of the usual snarl-up around Porta Ves-
covo, I decided it was foolish to put off a proper discussion of
the financial side of the matter merely out of embarrassment. I
said, in my most businesslike manner, "Gigi, I, er, what's the,
um, arrangement for, well, for getting, you know, paid?"

"Oh, yeah." He took his hand off the wheel and delved into
his sky-blue jacket. He threw me an obese leather wallet. "I
guess a million should do you for the moment, no?"

"Oh, yes, sure. I, um, just take it then?"

"Dig in, mate."

I dug in, plucking the hundred-thousand-lire notes from

their cosy cocoon of cash and credit cards. I put them into my own shrunken plastic purse, where they found themselves jostling rudely against rough telephone tokens and loose change.

I put my purse back in my shoulder bag, and his wallet on the window ledge. "Thanks," I said, trying to make it casual. It was nice to have it, of course, but it also made the whole thing suddenly seem real—and not just a new way to put off thinking about my next lesson. Money's funny like that—especially when you're not closely acquainted with it.

It also definitely tied me to my brother—and only an hour beforehand, if anybody had asked me, I'd have said that I would rather be tied to a cactus plant. There were still a good many things about that previous affair which no mere apologies were going to wipe from my mind. But taking the money like that did seem to imply that they'd at least got blurred. Did this make me a mercenary swine?

I decided to distract myself from these unprofitable doubts by learning something about the location of my bed that night: San Giorgio Veronese.

I looked up the relevant page in my Touring Club guide to the Veneto: *"ridente località di soggiorno estivo"*—laughing locality for summer stays. Well, you couldn't ask for better than that. Overlooked by the remains of a castle (thirteenth century). The church of Sant'Egidio, gothic *rimaneggiato* (adapted), with two paintings by Fel. Brusasorci, and the chapel of San Giorgio with remains of fourteenth-century frescoes. Museum with copy of legendary statue of St. George which disappeared in World War II—popularly believed to be of eighth century, but more likely eleventh. Nearby the seventeenth-century Villa Malberti. Notable the local craftsmanship in wrought iron. Nothing about local skills at drug-peddling or neck-perforating.

Gigi said suddenly, "Christ!" and the car juddered momentarily.

"What's up?"

"I was just finking, maybe you oughta hire a car, and then I fought . . ." His voice trailed off significantly.

"Yes, you're right," I said.

"You still haven't learned to drive, have you?"

"Well, I've had a couple of lessons."

"Yeah?"

"But that was in Rome. I don't think the same rules apply up here."

"I can't believe it," he said. "I really just can't believe it."

I said, "I'll try to avoid car chases."

"Christ, good fing we didn't mention this to Sir Alf. I mean, talk about bleeding amateurs. Well, you'll just have to make do wiv a bike or whatever."

"Did they drive out there—Rita and Piers?"

"Nah. Bus. Pretty expensive, hiring cars in Italy."

"And Piers doesn't have that much money."

"I don't fink his dad frows the stuff at him."

"Only for breaking up restaurants."

"Kids have got to have a bit of fun somehow," he said indulgently.

We reached Caldiero, a straggle of buildings along either side of the road, and he turned off left. We headed for the hills, a misty grey in the early evening light. We found ourselves chugging along behind lorries heaped high with grapes. After a mile or so they turned into a huge *"cantina,"* a concrete building where bare-legged maidens were no doubt waiting to tread them. The traffic and the houses became more sporadic. After a few minutes there were only vines and cherry trees on either side of the road, and one old lady on a motor scooter in front of us. The road began to get steeper and we overtook her. She accepted this philosophically. We drove for another fifteen minutes or so, rising all the time, and passing through occasional villages. The sign for San Giorgio Veronese appeared after a sudden bend.

Gigi said, "I'll put you down in the centre and then drive on. So you can seem like a hitchhiker, right?"

"Okay."

"Give us a ring at the hotel—let us know how fings are. Round two-firty?"

The first hundred yards or so there were modern houses with

gardens and wrought-iron gates—lions and eagles and spears and an occasional St. George-cum-spindly-dragon. Then the road narrowed and the houses were older and closer. There were shops, then a church, and then the piazza.

Gigi stopped and I got out. I dragged the bags out from the backseat, thanked him and waved. He said, "Good luck, mate" and drove off. I was on my own.

I looked around the square. A fairly standard Veneto village square: church with absurdly grand classical portico, *palazzo del comune* with a baroque facade, acned by peeling election posters and black-rimmed death announcements, a restaurant, a bar, and in the middle, a modern monument—to the war-dead, I guessed—in wrought iron. A few youths were lounging on motorbikes around this monument, with a radio thudding out disco music; they filled any gaps between drumbeats by revving their engines. They turned to look at me, but it was just an idle glance; I doubt their brains could have sustained any-thing longer than a second's curiosity under that rhythmic pummelling.

I felt a moment of relief. I wasn't going to be the stranger walking into the sullen town, silencing crowded rooms by my mere appearance. Two old men, I noticed, were sitting at a table outside the bar with glasses of red wine, and both had their eyes on me, but again there was no visible curiosity; I was simply the only moving object in the square at that moment.

I let my eye rove beyond and above the square to take in the hills that surrounded the village—presumably the laughing ones of the guidebook. The most obvious one seemed pretty gloomy to me, not to say frowning—darkly wooded and crowned by a jagged castle. The one looming over the opposite side of the square was a bit lighter in its greens and had a Pal-ladian villa halfway up its slope; smirking would have been the best I would have said about it.

I swung the rucksack onto my back, picked up the hold-all and made for the bar. Always a good place to start any enter-prise. Or not to start it.

There were about twenty people there, all male as far as I

could see, playing cards, video games and/or shouting. A fan above the counter did its feeble best to keep the cigarette smoke circulating. Nobody paid any attention to me—not even the barman.

I took the rucksack off and propped it against the bar and waited. It was clear that the village wasn't paralysed by horror at the recent events, nor plunged into deepest mourning. There were several conversations going on—all at top volume and many of them among the same people at the same time—and they all sounded like the *osteria* chit-chat of any Italian village: gossip, politics, television, sport and food. The barman himself was a big slow man and he was explaining, with big slow words, just what was wrong with the present government. This was a subject that could take some time to exhaust, I felt, so eventually I coughed. In mid-sentence the barman made a ponderous about-turn and announced rather than said, *"Signore, buonasera."*

"Glass of red," I said. I used a heavy English accent.

The wine was poured and then the barman returned to his oration. I retired to a chair in a corner. There was no better way to get the feel of the villagers' collective soul than by just sitting quietly among them while they drank. And sooner or later the subject of the murder was bound to come up in someone's conversation. If it didn't, I could only presume that the Mafia code of silence had crept right up the boot of Italy—or that they were exceptionally blasé in San Giorgio Veronese.

I sat there for half an hour or so, feigning intense interest in my guidebook, but trying to miss nothing of what was going on. The real risk was of a fractured eardrum: there was a group of double-chinned, double-drinking card players, and their bidding calls suggested a stock exchange crisis. There was a cluster of younger people around the video machines in a back room, and their noise suggested a Middle Eastern crisis. And at no point did the barman's voice ever falter: no matter what the subject, his opinions came steadily steamrolling out.

Eventually I realized the conversation around the bar had moved on to the question of journalism, on which topic everyone had a word to put in. The barman was explaining just what he'd said to the man from the *Corriere della Sera* who'd asked him what it was like to live in such a violent place; his interlocutors—five of them—were all explaining (and much faster too) what they'd said to the journalists from *La Repubblica, La Stampa,* and *L'Arena*—or what they would have said if they'd been asked. As ever, it was obvious that the barman, for all his slowness, was going to get the last ponderous word.

"And then he looked at me," the barman trundled on, "and asked what my solution would be, and I told him, I told him straight out, no hesitation, I told him, we need the death penalty for that sort, and I told him he could quote me on that, put my name in his paper, I wasn't afraid, and I told him that I wouldn't be afraid to say the same to the president himself, and that I knew that most honest people would back me up on this, and he didn't know where to look then, this journalist, and I told him, print it like I told you, don't tart it up, let your readers know that some people aren't afraid of speaking out. . . ."

After a minute or two his interlocutors were already flagging, none of them able to match his magnificent certitude and relentless repetitivity. Then I saw one of the men round the bar nudge his neighbour, who passed the nudge on. The nudge did the rounds of all the nearby elbows and the nudgers carefully avoided looking at an old man who'd just come in at the door. The topic of conversation was officially changed by the barman himself: "Bad about Verona last Sunday; that second goal was a real freak."

The old man, dressed in shabby grey trousers and an open shirt, shuffled up to the bar. Without being asked the barman poured him a glass of red wine. The old man looked at nobody, picked up the glass and mumbled something, and then made his way out.

The voices round the bar became urgent again, but sibilantly so, and the men's heads all leaned in conspiratorially. Even the barman dropped a few decibels.

I asked for another glass of wine myself and took it outside. The old man was sitting by himself at the furthest table.

I went and sat at the table next to his and tried to look casual.

"Journalist?" he said.

I spun round to him. "What? Oh, me?" I thought about it. I'd tried the ploy once before but not very successfully. His expression was one of deep distrust, if not dislike. I said, "Well, no. Not really. I'm a tourist."

"Foreigner?"

"Yes." I'd maintained my English accent. "English."

"And not a journalist?"

"No, no. I swear."

"I've had enough of journalists and their filthy snooping ways." He spoke in gap-toothed dialect, and I had to listen hard to fish out recognisable words from the flob-foamed flow.

"Well, I'm just a tourist," I said again.

"All their sneaking questions and then they write just whatever they want."

"Yes, I know," I said. I guessed my best ploy would be just to lend a sympathetic ear, even if it did get damp in the process.

"Pack of lies, most of it," he went on. "My son was no delinquent."

I'd guessed right. "Oh, I'm sorry. You're the father of the young man who—"

"That's right. And I'm not ashamed."

I looked at him more closely. He had a leathery face, with a two-day growth of hard stubble; the surface toughness was offset, however, by a red mushiness in and around the eyes, which could be due to grief or to drink—or more likely both. The only emotion in the voice, however, was defiance.

I felt a sudden qualm about my present role. I did my best to crush it by telling myself that at least I wasn't a journalist asking him how he felt and that anyway I had a duty to another father. "Why should you be?" I said.

"No reason. My son wasn't a delinquent," he repeated. "All right, so he was a bit wild, high-spirited. So what?"

The paternal protectiveness—though expressed in wine-and-saliva-slurred dialect—was identical to that of Sir Alfred. I felt

I could place as little reliance in it as a testimony to the son's character. I was, however, far more moved by this man's sentiments—and not just because his son was definitely dead: no, it was the fact that here I had no sneaking doubt that the speaker was more concerned with his own position. (But maybe the comparison was unfair to Sir Alfred: this Veneto *contadino* probably hadn't been sent to an expensive school to have all his personal feelings scoured out of him with cold showers and dormitory derision.)

"What have they said about him?" I said.

"Drug-pusher, delinquent, gangster. You'd think this was Naples."

I had better take extra care not to let my Neapolitan accent slip out. "And he wasn't any of these?"

"Of course not. All right, so the police had found marijuana on him once or twice." He pronounced it "Maria Uanna," as if it were some flashy film star. "Or perhaps a little something else. So what? He'd got into bad company. And it wasn't my fault. I brought him up right. But young people today—they have to go their own way. They know better than us. And they all take these things. They see those people on television and so . . . But anyway, who says my Zeno was ever selling the stuff? Who says so?"

I made a noncommittal noise, feeling that it wouldn't be right to say I didn't know, who did? He took another swig of wine and I asked, "Who do you think did it then?"

He spat, noisily and voluminously. His consonants remained as slobber-coated as ever, unfortunately. "There are a lot of bad people around here. And not all drug addicts. There are other things than drugs going on in this village."

"Really? What sort of things?"

"Other things," he said. "I could tell stories. . . ."

I didn't say "go on." I just tried to look encouraging. However, he seemed to think he'd said enough with this dark hint.

"Well, I'm sure the police will get to the bottom of it," I said.

"If they dare," he said. "You know what always happens. They pick up some little man, and the big fish get away."

"You sound as if you're talking about the Mafia," I said.

"There are other things than Mafia. Bigger things."

I guessed this was all drunken rambling. Or at least I strongly hoped it was. I said, "Did Zeno say anything to you about these things?"

He looked at me as hard as his wine-rimmed eyes permitted. "Why do you want to know?"

"Well, I, that is, I don't really, I mean . . . ."

He'd already lost interest. He said, "One thing I can tell you is that he would never have thrown any Molotov bombs."

"Why? Do they say he did?"

"And he wasn't really racist. He just said that the blacks should stay where they were, like we stay where we are. That doesn't mean he would throw bombs at them, does it?"

"No," I said, "I suppose not." This village was beginning to sound a lot less *ridente*. "But somebody has been throwing petrol bombs then?"

"Yes. Up there." He gestured towards the castle-crowned hill. "At the house where those blacks are. But it wasn't Zeno. Nor my other son either."

"You've got another son then?"

"Two. And he's got nothing to do with all this either. I've had enough of all these questions." He stood up abruptly— well, more abruptly than I would have expected. "You tell your paper that we're an honest family. If you want to find scandal in this place, there are other people you could start looking into. More important people."

"Right. Only I'm not a journalist. . . ."

He merely snorted at this and shuffled off, brushing past a blond young girl who apologized breathily and pinkly for being in the way.

I finished my glass of wine and went inside to pick up my rucksack and hold-all. They were talking about some recent scandal to do with a secret arms horde that had been discovered hidden in a cemetery near Milan; all the authorities in the country—the government, the army, the Secret Service, the police, the Mafia —were disclaiming all knowledge of it. They obviously should have come to this village, since it seemed everybody here was an expert: "Obvious it was the Red Brigades," boomed the barman.

"No," said an equally certain customer, "the Secret Service, you mark my word. Gladio—something like that."

Gladio was the name of the secret anti-Communist army whose existence the government had been forced to disclose to public scrutiny in 1990. The mere name is enough to throw any group of Italians into rancorous and endless arguments over the last fifty years of their history. I thought it best to get my request in before the bottles started flying.

"Excuse me, is there a pensione or hotel anywhere here?"

The barman looked at me, as if assessing the likelihood of my being a Red Brigade infiltrator, and then made his pronouncement: "Straight across the square, continue up the road for a hundred metres." He made it sound as if I'd need native porters.

"Thanks," I said, and made towards the door. I heard him take back the reins of the conversation: "Well, if it was Gladio, remember it's thanks to them that we're standing here and not behind the Berlin Wall."

I set out across the square in the direction the barman had told me. The youths were still busy pile-driving decibels into the afternoon air and whatever was left of their brains. I found I'd come to accept the *thud-thud-thud* as a natural part of the local atmosphere: it went with the petrol bombs and the neck-splattering, I suppose.

I passed quite close to the monument they were gathered around. Their eyes flickered toward me again with the same lack of curiosity. I looked at the wrought-iron design on the plinth: it represented in a highly stylised manner a man moving forwards in a low crouch. The rifle in his hands gave the necessary belligerent touch, to make it clear that it wasn't a monument to strawberry pickers or indigestion sufferers. In large letters were the words: "TO GIORGIO MALBERTI, 1922–1944. Not unworthy to have held the sword of Pipino."

This meant nothing to me. Pipino sounded like a dog. Malberti I remembered was the name of the villa on the hill—and the square itself, I now noticed, was called Piazza Malberti. I took a steep road out of it and walked up it for about a hundred yards. Then I saw a large sign on the left-hand side: "Hotel Las Vegas." It seemed a little unlikely.

A big gateway gave onto a gravelled courtyard, obviously once that of a farm. Opposite me was an ex-barn with great pillared arches, worthy of a cathedral chapel, under which were parked four cars. The hotel entrance was to my right, with another sign, in neon this time.

The entrance hall was lit and furnished like a funeral chapel: there were heavy velvet curtains, a dark oak desk by the staircase, and a dim electric light which contrived to flicker like a candle. A man came out of the shadows behind the desk and said, *"Buonasera"* with the gentleness of one who doesn't want to intrude on private grief. The expression of his face seemed determined by the droop of his large grey moustache: his eyes, mouth, and even his shoulders all sagged in sympathy.

I said, "I'd like a room without a bath."

"Single bed?" he said.

"Yes," I said, wondering if I should specify without a lid.

"Room twelve-B," he said, and handed me the key.

I waited for the usual request for documents, and when it didn't come thought that maybe he'd ask the next of kin for details later.

He said, "Second floor. We close the front door at midnight. No washing clothes in the basin. No radios. Showers two thousand lire extra."

"Thank you. Er, which way?"

"Second floor. *Di nuovo, buonasera.*" And he bowed and stepped back into the shades again.

Welcome to Las Vegas, I thought.

I made my way up the stairs and came to the second floor. Last door on the corridor was 12B. I turned the key and went in.

If the entrance hall had resembled a funeral parlour, the bedroom was a mortuary: cold, bare, and clinically clean. The sheets on the bed were hard and white and pulled tight to give the impression of marble; a smell of antiseptic hung in the air as if the whole place had been scrubbed after an especially messy autopsy. There were no pictures on the wall, just a crucifix above the bed. An empty vase stood on the chest of drawers, waiting for wilted chrysanthemums.

I slung my rucksack onto the floor, opened it and let a few socks and underpants dribble out, to make the place look a little more lived-in. It didn't work. They shrivelled in on themselves, to look like dead plague rats.

Well, I hadn't come here to live it up after all. I sat on the bed (it *was* marble) and pondered my next move.

A stroll round the village might be in order, and a discreet question or two to any likely-looking yokel. And a glance at the castle and any chapel nearby. And of course an inspection of the scene of Zeno Menegallo's demise—wherever that was.

My first task as private detective: find out where the crime had taken place. Discreetly.

After quarter of an hour or so of idle pondering (I'd slipped to a horizontal position on the slab by then), I got up and left the room again. As I walked down the corridor, I wondered idly which room Piers and Rita had stayed in—or at least Piers had. Rita, of course, had cleared off only a few hours after arriving in the village. It would be worth asking the bogeyman at the desk.

He materialised as I came into the hall and took the key from my hands. I said, "I was wondering whether I might find a couple of English friends of mine here."

"Ah, yes, sir?"

"Yes. They said they would be staying here this week. A young man with dark hair and a girl with blond hair—usually wearing shorts."

"Ah, yes." He definitely remembered her.

"Are they still here?"

"No, sir."

"Oh. You don't know where they've gone, by any chance? Or why?"

"Well, no, signore. It was after the murder."

"The what?" I gave a good impression of alarm as if I expected the corpse to be in a back room.

"Some unpleasantness with drug-pushers last week."

"Who?" I said, pretending not to understand the expression. I had to be careful not to let my rudimentary Italian slip into fluency.

"People who sell drugs, signore. You know, heroin, cocaine, marijuana, crack." It sounded as if they had quite a time in San Giorgio.

"Oh, yes. Who got killed?"

"A local delinquent." That seemed to him a sufficient explanation.

"Why? How?"

"He was shot in the woods here. Below the castle."

Well, that was point one cleared up. "And did they get the murderer?"

"No. But don't worry, signore. Such things are very rare here. Now down south . . ."

"Ah, yes. The Mafia," I said in my informed-tourist fashion. "But when did these friends of mine leave? Did they say when they were going?"

"No, signore. To tell the truth, I only saw them arrive. On Sunday, I think it was. And the next day a friend of theirs came to pay for the room and collect the luggage."

"Really. Who?"

"I don't know who he was, signore."

"Was he English?"

"Oh, no. From these parts."

"You couldn't describe him?"

"I beg your pardon?"

My line of questioning was undoubtedly a little odd. I said, "I'm just wondering whether this Italian might be another friend of ours. Was he, um, short with a moustache?"

"No, signore. Quite big. A big beard and dark glasses. Wearing jeans rather—rather like yours, signore."

Tattered. "I see. Ah, maybe it was Claudio. Did he speak Veneto?"

"Oh, yes, signore. From these parts, as I said. He told me your friend had decided to stay with them for a few days."

"From these parts. This village?" Many Italians pride themselves on a Professor-Higgins-like ability to place an accent to one end of a street or another.

"Well, I couldn't say for certain, signore. I'm not from these parts myself."

"But would he have been from around Verona?"

"I should say so. We haven't lived here very long, signore."

"I see. What time did he come?"

"Late afternoon, I think. It seemed all right to me, even if a little odd. After all, he did pay for the room."

"Oh, yes, I'm sure it was all quite regular. Well, maybe I'll run into him. Good-bye."

"Good-bye, signore. Please remember we close the door at midnight."

"Yes. See you later," I said, and slipped out.

I made my way briskly down the road to the square. I wanted to go and have a look at the castle and its surroundings before it got dark. Who knew what might be the scenario there after nightfall—drug parties, arson attacks, mad axe murders—or the hotel manager himself flitting around in search of succulent necks.

A road led out of Piazza Malberti in the direction of the castle. It went past a few houses and then petered out and became a rough path. A rather battered *Cinquecento* was parked to one side in the grass. The path rose steeply between the trees, often turning into much-scuffed stone steps. After a minute or so I came to an ancient-looking barn-type building, with a rudimentary wooden door and gaping windows. A tall black man came out of the doorway and eyed me as I walked up.

"*Buonasera,*" I said chattily.

"*Buonasera,*" he said, in a thick accent. He stayed watching me and I heard voices behind him speaking rapidly in a foreign language.

"Do you live here?" I asked, still in Italian. It looked even less comfortable than my hotel bed.

"Yes," he said. "Why not?" He was about thirty, dressed in jeans and T-shirt, like me.

"No, no—no reason why not. Been living here long?"

"You journalist?"

San Giorgio didn't seem able to get over its moment of notoriety. Then I thought that probably this was the building that had been firebombed. Well, I was glad he'd taken me for a journalist and not a bomber. I said, "No, no. Just a tourist."

"Nothing here to see," he said.

"No, I'm going up to see the castle."

"Okay."

Something made me want to ask a few more questions. I said, "Do you like it here?"

He shrugged. "There's good people and there's bad people."

"What sort of bad people?"

He looked hard at me now. "You know about the bomb, yes?"

"I heard something about it, yes," I said.

"And about the murder down there." He was pointing into the trees behind me.

"Yes."

"Well, that's bad people, no?"

"Do you think it's the same people?"

"We don't know anything. We got our ideas, but we don't know anything. But you tell your paper we're ready if they come again." A couple of voices muttered assent from behind. I couldn't see anybody; I could just get a glimpse of the bare stone walls in the gloom, and the hard earth floor, with sleeping bags laid out.

"Okay," I said. "But I'm not a journalist."

He nodded and went back in. I continued on up the path, beginning to wonder what there was about me that suggested the press: did I smell of alcohol or something?

I reached the castle about five minutes later. Despite the fact that it was evening and the path was all in deep shade, by the time I got there my shirt was sticking to my back and I was dying for a drink—water this time.

The castle was just an empty shell in the gloom, with irregular crumbling walls around a grassy field, dotted with broken boulders. Big notices warned of the danger of climbing on the walls. I chose the boulder that reminded me least of the hotel bed and sat down to let my shirt dry out and my mind soak in the place's suggestions.

The shirt took about two minutes. My mind took a little longer—though I doubted that the suggestions that came seeping in were at all relevant to the case. They were mainly to do with the way the shadows looked as if they were massing together in the castle's craggier corners to whisper their communal resentment at my presence there. And whenever I moved my head to keep an eye on some other shadow, the ones I'd just been looking at seemed to shuffle forwards—until I swung my head back, and they hulked there, motionless but menacing.

I tried to imagine what Piers and Zeno could have been talking about up here. Medieval architecture? Feasts and pageants of yore? Picturesque local legends?

I got up and went for a short stroll around the outside of the walls, looking in all the likely holes or secluded corners. Likely as what, I didn't specify to myself—just generally likely. I found old Coca-Cola cans, beer bottles, cigarette packets, torn-up porno magazines, used condoms and broken syringes. Not exactly Burne-Jones.

Now the wood seemed to be getting surly about me too. There were little scuttering noises, and sibilant leaf-swishing, despite the complete absence of wind. I went back to the big archway into the castle's interior, to see if I could catch the shadows out before they organized their massed attack. As I passed through the arch, a hand shot out and grabbed my shoulder.

FOUR

· · · ·

WELL, IT WAS A FAR-FROM-SHADOWY-PRESENCE, this one. A very big, very solid man of about twenty-five, with short hair and long arms. The hand was particularly unethereal, and at a guess I'd have said it was made of brick. He pulled me towards himself and then loosened his grip and just loomed over me. He was rather good at this, being almost a head taller than me, and I'm not short.

"What do *you* want?" I said in Italian, remembering to keep my English accent.

"What do you want?" he said, with a noticeably Veronese accent. I'd always found it a rather attractive cadence until that moment.

"I'm a tourist. Just looking around. This isn't private property, is it?"

"You another snooper? You come here to write dirt about the village?"

"I'm not a journalist, if that's what you mean," I said with resignation. Maybe it was just amnaesia on my part, and my real name was John Simpson. I looked at the stud in his right ear and wondered what had been used to put it there—a pneumatic drill?

"And what were you talking to those black bastards for? What were you asking them?"

"I just said good evening to the gentleman. What's it to you? Were you following me?"

"Listen, I'm fed up of shit being written about this place. This is a clean place—clean, follow me? At least it was till they let certain scum in. But nobody's going to get away with any more insults. And the scum's going to get cleaned away. And if you want to stay whole, you'll keep away from the scum."

"Look, I'm a tourist. Passing through. If you want me to get a nice impression of the place, you'll stop bothering me. Okay?"

Maybe I could have phrased this a little more tactfully. He moved forwards, suddenly accompanied by all the castle's shadows. I thought he'd been looming before, but it just showed I didn't know the full meaning of the word.

"I, er," I said, and not even this soothed him.

"*Oh, buonasera,*" came a new voice from outside the archway.

We both turned. A girl of about my age was standing there. She had short frizzy blond hair and pink cheeks.

The loomer stepped away from me, and I said to the girl, "Ciao."

"Ciao," she said, and her cheeks got pinker, as if she thought she must have said the wrong thing with "*buonasera.*" I could have assured her that any greeting from "wotcher" to "up-yours" would have been music to my ears. But maybe she was just embarrassed at having addressed two strangers.

And this led me to another guess: "Are you English?" I said in English.

"Yes, how did you know?"

"I just had a hunch." I glanced back at the big man. "Well, so long," I said to him in Italian. "I expect we'll see each other around."

He muttered, "You can count on it." He made his way to the archway and pushed past the girl. He turned and said, "And remember what I told you."

"I'll bear it in mind," I said politely.

He went off down the path to go and loom elsewhere. At home in bed I hoped. I breathed a long sigh and then said to the girl, "Thanks. You just saved me from the Incredible Hulk."

She was a rather unlikely saviour, being about a quarter the size of the monster, and looking duvet-soft and pillow-smooth to his brick and mortar. She was dressed in a pair of rather boyish blue dungarees, which didn't give a clear idea of her figure, but suggested gentle curves.

"Oh, was he, um, menacing you?" Her voice was breathy with a combination of shyness and eagerness, and there was a hint of hockey sticks about the vowel sounds.

"Well, I don't *think* it was just honest gruffness."

"Do you want to report him?"

"No, not worth it. It's complicated enough checking into a hotel here."

She smiled. "Yes, I know what you mean."

"So what are you doing here?" I asked.

"I like this castle in the evening. It's kind of—kind of atmospheric."

"Yes. Bit of a surprise meeting someone English here," I said. "I thought I'd got right off the beaten track." I felt I might as well keep up the dumb tourist act.

"Nowhere like that left," she said. "Unless you go right down south, to Calabria or places like that."

"Still," I said, "I don't suppose there are great hordes of day-trippers here."

"No." Now that we'd got off the subject of my assailant, she'd gone back to being embarrassed. Well, maybe she saw no reason to keep chatting to a dumb tourist. Perhaps I'd better play down the dumbness a little. She said, "Are you doing research or something here?"

"Am I what?" Had I been rumbled already?

"Into local history, I mean."

"Oh, er, no—not particularly, that is."

"Ah. No, it's just I think I saw you down in the square talking to Signor Menegallo."

"To who? Oh yes, the old man at the bar. Yes, that's right. But we just got chatting by chance."

"Oh. You see, he's the custodian in the local museum, that's why I—er . . ." The twin beacons lit up in her cheeks again, as if she'd made some appalling gaffe.

"Are you?" I said.

"What?"

"Doing research."

"Yes, how did you guess—well, I suppose it's clear enough."

"What's your research?" I asked.

"Oh, nothing special. Early medieval sculpture."

"Oh, right. Is that why you came up to the castle?"

"No, no. As I said, it's just a nice place to soak up the atmosphere." She had passed through the archway now, and was picking her way around the stones. Maybe she hoped that I'd have the tact to leave her to her solitary soaking. She might spontaneously combust otherwise.

But I didn't want to lose the chance of talking to a possible witness. There was a possibility she might have noticed Piers, and I guessed that she had a communicative enough nature, if I could just fight through—or beat down—the protective flames. I tagged along by her side and said, "Can you tell me anything about the castle?"

"Well, nothing special. Built originally by the Montecchi family—that's Shakespeare's Montagues—then destroyed by Ezzelino da Romano in the thirteenth century and rebuilt by the Scaligeri. But it's not really my period, you know."

"Oh. What is?"

"Well, from the eighth to the tenth century, or thereabouts." She obviously realised she wasn't going to shake me off, so she resigned herself to telling me all. "You see there's a statue that belonged to the village that has a really rather romantic legend attached to it. That's what I'm studying."

"The statue or the legend?"

"Well, both really." She laughed a little as she said this. "You see, as so often happens, the legend helps us to understand the object, if we just know how to read the legend."

"Oh, yes?" No other response seemed to be needed now. Her tongue had been untied and was skittering around quite happily, with no spurring from me. I was probably going to get every chapter heading of her thesis.

"It's a statue of St. George. It's made of silver and is encrusted with jewels. It's supposed to contain his finger and—"

"And a piece of the dragon's tail," I said.

"How did you know?" she said.

"I was guessing—well, I was joking actually," I said. "So is that the legend?"

"No, no."

"What, are those the historical facts?"

"Well," she said, with a dismissive wave of her hand, "there are lots of more unlikely saints' relics around the place: like the two skulls of St. John the Baptist—one as young boy and one as a man. That's not what makes the statue interesting. No: it's supposed to have been a gift of King Pepin to the village."

She stopped walking at this point and looked at me with an expression of triumph, and I realised I was supposed to gasp. I said politely, "Well, that's quite something." Then, I did a mental shoulder shrug and decided to come clean. "I know I'm going to sound very silly, but who's Pepin?"

She was the one who gasped—or at least dropped her mouth a centimetre or two. "Oh, but surely . . ." Then she realised that whatever she was going to say would sound rude, however well-deserved, and she blushed again: it was nice of her to do my blushing for me. She said, "He was Charlemagne's father." Then she darted a quizzical look at me.

I said quickly, "Yes, I've heard of Charlemagne." I wouldn't care to be cross-examined on my knowledge of him, mind you: history lessons at my school had been strictly insular, with just occasional references to such unfortunate foreign disturbances as the French and Russian Revolutions. I've always meant to fill in these gaps one day on my own, particularly the Italian ones, but was always getting distracted by some new science fiction novel.

"You see," she said, "Pepin was established in Verona for a long time, and the story goes that one day he went out hunting in the hills here and was attacked by brigands. Suddenly St. George appeared by his side and helped put them to flight. In gratitude Pepin ordered that a chapel be built to the saint on the site and personally ordered a statue of St. George, to be made by the finest silversmith in the city, which he then donated to the chapel."

"And that's the legend."

"Yes. Of course a lot of people don't believe that the statue is that old and say it's probably from only the eleventh century."

"And you?"

"Well," she said, glowing just the subtlest shade of bashful pink this time, "I have a theory based on the statue's curious appearance."

"What's so curious about it?"

"Well, it's noticeably short and squat—which is odd for a St. George, wouldn't you agree?"

"Well, I suppose one usually thinks of dragon-slayers as pretty hefty blokes."

"Exactly. So my theory is that maybe it was actually made in the likeness of Pepin himself. He was known as Pepin the Short, after all."

"And how are you going to prove it? Find his tailor's measurements?"

"No. It's a question of comparative analysis: gathering sufficient evidence to show that the statue's appearance is definitely anomalous, and then establishing my case that the statue was a deliberate act of homage to the king."

I thought of something. "And this chapel, is it near here?"

"It's up in the hills." She waved her hand to her right, indicating the hills which we couldn't see from within the castle, but which I knew to rise above the local prominence on which the castle stood.

"Is it interesting?"

"Well, it's quite sweet. It's been rebuilt since Pepin's time, of course. In Romanesque style. But it's entirely empty now—just frescoes on the walls."

"Could you take me there?"

"What, now? It's getting dark." She looked at me in some surprise—and maybe in alarm too.

I said, "You're right. I got carried away. It sounded all so fascinating." This was true: I was asking myself how likely it was that Zeno had been entertaining Piers with these local legends and artistic theories. The accounts I'd had so far of his character suggested that it wasn't very likely—*but* I mustn't forget that he was the son of the custodian of the local museum.

"Well, I'm glad you say so," she said. "I do tend to get a bit carried away myself at times."

"And this statue, where's it kept now?"

"Oh, don't you know?"

"No," I said. "Surely you've worked that much out by now."

"No, I thought you might have . . . Never mind. No, it's lost." And her big blue eyes looked into the castle's massed shadows and for a moment I thought a tear was going to form.

I said quickly, "Oh, how did that happen?"

"In the war."

I suddenly remembered something. "Pipino—is that Pepin?"

"Yes."

Not a dog then. " 'Not unworthy to have held the sword of Pipino,' " I quoted in Italian.

"That's right," she said. "On the monument in the piazza. Giorgio Malberti." And suddenly she sounded brighter. She looked around the place. "Maybe we'd better be getting back before it gets completely dark."

"Yes," I said. "Before the brigands come out."

"Oh, gosh," she said, "that man. Do you suppose he's gone?"

"Yes, yes. He was obviously just some local lout."

"I've seen him in the bar, actually. I think his name's Mauro. What did he want?"

"I don't think he's too fond of foreigners, that's all."

"Oh."

We made our way back to the arched entrance. I gave one last backward glance as we left, but I wasn't quite quick enough to catch the shadows out: they were all hovering there in casual poses that didn't convince me for a second.

She said, "That's another amazing story."

"What? Mauro's xenophobia?"

"No. Giorgio Malberti."

"Who was he?"

We started down the path, with her leading the way. There was just the faintest of grey light to show us where to walk. Tiny tickling creatures of the twilight darted around us, and cobweb tendrils took unwarranted liberties with our faces and hair. She started to recount this other story, making occasional brushing gestures with her hands and frequently looking back at me, to check I was still following—both the story and her footsteps. "He was a local partisan leader who got killed by the Nazis. He was evidently a really charismatic leader, and did some really heroic things."

"Oh, really?" I said, not meaning to parody her favourite word.

Anyway she didn't notice. "But the thing that really made his name for the people around here was to do with the St. George statue. You could say it was his most heroic action." There was no mistaking the breathy enthusiasm in her voice, and when she turned round to look at me I could see, even in that dim light, that the glow in her cheeks had passed upstairs to her eyes. She went on: "You see, it seems that the Nazis raided the museum and took away the statue, and then this Malberti organised a raid and managed to get it back."

"So why's it lost, then?"

"Well, that's the tragedy. You see, he took it to a partisan hideout in the hills—just an empty farmhouse—but then the Nazis got a tip-off and surrounded the house. There was a shoot-out and it ended with the Nazis setting fire to the place. There were ten partisans and they were all burnt to death. And the statue was never found."

"I see. So how are you carrying out your research then?"

"Well, there's a copy of it in the museum, which is supposed to be perfect. It was paid for by the Malberti family. Like the monument in the square. But don't you think it's a really thrilling story?" She turned round again, those big eyes still aglow.

I said, "Ye-es. It doesn't seem to have been a great military move, mind you—seeing that it got them all killed."

"Oh, but you've got to think what it meant to the morale of the local people—knowing that the Nazis didn't get away with it. I mean, this village was really proud of that statue. Their most famous possession. It's in all the history books and art books. You've only got to think that Malberti was a Communist—" and her voice hushed as she pronounced this word "—and risked his life to get it back."

"Not risked—lost it. And the statue too."

"But it was a wonderful symbolic act."

"A truly heroic pointless gesture."

She smiled. Nothing I said was going to dull her hero's lustre for her—and I suddenly felt a trifle wormlike for trying to do so. I was obviously getting cynical in my dotage. I said, "So a village square dedicated to a Commie—here in the Christian-Democrat Veneto." I remembered the bar conversation about Gladio: it was villages such as this that had supplied many of Gladio's most dedicated secret soldiers. "Well, I suppose he's dead."

"And connected to a big family in the area."

She'd said this, not me. "Oh, yes?"

"The Malbertis own the villa on the hill there." We'd come out of the trees and were standing on a bluff above the rooftops of the village. She pointed to the villa I'd noticed earlier, halfway up the hill on the other side of the village, preening itself in its Palladian perfection. "Giorgio Malberti was the elder son and broke away from the family. But when he died his hero's death, they obviously forgave him everything and paid for the monument."

"Even his communism?"

"Well, the whole family was anti-Fascist, and that was what counted after all. Then at any rate."

"I see. Where did you pick all this stuff up on the family?"

"Well, from the count himself."

"The count?"

"Oh, yes, the real thing. Conte Malberti. Not that he cares particularly about it. But also from Signor Menegallo. You see, he worked for them in the garden as a boy—and he even joined Giorgio in the hills as a partisan. More from hero-worship than from any real political or patriotic conviction, I think. In fact, after Giorgio died, as far as I can make out, he just went and hid in a cave somewhere in the woods for the rest of the war."

I noticed she was on first-name terms with the dead hero. We continued on down the path in silence. We passed the barn where the African immigrants were housed, and a figure came to the door and observed us, then quietly withdrew. When we came to the road into the village square I said, "Solid silver, you say?"

"No, not solid. I told you, it's a reliquary. But a good deal of silver all the same."

"And jewels."

"Yes."

"And never found."

"That's right. And yes, there are lots of rumours about it still being around somewhere. And yes, it would be worth a lot of money."

"I expect quite a lot of people would be interested in finding it," I said.

"Yes, I expect so."

"And you?"

"Well, we've all got to have some dream, haven't we?" she said, trying to sound merely jocular. "But it's not the jewels or silver I'd be after."

"No, no. St. George himself. Or Pepin the Short." I thought of something. "And how tall was Giorgio Malberti?"

She laughed. "You've got me marked down as a really silly hero-worshipper, haven't you? But actually, you've got a point. Apparently he was quite small."

"But walked tall."

We reached the village square. Giorgio Malberti's monument was for the moment a monument, and not a motorbike stand; the youths had all left, presumably for dinner. There was nobody sitting outside the bar, and the only noise was the sound of the evening television news coming from open windows all round the square.

I said, "Where are you staying?"

"At the hotel Las Vegas," she said. "Are you?"

"Yes." We had stopped near the monument now, and I wondered what would happen to her cheeks if I suggested dinner together.

Then she said, "Well, I really must go back and get some work done."

"What, now?"

"Yes. I work best in the evening. And I never eat dinner."

That was what's known as a preemptive strike. I said, "What's your name?"

"Oh, yes, sorry, Linda. Linda Housman."

"Jan." I didn't offer my surname. Before she could slip away I said, "Did you by any chance see an English couple who were here a few days ago? You see, I had this vague arrangement to meet them here, and I think they may have got the days wrong, or I did. She's a really striking blonde, kind of flashily dressed, and he's sort of dark and quiet-like."

"I remember them," she said. "Skimpily dressed, I'd say. I was there when they arrived. They were in room eleven, just next to mine."

"Did you get to speak to them?"

"Well, I saw him the next day, but not her. I just nodded to him."

"Oh. You don't know when they went or where then?"

"No, sorry."

I said, "Oh, well, it was a very vague arrangement. You know, we just picked this place out of the atlas with a pin. Pure chance. It seems nice enough though."

"Yes, it seems so, doesn't it? Well, I expect I'll see you around. Ciao." And with a sudden decisiveness that was rather surprising, she turned and set off in the direction of the hotel. Only when she'd gone did I realise how much I'd been hoping for her company over dinner—and I couldn't then decide whether I specifically wanted *her* company or just didn't want my own.

I also found myself wondering whether it was just my imagination that she'd emphasised that word "seems."

FIVE

. . . .

I FOUND A RESTAURANT JUST OFF the square where I scattered a bit of largesse—well, more than a bit, in fact. These unassuming country restaurants are never quite so unassuming as one assumes—at least not in their prices. Still, there was plenty more largesse going to get scattered in my direction, I told myself, once I'd picked Piers up.

After the meal I looked in at the bar and phoned up Simon. All my fine sarcastic phrases left me the moment I actually heard his voice, groggy with late-night semiotics, and I found myself stammering out apologies while he snorted and asked what about the text books I'd borrowed. I told him I'd post them back and not to worry, I wouldn't be wanting a reference, and then he hung up with a final snort and a click.

The barman gave me a grappa and a disquisition on the penal system while in the background the video game machine emitted playful noises of saturation bombing and nuclear holocaust. Mauro the Hulk was one of the youths playing the machine, but he studiously ignored me and I certainly didn't tug his sleeve. Wednesday evenings were obviously a real riot in San Giorgio Veronese. I finished my drink and set off back to the hotel. No bomb throwers or gunmen were to be seen, and the castle looked no more than picturesquely sinister in the moonlight. I may even have broken into quiet song.

I woke up that night to the insistent wheedling note of a mosquito. I turned over and tried to find a more comfortable nook for my head between the pillow's lumps of coal. The sheets, as ever, resented my moving, and made their opinion clear with a stiff crackle of disapproval. The mosquito continued to sing.

For a few minutes I pretended not to notice while it made continual whining assaults on my eardrum. But when these attacks began to be accompanied by all the existential problems I'd shoved to the back-cupboards of my mind during the day (who am I, where am I, what's it all about?) I knew I'd have to do something about it. And it was undoubtedly easier to squash the mosquito than answer the questions.

I turned the light on—all fifteen bashful watts of it. My watch told me it was one-fifteen. I got up and patrolled the room, espadrille in hand. The surgically scrubbed walls and floor were entirely insect-free as far as I could see. And the light seemed to have stunned it into silence too. After five minutes of fruitless search I decided to go to the loo—more as something to do than in answer to any message from my bladder. I pulled my pyjamas from the rucksack and put them on, and then stepped into the corridor. There was a dim night-light halfway down the corridor so I didn't need to grope for a switch.

The bathroom glimmered with moonlight, rendered even more ghostly by the frosted windows. I entered the men's cubicle, again without turning the light on. Feeling groggy with sleep (and existential doubts), I dropped my trousers and sat on the cold porcelain. It was perhaps fractionally more comfortable than my bed. I may even have nodded off for a second or two in that regal position. Then I heard a noise at the window.

Instantly my every sense was on the alert—as keen and finely wired as they had been at each mosquito attack. Maybe I'd been expecting something to happen.

Well, no, that was nonsense: how could I have been? But what *was* true was that I obviously welcomed this intrusion of the unexpected as giving my chafing brain something new and more satisfactory to concentrate on—something far more chewable than my addled adolescent angst.

I sat dead still, staring at the door of my cubicle, which I was glad I'd locked, and I listened hard. The noise was that of scratching and fiddling. My keenness slid naturally into nervousness, as my imagination got to work; something hard and sharp was prying at the window catch—and my mind's eye saw in turn a sharp-nailed hand, claws, hooked talons, stilettos, and a horror-film combination of the lot. Then there was a crack and the window swung open.

Maybe it's just a guest who didn't dare ring the doorbell, I said to myself wishfully.

There was a moment's wheezing, and the horror-film vision seemed that much more likely: something black and faceless with hooked silver talons and bad breath. Then the thing shuffled on the sill and entered the room with a soft thump.

I suddenly realised my bladder was passing urgent messages, but I didn't dare reply. I squeezed my legs together. The thing reached the door to the corridor and opened it slowly and carefully. There was a pause and I imagined beady eyes peering up and down the corridor. Then it padded across the corridor and seemed to halt at the door opposite: Number 11, where Rita and Piers had stayed. By now I was leaning right forward so my face was almost touching the cubicle door, and I thought I could make out the noise of the distant door handle being tried. Then there was the faint padding of the footsteps towards the staircase—presumably to fetch the key.

At this point I released my bladder muscles together with a long sigh. Then I gently eased the bolt back and peered out of the cubicle. There was a clearer and colder silver light on the floor and wall of the room, now that the window was wide open to the moonlight. I walked over and peered out cautiously. There was no ladder, but there was a convenient balcony on the floor below, from the parapet of which one could easily reach the stone sill of the window I was standing at. This window had been chosen because it was unshuttered, I guessed, rather than because of its closeness to Room 11. It suddenly struck me that there might be an accomplice outside and I drew my head back in quickly.

I went to the door and wondered just how stupid it would be to peer out of it. Pretty damn so, I decided, and started to return to the cubicle. Then I thought that sitting there wasn't a great demonstration of genius either. I made a quick mental calculation of the time needed for a cautious padding Thing to go down the stairs, reach the entrance hall, pick up the key for Room 11 and come back again, and I decided I had a few seconds in hand.

I opened the door to the corridor, listened hard, heard nothing, and I slid along the corridor to my room.

I would have liked to lock the door but was afraid of the noise that would make, so I merely stood still, listening above my heartbeats and rapid breathing. I was getting rather good at this. All I heard was the mosquito's bel canto.

Then there was the scrape of a lock turning, and after a second or two the faint click of the door being closed again. The Thing was now in Room 11.

I decided to get dressed: whatever action I was going to take—and I really didn't know what yet—would be better taken in my full clothes. It forced me to calm down too: I knew that an over-hasty assault on my jeans in the dark would break the last resistance in the patch in the left knee.

I slid delicately into jeans, T-shirt, and espadrilles. I was now ready to take on anything—or any Thing.

I went over to the window and opened the shutters the tiniest crack: the moon shot a shaft sharply into the room and I realised I didn't dare put my face to that searchlit gap. I went back to the door and listened: still no noise. Maybe I should go for the confrontation direct. It might even be Piers in the room, and that would be my mission over. Off we'd go to the nearest phone, and then we'd have a coffee and a chat while waiting for his father to turn up. And then I'd be ready for my next case.

I opened the door and heard my heart thump away in protest. I padded down the corridor and stood for a second or two outside Room 11. I could hear the fumbling and creaking and rustling of furniture being disturbed: a search was going on, it seemed. My hand was a few centimeters from the handle, and then it struck me I had no weapon—I didn't even have a jacket pocket I could push two menacing fingers through.

I heard a sudden intake of breath and the fumbling and creaking stopped. Then there was a quiet rustling of paper. It seemed as if the search had yielded some kind of result. Two-thirds of a second later I was in the bathroom, and in the remaining third I was back in the cubicle. A homing instinct.

The bathroom door opened and footsteps crossed to the window. Then there seemed to be a change of mind and he padded back. Maybe he was wanting a pee. I suddenly realised I hadn't shot the bolt across. All would depend on whether he took any notice of the little symbols on the door or not. Or on whether it was a woman, I suddenly thought.

I realised I was curling in on myself, but however foetus-like I became, if he opened the door he would have to be fairly unobservant to miss me. My fingers were gripping the cold side of the porcelain. . . . Then I heard the door of the other cubicle open.

My eyes dropped to the gap below the partition. I could just see one tennis shoe. Then something rectangular and rigid like a book or a folder was propped up against the gap, with its top leaning against the other side of the partition, hiding the shoe. I squinted harder in the gloom: yes, definitely a folder. Was this what the Thing had found in the room?

I heard a zipper being lowered, and in that length of time— two and a half inches, one and a half seconds—I made a decision. It was a decision that called for instant action, without a second's further thought: the kind of decision that has given me some of my most wonderful moments of triumph—and landed me in some of my deepest bogs of crud.

One second later a noisy Niagara echoed round the bath-room and I bent down to the folder and whipped it through the gap. There was a gasp from the occupant (who definitely *wasn't* a woman), but the Niagara continued to flow and before it stopped I was out in the corridor and running to my own room.

As I reached my door I heard the loo door being pulled open. I was inside the room one tenth of a second later; I suppose I must have opened and closed the door, but I couldn't recall doing so. In the remaining nine-tenths of the second, my brain told me that the noise resounding in my ears was in fact the slam—which was presumably also responsible for the way the walls and floor were all vibrating. A second or two later, I started vibrating too, but that was just my heart knocking against my teeth.

I stood as still as was possible in this general situation of delirium tremens and listened to the corridor. The hum of reverberating bricks and mortar died down and silence reestablished itself. I hoped this meant he hadn't seen me, and hadn't been able to identify the slammed door. Once again I didn't dare turn the key. I listened and listened.

Silence—as utter as ever.

And then footsteps started padding down the corridor—in my direction. They paused once or twice, presumably to listen into the rooms on either side. I was going to have to use that key.

I put my fingers to the cold metal and started to turn. Suddenly the footsteps were pounding and my fingers were fumbling; the key jammed. Something hit the door like a mini-tornado and it burst inwards. I fell backwards, and a hundredth part of my brain remained cool enough to direct my right hand which sent the folder skidding under the chest of drawers by the wall. Then that hundredth joined the rest of me, which lay on the floor a prey to gibbering panic.

The doorway framed a crouching thug, who was revealed by the corridor night-light to have a knife and no face. I wasn't in the best tactical position for dealing with this kind of problem, being horizontal, winded, and pretty well out of my mind. But for half a second or so he couldn't decide what to do either, and my brain took advantage of this respite to send disciplinary orders to most parts of me, along the lines of "Now just stay cool"; they might not have been very convincing orders, but strangely enough when he finally did throw himself on top of me I found I was ready. I brought my knees up suddenly, and they caught his stomach in mid-flight, and at the same moment my arms grabbed up at his knife-holding wrist and heaved. He went further than he had intended and I found my face somewhere underneath his thighs. With quite irrelevant distaste I realised he hadn't rezipped his fly.

I squirmed out from underneath him and scrabbled to my feet. He was pulling himself up but extremely slowly. I realised that he must have smashed his head into the foot of the bed. While he was still only kneeling, I grabbed again at his wrist and wrenched the knife out of it, then jumped back with it. He got to his feet and put his hand to his head. He still had no face, I realised: it hadn't just been my panicking brain that had created the illusion. The light from the corridor and the moonlight through the crack in the shutters were sufficient to show me the black featureless oval of a balaclava, gashed across with a slit for the eyes. I didn't need the media-created association with terrorism to find it terrifying, however groggy he might be underneath it. I picked up the chair by the bed in my other hand and stood ready to use it as a shield—or a club. My pyjamas slid onto the floor.

Then we heard footsteps in the corridor, and a sleepily truculent voice saying, *"Insomma, ma cos'è 'sto casino?"*

The thug turned and pulled open the shutters. Suddenly he wasn't groggy anymore: in one wiry swing and twist of his body he was hanging from the sill, then there was the distant thud as he landed on the balcony below. I dropped the chair and went to the window and stared out, just in time to see him drop again down to the gravel and run crunchingly off.

Then there was a knock at my door which had swung to in the meanwhile. I closed the shutters and said, *"Avanti."*

The door opened and the hotel manager was revealed, drooping upwards in the gloom like some viscid and unwelcome apparition in an Edgar Allan Poe story. "Signore, what is all this noise?"

"Oh, er, sorry. There—there was a mosquito."

"A mosquito?" He turned on the light and stared at me in

some wonderment. Only then did I realise I was still holding the knife.

"I—er—"

"Signore, are you hurt?"

"What?" And I suddenly felt a hot stickiness trickling down my temple, where the knife must have grazed me as he and it went flying over me. "Oh, that—I was, was just trying to dig out the venom. I react very badly to mosquitoes."

"So I see, signore." And his eyes looked around the room, at my scrumpled pyjamas on the floor, the overturned chair, the bedclothes hanging drunkenly off the bed. . . .

"And I sleep very badly. I'm sorry if I disturbed anyone."

"My wife was worried," he said. "But if you are all right now, signore. Or would you like a plaster?"

"That's all right. I've got my own. I'm sorry again. But everything's all right now."

"If you are sure, signore." He turned towards the door.

"Yes, yes. Goodnight. I won't disturb your sleep again."

"Once woken, I rarely get back to sleep. Goodnight." He went out, closing the door behind him.

I waited in silence while his footsteps padded back down the corridor. Somewhere in the distance I heard a motorbike snarl to life and then go growling off.

I knelt down and pulled the folder out from under the chest of drawers. It was made of hardboard and was secured by an elastic strap. I eased this off and a collection of A4 photocopies slid out onto the sheets.

My first moment's disappointment was rebutted by the prosaic thought that nowadays even Long John Silver would take a photocopy of the map with him—if not get it sent by fax. It was only after this moment's disappointment that I realised that I *had* been expecting something like a time-yellowed map with scrawled skulls and crossbones and a big X for the treasure.

It must have been the obviously sensation-loving nature of Piers that had fuelled these expectations. Together, of course, with all those rumours of bejewelled silver statues.

But anyway what had I got? The photocopies were all of ruled pieces of notepaper, presumably from an exercise book. They were all in handwritten Italian. The handwriting was neat but nonetheless difficult to read on account of the poor quality of the reproduction, which was due either to a worn-out photocopier or to the faded ink of the originals. I skimmed quickly through them; there were ten sheets, and only one was in a different handwriting. This was a photocopy of a smaller sheet of paper and was in the form of a hastily written letter:

G,
Vieni alla cappella. Dopo mezzanotte. Starai al sicuro lì—il solito posto, ti ricordi? Sopra il castello, la pietra con l'anello. Verrò io a prenderti quando tutto questo casino sarà finito. Potrai anche lasciar la roba lì quando te ne vai. Non la troveranno mai.

The handwriting betrayed haste, but the actual message could not have been simpler or clearer:

Come to the chapel. After midnight. You'll be safe there—the usual place, you remember? Above the castle, the stone with the ring. I'll come and fetch you when all this mess is over. You can leave the stuff there too, when you go. They'll never find it.

This called for a bottle of rum.

SIX

· · ·

WELL, OF COURSE THERE WAS NO RUM, which was a pity. It would have served as a kind of cross between a celebration and a stimulant. I just had to make do with warm chlorinated tap water, and a liquorice tablet.

Then I sat on the bed and started to read the other sheets. It became clear very quickly that I was reading a kind of last testament from Giorgio Malberti, the saviour and subsequent loser of the silver St. George. He wrote in an unstilted Italian, with hardly any crossings-out. It gave the impression of being an unpremeditated, unself-conscious flow of thought, but this may have been the result of carefully premeditated self-consciousness.

These words are written late on the night of April 25th, 1944. I am with my comrades [the word in Italian here was *compagni,* as opposed to the Fascist *camerati*] *in our hideout above the valley—and here "military considerations" require that I be vague. However, there seems to be no point in concealing the fact that the nearest village is San Giorgio Veronese, since if these words are ever found, it will be on my corpse somewhere in or near the village. I will of course refrain from naming any of my comrades.*

Why am I writing anyway? And who for? Maybe

tomorrow night I'll read these lines and just laugh at them and tear them up—I suppose it is what I must hope. But I can't shake off a sense that things are coming to some sort of conclusion for me.

I don't say this out of despair or even out of mere exhaustion. I am in no way longing for an easy way out. I am still bitterly aware that I'm young—too young to die. But then I've seen so many younger people die round me in these last few months that my own life seems the result of mere luck. Maybe that's what I feel at bottom: that my luck's running out—and that it is not reasonable to expect any more of it.

This might prompt the question: why, if I feel like that, am I planning what I am *planning? Surely the enterprise I have in mind is one that calls for an extra dose of luck—a real dose of fortune from heaven. And yes, it's true: we will pull off the mission only if helped by St. George himself. (Let's hope the real red ones among my comrades don't look over my shoulders at these lines: it was hard enough to convince one or two of them of the importance of this strike against the Nazi-plunderers—I had to put it all in terms of political symbolism and morale-boosting of the common people. If they see me invoking the saints, they'll really think I've gone mad.)*

There are too many questions in this "last message" of mine so far—and they all begin with "why?" I haven't got round to answering any of them yet. But maybe this answers the first of these questions—why am I writing? I suppose I'm doing so just in order to find an answer to all these doubts. I'm hoping, that is, that the mere action of pushing the pen across the page will clear my mind for me. Because the worst thing for a soldier is to have doubts. That's probably why the intellectuals among us need the doctrine of Marx and Lenin before picking up the rifles. My farm-working and factory comrades seem to find a good dose of hatred quite sufficient.

*And as for who I'm writing for: well, I suppose as ever
I want the biggest audience possible.*

I put the paper down and took another sip of warm water.
That last sentence seemed pretty ironic: fifty years on his audience consisted of one confused semiforeigner in a hotel room in
his native village.

*I've always wanted universal approbation, right from
childhood. Or at least, universal attention. I've been
accused (by comrades, no less) of taking up communism
for this simple reason. What easier way to distinguish
myself, the local aristocrat's son, than by preaching
Marx in the local bars? Particularly in dangerous times
for such opinions.*

*Is that why I took up communism? Or was it to get at
my parents? Do I really believe in all that stuff about the
proletariat and the masses? Do I want to be governed by
Bepi here? (Who is at this moment cleaning his
fingernails with the bread knife.) Well, rather him than
the Duce, of course. And maybe one extremism needs to
be fought with another one. When the fighting's all over,
we can see about the revolution. And does Bepi really
believe in the revolution himself—beyond his pride in
having the same name as Stalin ("Bepi del Giasso," as he
calls him)? The fact that he persists in calling me Signor
Conte would suggest not. In fact, I find it hard to believe
that the Italians will ever do anything really
revolutionary—but then a year ago I would never have
believed that we would be fighting the Nazis and Fascists
in the hills.*

*What did I believe a year ago? While I was still a
student waiting for my call-up papers, to be sent to
Greece, Albania, North Africa, God knows where? I
suppose, like so many of my age, I just accepted the fact
that I had no control over my fate: I might make secret
speeches of protest, scandalise a few people in the bars,*

but like everybody else in the end I'd do what I was told—lackadaisically, unbelievingly—but I'd do it. The story of our nation.

The strange thing is that while I passed for the rebel, the fiery speechmaker, it was Federico who really believed that things could change: "You can only push people so far," he would say. "They'll turn." Speaking reasonably, quietly, as his way has always been, but truly believing it. And of course he's been proved right—even if it did take a full-scale invasion by the Nazis to bring it about.

Am I writing these words for Federico perhaps? Knowing how much he would like to be with us? It's funny: in most families it's the younger brother who plays the part of the rebel and balls-breaker, but in ours it's always been me, and "little Federico" has always been the quiet one. Except, of course, as I've just said, maybe Federico is the real rebel; he's just never felt the need to make a fuss about it, to wave any red flags. And maybe that's why Federico was the one to get beaten up by the Fascists—even though everyone said it was because he was my brother.

If you're reading these lines, Federico, know then that I was thinking of you and your broken leg as well, when I went into action. I know you don't believe in revenge, but I do, and I'll avenge that leg.

And there's no getting away from it—despite all our rows and all the bitterness, I'm thinking of you too, Mamma. It seems that I calculated correctly and this pen-pushing has helped to clear my mind. I realise that I'm going after that statue for you as much as anything else. I know how sad it made you when I stopped going to church and when you found us treating the family's own sacred relics without due respect: I suppose I'm hoping that a gesture for St. George will make up for a few things.

We may be Marxists, but we're still Italians, and when

*an Italian does something crazy you can bet your life
that in some way—maybe some entirely screwed up
way—he'll be doing it for Mamma.*

*I hope to God it's a good enough reason to risk ten
men's lives. But whatever happens, it will have been
entirely my responsibility.*

*Should I make some kind of will now? At this time it
seems hopeless to think of such things, which imply
some kind of belief in an operative legal system. And
come the revolution, what will I have to leave to
anybody anyway? My collection of Salgari novels? So
let's stick to salutations. I send them to my mother and
hope you will forgive whatever was merely petulant and
silly in my "rebellion." I know you've always hoped that
by ignoring all political matters they would go away, but
by now you will have realised that this war is rather too
large to be kept entirely out of the Malberti villa and
gardens. (And I hope the gardens are not suffering too
much from the want of a gardener. Bepi seems to miss
the place more than I do.)* [There was an asterisk at this
point, referring to a scrawled footnote at the bottom of
the page: *"Rereading this I see it might be hurtful to the
person to whom it's addressed: well, Mamma, you know
I've never pretended to be a homeboy—you spent all my
childhood looking for me at mealtimes, and you can't
expect me to have changed much since then."*] *Whatever
else we may have disagreed on, the one virtue you taught
me was loyalty: maybe you were thinking of loyalty to
different things, but take comfort from the fact that I
died loyal to my ideals—and ultimately to my family.*

*I've been loyal—and I know people have been loyal to
me. Here perhaps is the final motive behind this sudden
urge to commit things to paper—to acknowledge all
those who have stuck by me. I know that from my
childhood (another recurring phrase) I've been able to
inspire loyalty in people: whether in bands of
schoolchildren, or university students, or as now,*

freedom-fighters in the hills. But it's a gift that can work for good or ill: and I suppose that until July 25th, Mussolini himself had it—and for some, still does. So maybe for the first time in my life I'm realising that it's a responsibility rather than just a pleasure.

Have I used it well? That little boy, for example, following me all the way here, and then following us up into the hills? Should I have sent him away sooner? True, he has no one else to turn to here—but am I right to be encouraging him to follow me—to take me as a model? It's hardly a path to fortune. And Bepi himself: it would never have crossed his mind to take up arms, if "Signor Conte" hadn't done so first. Maybe I'll find some excuse to get him away from the action tomorrow. Like send him with a message up the valley.

Again questions, questions. . . . Let's stick to salutations. I send them to Federico, again—now hors de combat physically, but not spiritually or mentally, I'm sure. Forgive me for any time we argued (though I know it was always I who did the shouting, the taunting). I think I've come to appreciate your quiet qualities only now, when there are far too many people shouting.

I don't know how to finish this letter—but maybe it's better to leave it open-ended. I don't want to be too conclusive; I don't want to go into battle tomorrow, weighed down by too definite a sense of finality. So I'll stop here.

And he did. There was nothing else—no dramatic bloodstains or scrawled last gasp. Just a signature: "Giorgio Malberti."

It was enough to be going on with. I undressed, turned out the light and settled myself for a really good ponder.

I fell asleep almost instantly.

SEVEN

. . . . .

WHEN I WOKE UP IT WAS GONE seven o'clock. I swung myself out of bed. It would be best to get out of the hotel as early as possible. I was now the possessor of something that somebody had broken into the building to get hold of. That somebody could well now decide to break into me—via the skull, ribcage, or testicles—unless I foiled him by some dazzling display of professionalism, like getting up before eight o'clock.

I dressed and shaved—and then paused before packing. I couldn't leave the village so soon—and there was no other hotel. There wasn't even a left-luggage office anywhere nearer than Caldiero station. After thinking it over, I did the reverse of packing: I took everything from my rucksack and scattered it in the furthest corners of all the drawers and cupboards the room possessed: it lessened the chances of a smash-and-grab raid on my belongings. Then, on a last-minute inspiration I took the papers from the folder and replaced them with a series of notes that Simon had given me on "Structuring a Didactic Unit for the Classroom Situation." I then placed the folder on top of the wardrobe. It seemed churlish to leave them nothing. I slipped the original documents inside a Terry Pratchett novel and then went along to the loo—my answer to so many of life's crises.

I stood up on the rim of the bowl and put my hand around the back of the water tank. It was secured to the wall by two metal brackets, which were reassuringly dusty rather than gooey or gungy. The Terry Pratchett novel rested there securely and invisibly. I'd just have to hope that my intruder, if he came back for another search, had not seen *The Godfather* too recently.

I was out of the building by seven-twenty. I saw no sign of the hotel manager: maybe morning sunlight would shrivel him to dust and dentures. The front door was still double-locked; I had a quick look out of the window first and saw no obvious lurkers in the courtyard. I opened the door and slipped out. The street too seemed clear once I'd left the courtyard. I made my way towards the square feeling cheered: I was up against amateurs—mere muddling amateurs.

I called in at the news-agents-cum-tobacconist in the square and asked the man if he had any maps of the area. He at once offered me three different maps, a guidebook to the village, a guidebook to Verona, a guidebook to Italy, an assortment of postcards (Juliet's Balcony, Juliet's Tomb, the Arena, the Rialto Bridge, and Leonardo's Last Supper) and a book on the Veronese dialect. I bought a map and a guidebook to the village (*San Giorgio Veronese: Its Art, History, and Legends* by Silvio Pigozzi).

I went onto the bar and joined the wimps who were drinking cappuccino. The barman himself was talking away exactly as he had been the previous evening, and I wondered if he'd been left switched on all night.

But after a few sips at my cappuccino I realised that the topic of conversation was new.

"Did you hear it? Did you hear it?" he repeated to every new face—even to mine. "A sudden great *whoomf!*—around three o'clock I suppose, and I looked out of the window and I said, I said to my wife, that'll be them again: more trouble on the hill. I looked outside—could see the flames—more trouble, I said. Did you hear it?"

One or two bolder customers—mostly grappa drinkers—put a word in and said they had or they hadn't. "I heard the fire engine and the police too," said one little man, trying to establish a first.

"Well, everybody must have heard them," said the barman dismissively. "Their din went on for hours. But that first *whoomf!* Just like that—*whoomf!* Like—like a sudden great *whoomf!* You know, like a sudden great sheet of flame. Well, that was what it was in fact. A sudden sheet of flame. I said to my wife, did you hear that? Did you hear it? And she said—she said—well, then I said, that'll be trouble again, you mark my words, that'll be trouble, I said."

I'd obviously slept too well. I'd casually assumed, as I slipped back into the laminated sheets, that the night could have nothing more in store—but I'd underestimated San Giorgio Veronese: never call it a day without a bang.

I kept listening in. I gathered that there had been another incendiary attack—this time on the second-hand car that some of the immigrants had recently bought. Nobody had been hurt, but the car had been destroyed.

Several people ventured a "Shocking," and a "What's San Giorgio coming to?" and the barman stated, "Of course there was none of this sort of trouble before they came," and several heads nodded. One decaffeinated coffee put in a mild protest: "You can't really blame them. I shouldn't think they like having their car bombed."

There was a mixed reaction to this. A few sympathetic *cappuccini* said, "Yes, poor bastards," "Not their fault," but most of the grappas and one or two *espressi* voiced utter contempt. "Where'd they get the money for a car anyway?" said one. "Bet they hadn't got a licence," said another, and the barman sealed the argument: "There was none of this before they came."

I finished my breakfast and left the bar. I went towards the castle end of the square, remaining vigilant for any possible shadowers or observers. Nobody followed me out of the bar, and there seemed to be nobody hanging around in the square. I made my way along the road at the foot of the hill. I could see the blackened shell of the *Cinquecento* ahead of me; two Carabinieri were standing next to it, talking to the black man I'd spoken to the previous evening. Three villagers stood at a distance, gawping. One of them was Mauro the Hulk.

Faces turned as I approached, and I did my best to look no more than a casual tourist whose only interest was the date of the castle. Then it struck me that even the most medievally minded tourist would be distracted by the sight of a burnt-out car, and I let myself glance at that too. Then I thought maybe my switch of attention had been a little too artificial and I looked back up at the castle with studied naturalness. Then I thought that this to-and-froing was a giveaway too. . . .

Then I told myself angrily that this was all crazy: a giveaway to what? I hadn't done anything. I gave a casual nod and smile to the Carabinieri, the black man, the smoking wreck, the villagers—Hulk included.

The black man called out, "Seems we weren't ready enough."

I nodded again. "Bad story."

The Carabinieri looked at me. "You know this man?" one of them asked.

"Well, we got chatting yesterday," I said, maintaining my English accent. "I'm just a visitor here."

Mauro the Hulk moved forward. "He was snooping around last night. I saw him."

"I was going up to see the castle. As I am now."

The Carabinieri fortunately weren't overimpressed by Mauro as a witness. Nobody else said anything so I kept walking. I felt my T-shirt sticking to my back, and I had to force myself not to look back.

I passed their barn-type house. There were four or five black men and women standing by the doorway, talking seriously. They did no more than glance at me—but it was not a casual glance. I proceeded up the hill.

The castle looked a lot less sinister in full daylight: there were butterflies, not bats, aflit around its towers, and the scuttering noises in the undergrowth suggested rabbits rather than vampires.

I pulled out my map. I had to keep on up the same path, it seemed, to reach the chapel of San Giorgio. It turned out to be another ten minutes' walk, with the path getting rougher and occasionally turning into rocky steps. Eventually these steps twisted and rose steeply towards a small flat clearing, where a simple stone building stood, with a stubby tower abutting at the back.

Very sweet—just as Linda had said. There was a rough Romanesque arch over the entrance door, with two protruding stone shapes on either side, which could have been anything from lions to lambs. In the lunette above the door, there were muddy stains which, with some imagination, I was able to interpret as a frescoed St. George and dragon.

At the bottom of the door there was an ancient bolt. I pulled it and the door opened with a squeaky scrape. I walked into the musty interior. There was nothing but a simple altar and two wooden benches with kneelers in front of it. The walls were stained with vague shadowy shapes which must have been remnants of frescoed saints: I could just about make out another stiff St. George with languid dragon.

I thought back to the cryptic message, presumably addressed to Giorgio Malberti: "The stone with the ring." I looked around the walls and the floor and could see no stones which had anything resembling a ring. After a few minutes of careful perusal—I even got down on hands and knees—I walked out into the sunshine again and closed and rebolted the door.

I walked all round the building. There were no large stones anywhere—certainly none with any rings on. I kept prowling for another ten minutes or so, continually extending the radius of my search so that I had to do a good deal of clambering, crawling, and jungle clearing.

Eventually I returned to the church, wiping the back of my neck. It was getting sultry. I sat on the ground leaning against the church and pulled the guidebook out of my shoulder bag.

It was a cheaply produced paperback volume: the publication date was 1985, but the whole book had a postwar-shortage feel to it, from the cheap paper to the blurred black-and-white photos. These showed the village seen from the hills, Piazza Malberti, the Villa Malberti, the Malberti Museum—and the statue of St. George.

I studied this last. He wasn't shown in a vigorous or violent pose: he held a chipped sword upright and stared straight forwards with one foot slightly advanced. He was impressively belligerent in attitude but, as Linda had said, was squat rather than towering. I wondered why he reminded me of Mauro, and decided after much staring that it must be the pugnacious grimace. The photo, I noted, was a prewar one of the original statue, not the copy that now stood in the museum. The silver did not exactly gleam from the picture, and the jewels—studding his sword-hilt and armour and helmet—could have been from Woolworths, as far as I could tell. Nonetheless, it was a statue one knew one would remember.

Silvio Pigozzi, the writer of the guide, was clearly an enthusiast: he described the statue from helmet to pedestal and savoured the name of every precious stone. He finished his description with words of hope: "Although we can but mourn the tragedy of this statue's disappearance, at the same time it seems inconceivable that anyone could be of so barbaric a frame of mind as to have destroyed such a masterpiece: we must hope that some day the statue will emerge from its hiding place—or that those conserving it will realise their duty to the world."

He reported in full the legend of the statue's origin, and was obviously a supporter of good legends over dull history. At the end of the tale, he asked a couple of rhetorical questions: "Although no historian will guarantee the authenticity of this story, can we doubt that such a striking masterpiece had its origin in some striking, even if not miraculous, event? And who knows but that some equally striking event will bring it back to light again one day, so that it may continue to watch over the village of San Giorgio Veronese?"

He then recounted the story of its disappearance, very much as Linda had done, but in a rather less rapt fashion. Events of fifty years or so back clearly didn't stir him quite so much as those of ten centuries. He paid dutiful homage to Giorgio Malberti and said that the Malberti family, "as is well-known, continues in its tradition of dedication to the public good, as in their generous donations to the museum." Silvio Pigozzi, the back cover told me, was the director of the museum.

He had little to say about the chapel itself: he gave it a date, mentioned its faded frescoes and called it *"deliziosa."* I wondered whether he'd talked to Linda about it.

Well, this was all very pleasant, I thought, stretching my legs out fully. If I wanted I could now doze off in the sun, my back against St. George, my book by my side and the crickets chirruping a squeaky chorus in the background. But unless the saint dropped in on my dreams to enlighten me, I wouldn't be getting any closer to those four thousand pounds—to discovering the whereabouts of Piers, that is.

I pulled myself to my feet. If the saint wouldn't come to me, I'd have to go to him. I set off down the hill.

EIGHT

. . . . .

THE MUSEUM WAS IN A BUILDING to one side of the parish church, the kind of annex one would expect in England to see advertising a jumble-sale or over-sixties coffee morning. A notice told me to ring at Number 5 if the door was closed, which it was. There was no added notice about it being closed for family mourning, so I rang the bell indicated and the door was answered after a minute or so by Signor Menegallo. He was dressed in the same grey trousers and open shirt, and the face stubble was definitely not designer now. He gave no sign of recognising me, merely grunting when I asked if he would mind opening up the museum. He shuffled across the road, turned the key and said, "The lights are over there. When you want me, just open one of the glass cases."

"What? Why?"

"That sets off the alarm in my house. I'll be along straightaway."

"With the Carabinieri?"

He just grunted and shuffled off home again.

I switched on the lights in the museum's main room. There were rickety glass cases all round, mostly containing church treasures: chalices, crucifixes, vestments, reliquaries. I should have brought along a big bag: by now Gigi would be bound to have run into someone in Verona who'd know how to place this sort of stuff. Above the cases were a few seventeenth- and eighteenth-century paintings of saints posing in what generally appeared to be coal pits. The labels were written in faded ink on curling slips of yellowed paper.

I moved into the next room and switched on the light there. It was in complete contrast: there was concealed neon lighting and the cases were of light brown against cool white walls. There had obviously been the hand of a designer in this room, arranging things so that one's attention fell at once on the central glass case which stood on a simple metal stand. There was St. George.

Three feet of solid-seeming silver and jewels: imposing, threatening, stern and eye-catching. Unfortunately he still reminded me of Mauro.

It wasn't the only eye-catching thing in the room: the back wall seemed less of a wall than a billboard placed there to hold a big notice in red letters on a white background: "AULA MALBERTI."

My eyes returned to St. George. There was a placard set in a little marble plinth in front of the case: this recounted the story of the statue and stated how the Malberti family had ordered and arranged the construction of this extension to the museum to honour the memory of Giorgio Malberti, who had died fighting against tyranny *"per la patria."*

There were several other items that celebrated the Malberti family. On the walls were a few eighteenth- and nineteenth-century portraits, several views of the villa and a family tree. I studied this last and saw that the line looked on the point of petering out—hence, perhaps, all this desperately public gathering of mementoes and keepsakes. The last teetering twigs of the trees were thus laid out:

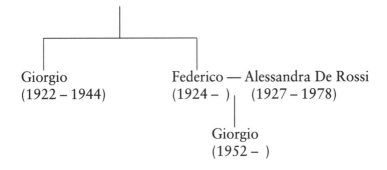

Giorgio
(1922 – 1944)

Federico — Alessandra De Rossi
(1924 –)   (1927 – 1978)

Giorgio
(1952 –)

This seemed to suggest that the enormous villa on the hill housed just a father and a son. I studied an eighteenth-century painting of it, which was very precise on architectural detail but a little looser on perspective: it represented the villa and the grounds as occupying two-thirds of the hill.

I pottered around a little longer, looking at the various "School of . . . ," "Workshop of . . . ," "Attributed to . . ." paintings, and the various obscure bits of obscure saints in flashy reliquaries, and then I lifted the flap of a case. I could just hear the distant tinkle-tinkle. I waited in the Malberti room.

Menegallo appeared after about three minutes. He'd been in the bathroom, he explained. I noticed with relief that his speech, while not likely to win any elocution prizes, wasn't quite so slurred as it had been the previous afternoon; maybe he hadn't been able to face the thought of the barman's voice at this hour.

"Nice little museum," I said chattily.

Perhaps not the most brilliant of conversation openers, and it didn't get much more than a grunt out of him.

"Do you know the Malberti family yourself?" I then said, with a jerk of my head to the family tree.

That was more like it. He said, "I should say so. Used to be gardener for them—up at the villa."

"What—that enormous garden?" I glanced at the painting on the wall, which depicted in meticulous detail the place's every status symbol, including stables, out-buildings, informal *giardino inglese* with formal chapel above it, medieval tower and sundial, and tried to imagine this little shuffling man in charge.

"That's right. Right back before the war."

Well, he'd probably been a little nimbler then. "So you knew Giorgio Malberti?"

"Knew him? Better than his own brother. He was a man, he was."

"Oh, yes? Deserves his fame, does he?"

"He was a man, he was. I'd have followed him anywhere. I did too. Into the mountains. I was with him. Those were heroic days." The red-rimmed eyes were fixed on the other side of the room and the century. I wondered how Zeno had listened to these stories: in admiration or mockery or just boredom?

"So you were a partisan?" I said.

He sat down on the chair by the door. "I was with them," he said. "Up in the hills. And then Signor Giorgio died."

"Yes. I read about it. Terrible. That was when the statue disappeared, wasn't it?"

"That's right."

"Were you there—when it happened?"

"No. They'd sent me with a message to another band further up the valley. An important message." He paused. "But I heard about it from the boy," he then added, as if to make it clear that he did know what he was talking about.

"What boy?"

His eyes screwed up in the effort to remember. He didn't seem at all curious about my curiosity: this stagger down memory lane clearly provided a relief from more recent events and thoughts. (Or so I told myself, in an attempt to crush those rising qualms again.) "Gianni, his name was," he said eventually. "Just a kid whose parents had died somewhere down south. Bologna or Florence or somewhere. Came to San Giorgio to stay with relatives and then joined up with Signor Giorgio. Followed him everywhere. He saw it all."

"What—the death?"

"Yes. He was coming up with provisions or something and he saw the Germans surround the house. He couldn't do a thing, of course—except watch it. Just a kid too. Terrible days those."

I didn't remind him that he'd called them heroic half a minute before. There wasn't really any contradiction. "And so the statue definitely perished?"

"Everything did. Ten men—the house—everything inside." He shook his head.

"Terrible," I said, and I meant it. "What did you do then?"

"I went and hid," he said simply. "I couldn't do much on my own, could I? I went to a cave in the woods above the village here, and my sister brought me food."

"What—for the rest of the war?"

"Yes. Terrible days. Never been so cold in my life. Mind you, in the spring it wasn't so bad. And I managed to make the cave quite comfortable, with straw and things."

"And nobody ever found you?"

"They never looked," he said. "And I'd chosen the cave carefully."

"I suppose you brought your children up on these stories," I said, taking a tentative step towards the present.

A grimace further creased the old leather of his face: whether of pain, distaste, or just surprise I couldn't tell. "I brought them up right," he said. "Nobody can say I didn't."

This was just automatic self-defence. Then he went on, "They always liked to hear of my adventures in the war. They really did." He put one hand to his eyes and wiped away something. "At least they did when they were little."

I found my mouth had gone dry, and remembered the same thing had happened when I'd had to force myself to ask Sir Alfred a brutal question about his son. But of course *any* question about Menegallo's son was brutal. I swallowed and said, "And later?"

"Well, all kids laugh at their elders a bit, don't they? Only natural. But Zeno wasn't a delinquent. Just high-spirited. All right, so he'd have his bit of fun now and then. . . ." Again he was talking to the world rather than to me.

"Was he ever interested in the story of the St. George statue?" I said.

He looked up slowly. "Why do you ask?"

"I don't know. It's a fascinating story. I thought maybe . . ."

"It's really strange," he said. "Strange. You know the day before he . . . before he got . . ."

"Yes," I said, sparing him the words.

"Well, he suddenly asked me about it, and he even asked to come and see it in the museum. And he asked me all sorts of questions, and I said if he was really interested he should talk to Signor Pigozzi. . . ."

"The director."

"That's right. So he did. He went round to his house straightaway. What made you think—"

"Nothing. I just wondered." I'd better not ask for Pigozzi's address. I tried to change the subject. "Do you keep up with Giorgio Malberti's brother?"

"Il Conte?" His communism obviously hadn't gone very deep.

"I suppose so."

"He's all right. Not like his brother was, mind you. Much quieter: Giorgio was the real lad. Pulled all the girls too." This even got a chuckle out of him—a rusty, not to say dilapidated one. "Federico never had a chance when Giorgio was around. But he didn't mind. More the scholar type, know what I mean? Reading books and that. I was telling an English girl—a blond one, you know her?—was telling her she should get in touch with the count. He'll have stories about Giorgio to tell her. And about the statue maybe. Or at least about why Giorgio was so keen on getting it back. I suppose a brother's most likely to understand such things. Family, you know." This touched off another memory. "Why did Zeno get interested in it? Do you think—do you think St. George will have put in a word for him? I mean, he wasn't a churchgoer—neither am I—but if he was getting interested, maybe . . ."

I felt more uncomfortable than ever about my intrusion on his grief. I could hardly tell him that I thought Zeno's interest most likely to have been in the saint's market value. I said, "Yes, I'm sure, I'm sure. Thank you for—for everything. Maybe I'll call on the count, as you say." I wasn't sure why I added this last. Acute embarrassment had befuddled me, and I think my main thought was not to let him know I was going to try and see this Pigozzi fellow: that would make my interest in Zeno too clear.

He was still mumbling away about St. George as he turned the lights out: the statue still hulked in the gloom. I wished it a final good-bye and we left the building. I had another moment of embarrassment while I wondered whether a tip was in order: it turned out that it was. Just before he shuffled back to his house, I pointed out that he'd left the keys in the lock.

NINE

· · · ·

THERE WAS A PHONE-BOX IN THE SQUARE which turned out still to have its directory. Silvio Pigozzi was in the book and his address was beautifully self-explanatory: "Il vicolo dietro il campanile, 9"—Lane behind the bell-tower, number 9. I thought there was no sense in trying to call him for an appointment: he might say no. And anyway the youth of San Giorgio Veronese had already begun their engine jam session around the Malberti monument.

Number 9 was a quietly crumbling house behind the apse of the church. As is often the case in Italy, although the building looked from the outside as if nothing had been done to it since Attila the Hun's last visit, it had a modern bell-push and intercom. Pigozzi's was the top bell-push of three, and his name was displayed thus: "Dott. Prof. S. Pigozzi." I rang and eventually a distant tinny voice answered: *"Sì?"*

"Good morning, professor," I said in my careful tourist-Italian. "I'm a visitor to San Giorgio Veronese, and I was wondering if I could speak to you about the village." Could I tell him I was one of his most avid readers?

"Why?"

"Well, I've read your guidebook and become very fascinated with the legends of the place." I emphasized the word legends. "I wondered whether we might talk them over."

The door clicked open. I walked up a musty staircase, lit

halfway up by a plastic shrine to the Madonna. At the top of the stairs a man in baggy trousers and pullover was awaiting me. He was already smiling and nodding as I turned the corner in the stairs. I shook his hand, which was dry and flakey to the touch (how come he wasn't sweating in that pullover?), and he said, "Welcome, welcome, Signor . . . ?"

"Brown." No point tiring my imaginative powers.

He ushered me into his flat, his eyes glowing with pleasure behind his glasses. The inside of the house hadn't been touched since Attila's last visit either. It resembled a library that had been hit by an earthquake. The books spilled out of the shelves, onto the tables, chairs, floor, and here and there were obviously making valiant attempts to climb up and open the windows—something else that hadn't been done since the Dark Ages. I breathed in the heady compound of dust, mildew, and mouldered erudition that passed for air in the room, while Professor Pigozzi fussed around trying to find a few square inches of buttock-space for his guest. Eventually he found a leather armchair in the corner; he shifted the books that it held onto the floor or shoved them firmly down into the chair's own crevices. He himself perched on the edge of a chair drawn up at a desk.

I suppose he wasn't much over sixty, if that, but he seemed ancient—or at least antique. It was in fact difficult not to compare him with his own volumes: there was something dog-eared and tattered about his clothes and something musty about his complexion; his slouchy posture suggested a loose binding—perhaps, on the evidence of the gleam in his eyes, a cracked one.

"So you've read my little book," he said.

"Yes, I have indeed," I said. "I'm particularly fascinated by the legend of the old statue."

"Aha," he said, and rubbed his hands together. He really did—and I could swear that there issued a cloud of dust. "Are you, erm, professionally interested in such matters? A scholar?"

"Well, er—" It didn't take me long to debate whether or not

to tell him I was a professor of Medieval History—just the time needed to review all my knowledge of the subject. "No. I'm just a passing visitor, but I'm very intrigued."

"Ah." His disappointment was clear: maybe he'd hoped I had a spare Chair on offer—or at least free essay space in some learned journal. But he recovered very quickly as enthusiasm took over. "The statue, you say. The gift of King Pepin."

"Well, yes, if we can believe it."

"Why should we doubt it? Why should we doubt it?" He put his hand out and pulled a large volume from the middle of a stack on the desk; the stack collapsed in a tottering clatter, one or two of the books apparently turning to instant powder. He took no notice. "Here we are: Pipino's residence in Verona— his visit to the surrounding countryside. As attested by contemporary evidence. The village of Illasi and the castles—Illasi, Tregnago, Cogollo . . . It's all here." He was pointing to a large page of Latin script, and I could do little but smile and nod. But at least his Italian was refreshingly clear and unaccented after Menegallo's slurred dialect. "Some would have it that this merely testifies to the tributes paid by the villages to his court, and they base this reading on these words here in this line, seeing them as, referring to his tithe-collectors' journeys rather than his. But really: would a contemporary witness—a monk, to boot—have seen any point whatsoever in reporting such humdrum circumstances? Is it likely?"

"No, I suppose not," I said.

"Furthermore, as I established once and for all in my article in the *Journal of Antiquarian Research* in '73, these trips were very much part of court practice. . . ." He talked for another ten minutes, his sentences becoming more and more entangled and his references more and more abstruse. He quoted from Latin texts, from German historians, and from his own essays on the subject. He fumbled among his books, showing unexpected vigour as he leapt up to pluck leather-bound volumes from the ends of shelves, from the depths of sofas, from underneath undrunk glasses of wine, and from the midst of fungus-furred journals; volumes that he would then flourish with an air of defiant triumph, as if he'd scored a definitive victory against hordes of unheeding scholars and hostile household objects. I gathered this wasn't the first time he had defended the truth of the legend: Pepin, he believed, had definitely visited the village, had definitely undergone some mystical experience there ("And who are we, we feeble modern sceptics and scoffers, to deny the possibility of such experiences?"), and had therefore commissioned a statue and a chapel to commemorate the experience. This was the central line of argument, and by learning to stay on this line and not trail after him down some of the boggier parenthetical side paths ("As I wrote to Professor Cerclin in '65, who made the fundamental error in his own essay in '62, simply because he ignored the evidence I'd presented in my article the year before . . ."), I managed to follow him through to his conclusion: "The so-called legend is—as is often enough the case, were we a little less blinkered and prejudiced by the modern taste for self-doubt—the legend, I say, is the history."

"So you think he really saw St. George?" I said, when he sat back still brandishing a volume whose pages were pasted together with (I think) *pesto genovese.*

"And why not? Why not?"

"But I mean, St. George—the dragon. Even the Church says—"

It was as if I'd cited *Men Only.* "The Church," he said, with a contemptuous wave of his hand (a leather-bound volume became an instant paperback). "The Church. Dismissing its own history. Demoting saints: not considered relevant—isn't that the excuse? St. Christopher and St. George didn't play the guitar or deliver a message about rain forests, so out they go. Everything has to be judged by our feeble twentieth-century perspective; centuries of faith and centuries of dogma and learning all go for nothing. How can we be sure of anything? is the Church's feeble modern wail, when they should realise that their job is to give people certainties. The people don't need doubts and qualms."

"But, well, dragons . . . ," I said, trying, as I sank into his nineteenth-century armchair and breathed his medieval air, to keep a modicum of feeble twentieth-century perspective. "I mean to say . . ."

"Did Pepin say anything about dragons?"

"No, but if you bring in St. George—"

"St. George is simply the type of the warrior-saint: virtuous, heroic, manly. Dragons can be taken as exemplary of the kind of dangers such a saint would be thought of as having faced."

"Symbolic, you mean."

"Another nasty twentieth-century word, but I suppose it might do. They believed in them, however, just as you and I are expected to believe in—in—greenhouse effects and black holes." There was a little more emphasis on the "you" than the "I" here. "Or UFOs. Or computer games."

"Do you suppose that's why the partisans considered it important to get the statue back—its symbolic connotations?"

He almost winced at the twentieth-century sound of this. But then he said, "I suppose some such consideration must have weighed with them. Indeed, on the other side, they say that Hitler himself had ordered the original sequestration of the statue."

"Hitler?"

"Well, yes. Pepin, who came to help the Pope against the Longobards, can be considered the defender of a new world order against barbarism, and this of course is the image the Nazis liked to have of themselves. And as I said, St. George has always been loved by warriors the world over. And quite rightly. We need things to look up to—whereas nowadays the Church would just have us looking at the dust. You may remember an essay of mine on this subject in—"

I broke in hastily. "What about the statue's contents? Isn't it supposed to be a reliquary?"

"It is supposed to be, yes." He repeated my words with a certain irony—at the expense of my scepticism, rather than the statue's contents.

"So where did the, um, saint's bits come from? I mean, if he was merely appearing to Pepin?" I had realised that gentle provocation worked better than mere lip-hanging in getting him to talk.

"There was an international market in such objects. If you were putting up a shrine to a saint, acquiring a suitable part of his anatomy was no problem if you had the money. I'm told that in these enlightened days pop-singers' sunglasses or cigarette ends can be similarly obtained."

I thought I should try and move a little closer to my real aims. "Do you often get people coming to talk to you about these things?"

"Well, it happens. It happens from time to time." There was something wistful in his voice.

Maybe, I thought, it didn't happen quite so often as he would have liked—or quite so often as it used to. There was no suggestion that I'd *interrupted* him in any way: indeed, the teetering, tottering erudition all around was not the clutter of a man hard at work on some academic project, but the chaos of a man with a million theories and nothing to apply them to. The scholarly wars that he'd waged without quarter in learned journals were all in the past: he'd cited no essay or article more recent than the seventies. Perhaps his antagonists had all died off—or had taken up computer games. "Is there a lot of local interest?" I said.

"Not quite as much as one might wish," he said. "Foreigners such as yourself seem more intrigued on the whole."

"But," I said, "it's a wonderful story. A village should be proud of it. You mean, they don't go to the museum? They don't learn about the legends?"

"The schoolchildren will occasionally be taken to the museum."

This, I gathered from his tone, was not an educational policy of his own choosing. "It's a fascinating place," I said. "I got talking to the caretaker. He told me how his own son had suddenly become interested in the story. He said he'd called on you, in fact."

"Ah, yes." His brow was furrowed: thinking back a day or two was clearly a lot tougher than a decade (or millenium) or two. "A strange young man. Didn't I read somewhere that he'd come to—come to an unfortunate end?" He looked vaguely around the room as if wondering which learned journal had touched on the subject.

"Yes. A very sad story. What do you think was behind his sudden interest?"

"Well, I don't like to speak ill of the—the dead—"

"No."

"But I fear his real interests were rather basely commercial. He kept insisting on the weight of the silver and asking me about the value of the various jewels. . . . He seemed to have no curiosity whatsoever in hagiographic tradition."

"Really?" I said. "Strange. Do you think he thought he might have a chance of finding it?"

"Well, I did wonder whether that was in his mind, but he was such an odd character. He wouldn't answer a direct question. And the whole time he continued to chew gum and look around himself in a most shifty fashion."

"But did he say *why* he was interested?"

"No. No." A pause. "Oh, he *did* say something about a friend of his being the one really interested, but I didn't give much credence to that."

"A friend?"

"Yes."

"Not a foreign friend, by any chance?"

"Ah, it may even have been." He was looking at me in some puzzlement. "I can't remember: which university did you say you're at?"

"Well, I'm not—not officially. That is, I, er, I studied at Oxford." Well, I took my O'levels there, after all. "But he didn't mention a name?"

"What name would he have mentioned?"

I decided there was little point in being over-discreet: it was unlikely that anything I ever said to him would stray beyond these four walls; the words would just hang around, adding a little 1990s tang to the room's medieval brew. "Does Ainsley ring any bells?" I said.

"Ah. Ainsley." He pronounced it "Aheenslee." "I don't recall it." He was more puzzled than ever. "Is he at Oxford?"

"Well, associated with it," I said vaguely. "The fact is, this chap, Piers Ainsley, seems to have disappeared, while making a study of this statue. And I've been wondering whether he might actually have come here."

"I see. So the university has sent you, has it? How curious."

"Well, after a fashion. But can you remember whether Zeno—the young man who was murdered, that is—said anything about Piers Ainsley—or anything that might indicate he'd met him?"

He thought very hard now. "He simply mentioned a foreign friend who was curious about the statue—but who was staying in Verona. Would that be right?"

"Well, yes."

He was looking very disappointed now. "So your real interest is in this Ainsley, and not the story of the statue?"

"Well, no. That is—well, the two things go together. Or rather, it's been most fascinating—and I certainly would like to learn more about the statue. . . ." I was burbling. I got a grip on myself. "For example, do you yourself believe it might have survived?"

"Oh, yes. I'm sure of it."

"Even though it's supposed to have been in a house that got burnt to—to cinders."

"The hideout was destroyed along with the men in it, but they may have put the statue in some secure place before going to the hideout." Then his expression grew almost pleading. "They *must* have done so. However incompetent they may have proved themselves otherwise, they surely can't have failed to ensure the statue's safety. A masterpiece like that . . ."

"Do you remember it? I mean, do you remember the event yourself?"

He shook his head. "I didn't live in San Giorgio then. I only came here in the fifties. But I came because of the statue."

"You came looking for it?"

"You might say that. I was teaching at the University of

Verona and my studies into King Pepin brought me here. I'm from the Marche myself."

"And have you ever looked for it? Looked for the safe place the partisans might have put it?"

"In my younger days I walked the hills often."

"Oh really?" I said. So fresh air wasn't fatal to him. Actually, I realised, he wasn't quite so frail as he first seemed. His skin might resemble old vellum in texture, but he clambered up his shelves with a spidery dexterity and held large volumes with surprising ease.

He went on, "But the person you should really ask on this subject—if you are truly interested—is the count. Count Malberti, Giorgio Malberti's younger brother. An enlightened man—unlike so many of his class. Unlike his own ancestors, indeed, whose respect for their possessions was minimal: pulling down their chapel, selling their paintings, their library . . ." He shook his head. "I believe, indeed, that the count's son is another such Hun. If our aristocracy is degenerate, what hope can there be for the people? But the count himself is a true historian and his concern for family history has led to his investigating all possible tales and rumours regarding the events of '44."

"I see. Are there so many tales?"

He absentmindedly picked up a piece of bread, which was beginning to sprout a delicate green fur, and bit off a piece. "I imagine where anything of such value is concerned there are bound to be tales. Who knows? Perhaps your Ainsley will have called on the count?"

I stood up. "Well, thank you for giving me your time and your expertise."

"Not at all. My best wishes to Oxford. Do you know Percy Falkend?"

"No."

"A complete cretin. A moron. Do give him my best wishes."

"Er, yes. Sorry for disturbing you, taking up your time." A thought struck me. "Have you yourself ever seen the real statue?"

"Yes," he said. He chewed another piece of billiard-table bread. "Yes," he repeated. Then he shook his head. "But only in dreams."

He then led the way to the door, beating back the books that seemed to have retaken possession of the path we'd hewn earlier. He shook my hand at the door and then put his other hand rather unexpectedly on my shoulder. "You'll excuse my rambling, won't you? I get carried away. You know, beneath this moth-eaten exterior there's the heart of a true romantic."

This threw me. I could only burble something along the lines of, "Yes, yes, thank you, I'm sure, yes—"

"Let me know how your investigations proceed," he said.

"Yes, of course."

"And St. George be with you." He gave my hand a final papery squeeze.

I made my way back down the stairs, past the plastic Madonna and out into the sunshine, feeling a little dazed. I stood still for a few seconds, enjoying the novel sensation of breathing.

There was a car drawn up onto the pavement—well, half on, half off. I'd noticed it before, but now the almost artistic badness of its parking made me look at it again, and I saw that the backseat was covered in books and journals: leather bindings, cracked spines, yellowing pages. So he does come out into the twentieth century occasionally, I thought. Amid the books one cheap volume stood out rather: it had a garish 1950s cover, depicting a pirate brandishing a sword, a choppy sea, and palm-tree-covered island: *I Tigri di Mompracem,* by Salgari— Italy's Jules Verne or G. A. Henty.

I wasn't sure whether this made me feel I knew him a little better or a lot less. At any rate it warmed me to him.

T E N

· · ·

As I came out into the square I saw Linda leaving the bar. She was dressed in the same blue dungarees as yesterday, had a capacious shoulder bag swinging by her side and was walking in the direction of the hotel. I caught up with her as she left the square. "Hi," I said.

"Oh, hello," she said. "I've just had a rather late breakfast I'm ashamed to say. They have such delicious brioches there."

"Yes. Heard about the new bomb?" In most villages, I suppose, one would be asking about the new bus route or bike path.

"Yes. Isn't it *awful?* Just too awful. Apparently they're talking about organising a demonstration for the weekend."

"Who is? The barman?"

"Oh, no, not him. A demonstration *against* the violence, you know. He's a bit of—well, a bit of an old Fascist, by the sound of it. Or at least, a little insensitive. No, there were one or two young people in the bar and the old parish priest, Don Luigi."

"Ah."

"He's particularly outraged. You know that the bomb's been claimed as the work of a group who have the cheek to call themselves the Knights of St. George?"

"The who?"

"*I Cavalieri di San Giorgio.* Isn't it—well, it's blasphemous surely."

"If you can blaspheme against a demoted saint. Talking of which, I've just been to the museum."

"Oh, yes? Signor Menegallo's still opening it up, is he?"

"Yes. Maybe it keeps his mind off things," I said. I only winced internally as I said this. "He told me I should go and see *'il signor conte.'* "

"Oh really? Are you that interested?"

"Well, it's got me quite intrigued, I must admit."

"If you like, I could probably fix it up for you. I think the count and I got on rather well. Shall I ring him for you?"

I said that would be kind of her. We were getting near the hotel now and I was feeling nervous. I could see no loiterers or lurkers, but nonetheless felt it would be tempting fate for me to go in with her—and fate didn't seem to need much tempting in this village. After all, the thugs could be waiting inside—happily laughing over Terry Pratchett and anything else they'd picked up in the loo. I told her I'd wait on the corner.

She came out after a minute or two, smiling. "He says why don't we go straight on up and have a cup of coffee or something?"

"Ah, great. By the way, was there anyone in the hotel?"

"How do you mean, anyone?"

"Anyone there hanging around?"

"Just the manager—you know, Signor—"

"Yes. Nobody else?"

"No. Are you still expecting your friends?"

"Well, you never know. Just wondered . . ." I let my voice trail away inconsequently.

We started up the hill out of the village, and by the time we reached the last few houses I was reasonably sure no one was dogging us. Linda, I think, was reasonably sure I was crazy.

The road wound up through vineyards and cherry orchards on the right and deep dark woods on the left. Every so often we would get a glimpse of the villa above the trees, and each time it seemed to have done another smirking backwards leap, to shimmer provocatively at us through the heat haze. However, several pints of sweat later (from my pores at any rate—Linda merely turned a shinier pink), we reached a great pillared gateway; through its wrought-iron curls and flourishes we could see the villa looking cool and unruffled on the other side of a raked-gravel yard.

Linda rang a bell which I could swear actually went "dingdong" somewhere in the depths of that austere marble pile. I panted and looked down the hill. Over the top of the trees I could just see the rooftops and the church tower of San Giorgio. I heard a motorbike beginning to snarl its way up.

We waited and the bike continued to snarl. I found my ears tuning in closer and closer to the noise. I was recalling the motorbike I'd heard driving off into the night just after the intruder had left my bedroom. This wasn't, of course, the first motorbike I'd heard this morning—their engines were a permanent *sotto fondo* in Piazza Malberti—but it was the first one I'd heard in isolation: distant but sinister isolation.

Then I heard the engine cut out.

"Ah, here's someone," Linda said and I said, "What, what?" switching my attention back to the villa.

The gate clicked open and we crunched across the gravel to the front door: this was a magnificent arched portal at the top of a double flight of steps, which flowed down towards the courtyard in two sexy sweeping curves; for the fullest effect they looked as if they needed rows of housemaids and footmen standing to attention all the way up, with a majestically rubicund butler crowning the whole lot at the top. Instead, there was a little old woman in a dirty apron peering suspiciously round the door.

Linda took the left-hand flight of steps, so, feeling that it would be silly to waste the possibility, I took the right-hand one. This, I think, made the old woman even more suspicious.

"*Cossa volé?*" she said in toothless dialect. What do you want?

"We've come to speak to the count," Linda said in Italian. "He's expecting us. I came yesterday, you may remember. And this is a friend."

The wizened features didn't give away whether they remembered or not. They turned to me, obviously unimpressed by Linda's choice of friends. Then she said grudgingly, *"Va ben,"* and opened the door another centimetre or two so that we could squeeze through. She told us to follow her.

The hallway was mostly marble and mirrors; in between the mirrors were dusty frescoes of hunting scenes. She led us through all this faded jollity to a room on the right. *"Ghè la signorina,"* she announced to the back of an armchair by the window, in a tone that suggested the armchair should know better at its age. She added, *"Ghè anca un'amigo."*

"Ah, come, come Miss—Miss—" the armchair said in English, and a hand fluttered vaguely in the air to one side. *"Grazie, Rina. Ci porti del caffè, per favore."* I put in a request for a glass of water as well and then the old woman turned and stomped off, as if undesirous to be a witness to whatever lascivious doings were now in store.

We crossed the room carefully. The marble and mirrors continued here, only the mirrors were so dusty and cracked they reflected nothing but blurs. I half-expected these blurs on closer inspection to resolve themselves into figures in ruffs and hoses discussing Ariosto's latest. There were two bookcases with leather-bound volumes that looked as if they hadn't been touched since Ariosto autographed them, and there was a central table covered with knick-knacks of varied and obviously valuable sort, such as vases and marble figurines and miniature portraits. A few photos tried to disguise their vulgar modernity by shrinking bashfully into heavy silver frames.

The man in the armchair was staring out into the garden. "Excuse me not arising," he said. "La signorina Linda understands why." He indicated two crutches leaning against the wall. Despite his affliction, he looked rather younger than his seventy-odd years, with a surprisingly unlined face and good head of grey hair. He took Linda's hand in an almost proprietary fashion and drew her down to a chair next to him. It was done undemonstratively but firmly. He was wearing a pale-colored suit, which Linda's cheeks were already setting out to contrast.

"This is my friend, Jan," she said. She took advantage of this introduction to free her hand so that she could indicate me. "He's interested in the story of the statue too."

"Is he indeed?" He took my hand for one moment and then waved vaguely around the room, intimating that I might take any of the other seats, but preferably one of the more distant ones. I tactfully sat down on a chair near the other window, so that I could in all politeness gaze at the view outside and leave the count to get up to whatever he wanted inside the room. The view was worth it too: there was a long stretch of lawn broken by occasional posturing statues and bordered by clipped hedges. At the far end, trees and bushes and statuary mingled more informally on the hillside, and the garden rose to another level lawn. The window was open, and I listened again for the motorbike, but its engine remained silent.

"And where are you from, young man?" he said. His voice was quiet and as oddly youthful as his face.

"Near Oxford."

"Ah, the dreaming spires," he said.

"Well, not quite," I said. "A little village with just one church steeple."

"I confess I don't know the English countryside as I would like, but your villages are charming."

"Yes," I agreed. His English was accented and a trifle antiquated, but undeniably good—and he was clearly proud of it. It seemed in order to ask, "Where did you learn your English?"

"We had an English nanny as children. And there was an English family that used to come regularly to the village with whom my parents were friendly. We played with their children—chums together. I remember how amusing they used to find Mussolini's tales of the English eating five times a day. Perfidious Albion of course was the cry then."

"And now we're just the nation of football hooligans."

"I fear indeed there is something of truth in that. Now, my dear"—he had turned to Linda again—"what can this foolish old fellow tell you now? By the way, did I tell you yesterday what a wonderfully witty nose you have? *Un naso davvero spiritoso.*"

"Yes," she said, and the witty item turned the same red as her cheeks. "You did."

"Ah. I had the feeling I had done so. Well, I can but confirm it." He turned to me. "Do forgive me. One of the advantages of old age is that one can make compliments that callow youth would never dare to."

Linda did her best to assume a businesslike tone: "My friend has been to the museum too, and is interested . . ."

I helped her out, forcing my mind away from that damned motorbike. "Yes. I hear that you've looked into all the various stories to do with the statue's possible survival." Then my mind instantly reverted to the bike: why had it stopped halfway up the hill? I couldn't recall seeing any houses on the way up to the villa.

"Very few of them bear much investigating," he said. "There seems little doubt that the thing must have perished with the partisans."

"But was it absolutely certain," I said, "that your brother had the statue in that house when the Germans got there?"

"Nothing, of course, is absolutely certain. But that house was undoubtedly the only hideout close to the village. At that time the partisans were still in formation and most of their activity was limited to the mountains. This, em, raid on the village was really exceptional."

"Yes," I said. "But is it definite that after the raid they retired to that house and stayed there?"

"So it seems. They had sustained some injuries and so they decided to wait there until their *compagni* could come down with a *barella*—stretcher, no?—for the injured ones. Remember, they didn't believe that the Germans knew about this house."

"And you don't think they might have hidden the treasure on the way to the house?"

"No, they definitely had the statue with them when they returned to the hideout. We know that from the boy who was there waiting for them." He turned to Linda. "You will remember I mentioned him yesterday."

"Yes," she said.

"He was in the hideout when they came back, and he saw my brother with the statue in a—a bag. The boy was then sent down to the village to get provisions. When he returned, he witnessed the—the end of it all."

"And there was no further communication with anyone?" I said. "No messages?"

"Nothing," he said simply. "The rest was silence."

"And nothing was found afterwards? No last messages or farewells?"

He looked at me in some perplexity. "No. As I said, the house was burnt to—to a frizzle."

So that letter I'd read from Giorgio Malberti had never reached its addressees—as I had already guessed, of course. "So you—your family—you all just heard of his death from that boy?" I said. "How did you feel?" As soon as I'd said it, I thought, my God, I *am* a journalist.

"How do you think?" he said. "Particularly since he had left the house in—in some anger."

Well, this gave me something to feel guilty about. But I couldn't hand over the letter yet—not until I'd worked out its exact connection with Piers's disappearance. I said, "So relations were strained in the family?"

"We were different—and my mother never understood him."

"You did?"

"I was probably the only one who did. Even though I don't think he ever realised it. And he certainly never respected me."

He stated this in such a matter-of-fact way that I almost blurted out a contradictory "No." But I held back. That's what being a pro is all about, after all: being a bastard. "Why do you think so?"

He shrugged. "He was the athlete, the winner, the leader, the joker. I was the book-reader."

Well, he'd get a boost out of that letter when it finally got to him, I told myself. Then I said, "And your mother—how did she feel?"

"It broke her heart," he said quite simply. "He'd left the

house after a terrible row and she never saw him again. And yes, even with her, despite the rows, the disagreements, the ways he worried her, he was the favourite. I could never replace him."

"Broke her heart?" I said. "You mean—"

"I mean it literally," he said. "She died very soon afterwards."

Linda was looking at me a little curiously. She was the organiser of the Giorgio Malberti fan club, after all. I said to the count, "Was he a bit of a rebel then?"

"Yes," he said. "More of a rebel than a Communist in fact."

"More of a—sorry?" Linda hadn't followed this.

"Oh, Communists weren't rebels. Or at least if they were they didn't last long. All that nonsense was, em, purged out of the real Communists. Giorgio was never one of those. He wasn't serious enough, I'm happy to say. You know, I sometimes wonder if the rescue of the statue wasn't just his last big jape. He would risk anything for the sake of a joke."

"And this time he risked too much," I said.

"I suppose so. But if there isn't the possibility of failure, you are not truly risking. And it was because people saw that he truly risked that they followed him. Right from a little boy. Wherever he was, he naturally took the lead. If we went on holiday somewhere, after a day or two he would be the leader of a gang."

The word "boy" reminded me of something. "What about this boy—the one who saw the whole thing, I mean? Who was he?"

"He was from somewhere in the south—Naples or Salerno, I believe. He'd been sent to stay with relatives for the war, and his dream was to go with the partisans. My brother—perhaps foolishly—did not discourage him. He would not allow him to be involved in fighting, but he did use him as a scout. He saw the whole terrible conflagration and came running back to the village to recount what he had seen—in a terrible state, of course, but clearly quite reliable all the same."

"Where is he now?" Linda asked.

"I have no idea. He left the village immediately after this shocking affair, as did his relatives."

"Oh," she said.

"I understand your eagerness, and it brings a pretty flush to your face—"

She immediately looked as if she'd swallowed an incendiary bomb.

"—but I really think you are destined to disappointment if you place too much hope in this treasure hunt. Remember, I've been looking into such stories for nearly fifty years now."

"Yes, yes," she said. "I suppose you're right. But would there be any way of tracking this boy down?"

"I suppose he would be in his fifties now. You could ask in the village if anyone remembers him or his relatives. I doubt it. They were only here for the war, you know. It's nearly half a century now. But this is all such sad talk—deaths and bombs and fires. I would like to know about yourselves. Are you lovers?"

"What?" she squeaked.

"Or is the expression boyfriend and girlfriend? *Insomma, morosi, fidanzati,* bed-sharers." He clearly enjoyed being quietly shocking.

"No," I said. "We only met yesterday."

At that moment my cocked ears heard a car approaching. It was a little way down the hill as yet, but its noise set me thinking about that motorbike again. Had the rider parked it in order to come furtively on up the hill towards the villa? A pity I couldn't see the front gate from these windows.

"That means nothing," the count said. "Not among the young people today, I believe. Though I exempt my son from this, em, discourse."

"Oh?" I said. "He's another Giorgio, isn't he?"

"Only by name," he said. "He has nothing else that is remotely, um, Georgian about him—although now that I think of it the word has no, em, saintly connotations in English."

"No, definitely not," I said, listening as the car drew up outside the house.

"But it has definite associations with architecture," said

Linda with a studious nod of her head. "And he is an architect, isn't he?"

"That is correct. You've seen the museum, haven't you?"

"Yes," I said. "Nicely set out, I thought."

"Nice," he said drily. "Not a word I love. But maybe it is suited to my son's work there."

"What words do you like?" I said, deciding I couldn't actually press with a question about his son.

"Passionate, inspired—revolutionary, even. This is what architecture should be about." He said this as quietly and unemphatically as ever. I remembered his brother's description of him: the quiet one, but maybe the real rebel for all that.

"Would you describe this house as being any of those?" I said.

"Of course not. It is in a different tradition—the tradition of classical perfection. But that is not an architecture for our age. We should be fighting to affirm ourselves, to send a message to a degraded commercialised world. A message of love and freedom."

I suppose I could have said, "Far-out, man" or something similarly sixties-silly, but his tone of quiet conviction made him sound quite unlike Allen Ginsberg. Instead I said, "And your son doesn't agree?"

"No. His is a respectable art, at the service of commerce and state institutions. Institutional architecture, in fact. An art of compromises and timidity."

"An art that respects the desires of my clients," came a new voice from the door.

Linda and I turned. The count merely sighed. A man in his early forties was standing by the door, holding a briefcase. He wore a formal grey suit with a dark blue tie on a white shirt. His hair was brushed over to disguise incipient baldness and he had pale eyes behind gold-rimmed spectacles. All he lacked was a copy of *The Financial Times*. Behind him stood the little old lady with a tray of coffee.

"I trust," he said in rather more heavily accented English than the older man's, "that you are not fatiguing my father?"

"It is very good of you to be so concerned," the count said, "but I assure you it is not necessary. Put it down on this table," he added to Rina.

"But let us remember that recently you have had a return of your liver problem."

Linda said, "Really, we don't want to be any trouble," and she started to rise.

The count's arm shot out and pushed her down again. "I decide when and if I am tired. Well, Giorgio? What news from the Town Council?" He continued to talk in English; I wondered whether this was just out of politeness towards us or because he knew that his English was better than his son's. He poured out the coffee.

"Always new obstacles raised by those red and green fools."

"Those what?" Linda couldn't help putting in.

The count said, "My son has a project for a large hotel on the hill above the castle—with saunas and massage parlours and perhaps hired concubines—"

"Don't be foolish, Papà." Giorgio Malberti placed his briefcase on a chair and addressed the nearest mirror. "A luxury hotel with the modern conveniences that people expect nowadays on holiday or even on business trips. And those fools—"

The count broke in suavely. "He has come up against opposition from the left-wing members of the town council and from the so-called Greens, who do not see the need for such a hotel on such a site."

"These people have no imagination, no foresight. Do they not see that this village could be a major tourist site? for Italians and foreigners? And we have only one hotel. Do these people not see that tourism will benefit everyone—everyone? But in this country there is always bureaucracy, there are always objections, nothing ever is done because everyone is too afraid of the new."

"The new," murmured the count with distaste. Not for the new, I think, but for his son's concept of it.

Giorgio Malberti continued: "And now they're coming up with objections because of some obscure little chapel that nobody ever uses anyway."

"You mean the chapel of San Giorgio?" said Linda, her eyes wide. She put down the cup of coffee she'd just been handed. I remembered that Pigozzi had described him as a Hun.

"That's the one, I believe. Quite unimportant architecturally. I've even offered to have it moved instead of just pulled down." He looked at Linda hard, and then at me. "You're not journalists, by any chance?"

"No," I said, as I took my coffee and glass of water.

"We have enough of the scandal-seeking ones," said Giorgio Malberti. "We certainly don't need any Green troublemakers as well."

"But—but—" said Linda, getting her power of speech back. "That chapel—that chapel—it's *the* chapel. I mean, King Pepin's chapel. It's—it's of great historic importance. . . ."

"Well, as I say, I'm prepared to have it moved. We could then include it in our brochures as one of the attractions."

"How would you advertise the village?" I asked. "Adventure holidays for the family? Bring your own bombs?"

"A lot of fuss about nothing," said Giorgio Malberti. "A little local friction, due to ridiculous immigration policies."

"And the murder?" I said.

He stared at me. "A local delinquent. But such things are no more common here than in other places. If the police—"

"My son is a believer in more rigorous punishment."

Giorgio Malberti continued: "We all know that in prisons today criminals are treated like guests in hotels. *Permessi* to go out for the day, to meet their wives and lovers, television in their rooms. And that is when they *do* go to prison. This young man who was killed should have been incarcerated already. He had been in trouble many times with the police."

"You knew him?" the count said in what seemed to me to be feigned surprise.

"Of course I knew him. You know he was old Bepi Menegallo's son. If you remember we took him on in the garden for a while, some years back. Until we found he was stealing the peaches."

"I remember. You wanted to denounce him to the police."

"Of course. And if he had been in prison the other day he wouldn't have been killed."

"How grateful he would have been to you," murmured the count.

"Drugs were behind the murder, of course, as always. And no doubt blacks were behind the drugs."

"My son has never felt the need for artificial stimulants for his imagination," the count told us. "But then that is perhaps because he hasn't any at all."

"I may not have," he said. "But at least I have made some buildings. I have achieved something. Not simply dreamt of achieving something."

The count's eyes glittered angrily. "And your next achievement will be to destroy your own village."

"To give it a commercial future. But I think I have heard enough nonsense for the moment," Giorgio Malberti said. "If you will excuse me, I have much work to do."

We excused him, but rather as if we were excusing ourselves, which was no doubt the point, and he picked up his briefcase and walked out.

The count said, "My dear son, as charming as ever. Well, at least I'll probably be dead before the hotel is built."

"Is it really being planned above the castle?" Linda asked.

"Yes, but 'in a style in keeping with the area's monumental and natural beauty'," he said, clearly quoting and clearly disbelieving what he quoted. "But enough of this. Can I show you the garden? Or would you prefer to wander it alone? More romantic perhaps."

"Thank you," I said, without looking at Linda. "That would be very nice—er, very delightful."

"Don't worry about the gardener," said the count. "He is quite mad, but harmless. At least generally so—just remember to say 'Buongiorno,' if you meet him; he does appreciate to be acknowledged."

I said, "Wasn't Signor Menegallo—the man in the museum—once the gardener here?"

"Yes. As a boy and young man. But his health was ruined by

the war and he had to take on more sedentary work then. Well, do enjoy your stroll."

We both stood up and thanked him and shook his hand, which was firm and slightly leathery to the touch. "Please wander as you please, and feel free to take a peach or two—well, no, a fig perhaps, considering the season."

I stepped outside and let Linda out first and the count said in a low voice to me, "You're a lucky boy." Fortunately Linda didn't hear. That would have reduced her to a frizzle.

ELEVEN

· · · · · ·

AS WE STROLLED ACROSS THE LAWN she said, "Well, he's very nice but, gosh!"

"Gosh," I agreed.

"The thing to do is not take him seriously, you know. He's a dreadful old tease."

I said, "I think he's just playing a role—the ageing rake. Probably to annoy his son."

"Yes," she said. She lowered her voice to talk about the son. "He's certainly annoying enough himself, isn't he? I mean—that hotel business. . . ."

"Well, that'll be up to the citizens of San Giorgio to decide," I said. I looked around myself. "I wonder where that gardener is? We don't want a pitchfork through our bellies just because we didn't spot him touching his forelock." I was also trying to see any signs of spies. If I was right and the man on the motorbike had been following us, he might simply be waiting outside the front gate—or he might be taking advantage of the garden's civilised clutter to sneak up on us. I had to consider every statue and bush as a possible enemy—without, if possible, alarming Linda.

She said, "I think that must be him," and indicated a man coming down one of the steep paths at the far end of the lawn. He looked like a cheap rag doll that had been put together by some bored child out of old leather (the face) and pan scourers (the hair and beard), and then tied together with scraps of old denim. He was coming toward us and we could already see his mouth muttering gnomish curses beneath the wild wires of his beard. He was carrying a spade, and the way he held it, it looked every bit as lethal as a pitchfork. Linda said, "Oh, dear . . . ," and her footsteps haltered.

"*Buongiorno*," I called, and hoped my voice was steady. I repeated it, "*Buongiorno, buongiorno*," and hoped the word really did have the magic effect attributed it by the count.

He continued to approach and continued to mutter. I wondered if it was just my imagination or the sky really had begun to darken.

"*Buongiorno, signore*," said Linda.

The title—or Linda's voice—did the trick. He lowered the spade and after dragging his arm, together with quite a bit of the garden, across his mouth and nose, said something like, "*orno.*" Then he stood still, considered the situation, jerked his thumb towards the house and said, "*Gavé parlà con lori, eh?*" You've spoken to them, right? He was obviously almost toothless.

We nodded and smiled and said yes, and I added another "signore" and then, as he turned down one of the paths, called out again, "*Buongiorno.*"

"All right, all right," said Linda, "it's all clear." We could hear him still muttering as he walked away and I hoped it was the thrips he was cursing now.

One danger was over, I thought, and looked around again at the garden's scenic effects. I could see no statue with extra arms and no unduly plump bush. I forced myself to be casually chatty. "This garden is amazing."

"Yes, isn't it? And it really is just that one chap who does it all. And in the house there's just that old woman. He was telling me yesterday how the Nazis searched all over this place after the partisans' raid, since they knew his brother was one of them, and his mother went rushing in front of them, telling them to wipe their boots before entering each room. And they did."

"He must have had some mother."

"But then they trampled all over the garden and through the bushes and really ruined it."

"Fifty years later it looks pretty good to me."

We were approaching the far end of the *prato inglese,* which was a rich velvety green, suggesting copious use of sprinklers to supply *pioggia inglese.* In front of us now the garden rose with winding paths between trees and bushes and statues of gods and goddesses clad in moss and bird-droppings. A marble balustrade some way up the hill indicated another level lawn, presumably with a fine view of the villa and the valley in general. It was strange to think that all this ordered peace, where even the birds seemed to twitter more respectfully, was under the control of that wild man of the woods.

"Shall we go on up?" asked Linda.

"Might as well," I said. We started climbing one of the little paths.

"Ugh, spiders," she said, brushing sticky tendrils from her face. The bushes were strung everywhere with shining webs, all as perfectly and as delicately formed as the garden seemed to require.

"Look at this one," I said. "Isn't that beautiful?"

"It would be without that thing in the middle," she said.

As we stopped and looked at it my senses, already on full alert, caught the sounds of distant footsteps in the woods to our left—and the gardener had gone off to the right. I stared hard but could see nothing—just bushes and trees and statues and millions of swinging silver masterpieces.

"What's up?" Linda said, staring in the same direction.

"Oh nothing," I said. "Let's go." We kept walking, our faces and hands occasionally caressed by tickling strands of web. I kept my ears and eyes cocked leftwards and was eventually rewarded by the sight of a distant shadowy figure scurrying between bushes. Well, it wasn't the crippled count was all I could say for certain. I said nothing to Linda.

We came out onto the next level lawn. There was a bench by the balustrade. We sat down gratefully and gazed over the trees to the villa, and below the villa to the woods and the just-glimpsed rooftops of the village, and then to the haze of the valley as it rolled down to join the murky steam of the Po plain. People who talk of the blue skies of Italy have never lived in Mantua or Padua, where the summer sky usually has the clarity of a Turkish bathroom mirror.

I kept my eyes on the nearby trees to see if the shadow was going to make another break for it. Nothing stirred, however.

"Let's go to that tower thing over there," I said at the top of my voice, indicating the hilltop above this lawn, where a small observation tower gave a yet wider view.

"All right," she said, "there's no need to shout."

"That tower, okay?" I decided regretfully that switching suddenly to Italian would not be very convincing; I pointed as clearly as I could, in case the follower was monolingual.

"Yes, okay, I understand."

We set off in that direction, but when we reached the next clump of trees I pulled her to one side, with a sudden "ssh." I indicated—in silence this time—an ivy-covered stone building to the right, and she followed me towards it. It had no door, just an open archway, and we entered its gloom.

"What is all this?" she whispered sharply.

I noticed she wasn't blushing, so at least she hadn't got the "wrong idea."

I said in a low voice, "There's someone following us."

"What?"

"There's someone following us. I thought that from here we might get to see who it is." I peered out of the doorway.

"All right, all right," she said. "Let's wait and see then."

I got the impression she wasn't taking me entirely seriously. She was looking around our refuge, which seemed to be a sturdy shed; it was filled with the Malberti family's junk from the time of Dante, and it all looked as if it had been through the wars: there were gardening tools which must have speared a few Guelphs and Ghibellines in their time, crippled chairs and tables from the Hundred Years war, broken-backed rocking horses that had faced the guns at Solferino and Magenta, disembowelled dolls, shell-shocked teddy bears, and puppets with glassy eyes that couldn't forget the trenches. All this stuff was stacked and balanced and jammed in precarious heaps, like the aftermath of an air raid, with twisted dolls' limbs and chair legs protruding at pathetic angles; it just needed a cobweb to give way and we'd be buried under a clattering avalanche. The little floor space that was left was covered by old sacking, but at the edges of the room I could see cracked blue tiles. The only light was from the doorway, since the windows were covered with ivy. "Gosh," she said, "what a lot of memories there must be here," and she touched one of the horses, which let out its first whinnying creak since the Congress of Vienna.

"Ssh," I said, looking nervously at the pile she was touching.

I looked back out of the doorway and saw the figure moving quickly alongside the hedge that bordered the lawn. He left its cover and ran towards the trees, bent low. He was a small wiry man of about thirty. He had a pugnacious ball of a face on which the tiny features were screwed up so tight that no expression could be discerned; I imagined James Cagney must have looked rather like that as a foetus.

Linda had joined me. "Hey," she whispered, "that's—that's—"

"Who?"

"It's Signor Menegallo's other son—Luca, I think his name is. What's he doing here?"

"I don't know, but he's interested in us. You believe me now?"

"Yes, but why—"

"Ssh."

He was now gingerly taking the path up towards the tower. He didn't like the spiders either. He winced and his face practically disappeared.

I backed away from the arched doorway, in case he should turn and stare in this direction. Linda said, "Now what?"

"Well, at least we've identified him." He seemed a little smaller than the man who'd attacked me in the hotel, but my powers of assessment and sense of perspective may not have been at their sharpest then. I wondered whether, having missed me outside the hotel this morning, he had then heard about my intention to visit the count from his father, and thus at once leapt onto his motorbike. I peered out again, but he had slipped out of sight now.

"Why's he following you?"

"Me?" I said. "I thought he was following you."

"Me?" Her voice went squeaky with surprise. "Why—"

"I don't know. This statue business perhaps."

"I don't believe you. You were expecting to be followed."

"What?" This caught me off-guard.

"Anyway," she said, "I think the thing to do is turn the tables. We follow him, and see where he goes next. And then maybe we'll find out who he is—if you don't know already."

"Look, I've told you—"

"Ssh. And come away from the door."

It struck me that she'd turned the tables on me pretty efficiently. Now I was the one being silenced and ordered around. How was I going to turn them back again? Or at least get some kind of control over the situation? Should I let her in on the whole business? Or some of it? How much?

My real desire, I realised, was to spill out the whole story there and then and thus secure myself an ally. But that would mean kissing goodbye to any last vestige of self-respect I might have: Philip Marlowe didn't turn to the nearest blonde and ask her to solve the case for him.

And anyway it would mean splitting the reward.

I decided to go on playing things by ear: improvisation (or muddling through) was my real speciality.

She went back to the rocking horse. "I expect you could write a whole family history from the stuff in here," she said.

"Toys and garden tools?"

"Well, certain aspects of the family history. You know, that's what most attracts me about history—when you feel you've got to *know* someone who's dead. I mean, really know him. Got to the bottom of him."

"Identify with him," I said.

"Perhaps that too." She picked up a wooden sword that lay on top of a pile of broken-spirited deck chairs. "I bet Giorgio Malberti played with this."

"The uncle, you mean—not the architect down there." I gestured in the direction of the villa.

"Oh, gosh no. He would have been busy with instructional games."

"Or playing Monopoly and building lots of hotels."

She shuddered. "Don't. Isn't he just too awful?" She peeled some ancient chewing gum from the hilt of the sword. "I wonder if he ever played at being St. George?" She lunged at an imaginary dragon.

I shook my head, wondering whether I could restore my self-respect by telling her sternly that this was no game—or would she just laugh right back in my face?

There was a sudden cry from below us—the blood-curdling cry of a crazed and toothless man: *"Lazzaron! Mascalzon! A romper le piante! Te romperò il culo."* Which could translate roughly: "Young varmint, breakin' trees, I'll larn yer." And the Mad Gardener burst onto the scene, shaking his spade in the direction of Luca, his hair and beard collecting cobwebs as he thrashed his way through the trees.

Luca's voice said nervously from above, *"Ma mi son vegnuo solo par—"* and then he obviously thought better of trying to argue his situation to the approaching hairy hurricane. We could hear a scurry and flurry of footsteps, scuffed branches and snapped twigs, a further frothy outburst of protestations and oaths, and then Luca came tearing down a path just feet away from us. The gardener attempted to force his way through a bush to reach and disembowel him, and when it was clear he couldn't make it, threw his spade like a javelin, and then turned back down the hill to try his luck on the level.

We left the building to watch the chase across the lawn. Luca had a good start and was making the most of it. The gardener eventually halted in the middle of the lawn, raised both hands to heaven and pronounced a series of curses on Luca, his parents, his present or future progeny, and his deceased relatives.

I was glad we'd said *"Buongiorno."*

"Well, it looks as if we've lost our chance to follow him," said Linda.

"I suppose so," I said.

Then there was a sudden yelp from the distance, followed by a thud. Luca must have tripped or fallen. The gardener, who had stopped his prayers to pick spiders out of his hair, set off in the direction of the cry with an air of gleeful anticipation. Seconds later we heard his voice saying something in dialect which obviously meant "Gotcha!" and Luca's voice pleading for mercy.

"Oh, dear," said Linda. "Do you think we should rescue him?"

"No. Look down there."

I pointed down the steep side of the hill, which descended through the woods to a bend of the road. We could just glimpse a motorbike drawn up among the trees.

"What about it?"

"Might be worth a look," I said. There was a wire fence a few yards below us, but it didn't look particularly difficult to climb.

"Are you thinking of pinching it?"

"No. Just looking at it. Identifying it."

"But oughtn't we to say goodbye down at the house?"

"I'm sure the count will understand. He'll either think we've been offered up in human sacrifice or—"

"Or what?"

"Nothing." It was probably better not to add that he might think we were too overcome by our passions. I slipped round the side of the stone building and Linda followed me. We groped our way along its ivy-covered side to the back, where it bulged out in a rough half-circle. The ground dropped steeply now and we half-slithered, half-climbed, grabbing at roots and rocks. We reached the fence and I joined my hands for Linda to step into. Once she'd grabbed the top of the fence I was ready to give her another helping heave, but she instantly swung herself over and dropped to the ground in one easy movement.

There was no one to give me a leg up, I realised stupidly. I made a wild leap towards the top of the fence. My hands grabbed it, but slipped—and then I fell back. The nearest paling, as if taking pity on my foolish tumble, gave a kind of shrug, then a lurch, and then tottered down towards me, wrenching itself from the soil at its base. The wire fence sagged and sprawled drunkenly.

It just remained for me to pick my way over it.

Then we walked over to the bike. I realised I wasn't quite sure why I'd wanted to do this—except that it had been a way of wresting the initiative from Linda's hands. So I had better now make my investigation look good.

She said, "It's a Suzuki. Not cheap." She was pink from exertion now, but her eyes were bright with excitement.

"No," I said. I think my knowledge of motorbikes was a fraction less profound than my knowledge of medieval history. I looked at the helmet, which was perched on the pillion, and hoped for secret maps stashed away inside. There was nothing, not even dandruff. So I had a look at the front wheel. I was vaguely aware—well, I was acutely aware—of Linda standing and watching me.

"That's pretty odd," I said, straightening.

"What?"

"Look at all this leafy mush and mud on the tyre here."

"Yes, well, look where he's parked it."

"And look how dry the earth is here."

She admitted the point, then said, "And so?"

"I don't know if it means anything," I said, "but we might as well bear it in mind."

We suddenly heard footsteps coming down the road at a run. We stepped back into the trees and held our breath. Luca appeared, his tiny features almost obliterated by sweat-beads. He seemed to have most of his limbs still attached. He ran straight to the bike, put the helmet on, and roared off down the hill.

"So are you going to tell me why he was following you?" she said as we left the trees.

"Well, if you must know, I'm a private detective." I started walking downhill and kept looking rigidly ahead.

She laughed.

"Thank you," I said.

"Come on, be serious."

"I am," I said. "I don't mind you laughing. After all, what good's a private detective that everybody immediately recognises as one?" I liked this: it struck me it could even be true. I went on, "In strictest confidence, I've been asked to look for Piers Ainsley—that English guy who was at the hotel. He's disappeared."

"And why you?"

I kept my eyes on the road. "As I said, I'm a private detective. Unofficially."

"And so why was Luca following you? What's he got to do with it?"

"Ah," I said, "I think he must have heard about my making enquiries and so . . ."

"You think he knows something about this Piers?"

"I'm sure he must."

"Gosh, this is exciting. So the murder must be connected too."

"I'm sorry. I really can't tell you any more." After a moment's pause I said, "Not without my client's approval."

"Who's that? The girlfriend?"

"Her and Piers's father."

"I see," she said. Then after another pause, "Gosh, how exciting."

"Please remember this is all strictly confidential. My—my clients don't want the police involved."

"And do you think it's all linked up with the statue?"

"It's one line I'm following."

"So what's your next step?"

Well, I didn't want to say, "I wish I knew," so I said, "I'm going to, er, look into this motorbike business. It might mean nothing as I say, but then again . . ."

"What business?"

"The mush on the wheels. It can only have got that by driving right into the woods, and these are the only woods around."

"So what are you going to do?"

"Just look for tracks that lead off the road."

"Oh."

We kept on walking and I tried to make myself look that much more seriously vigilant. After a while she said, "So do you use disguises? And do you carry a gun? And is it mostly divorce cases?"

" 'No' to all of those," I said. "I might as well tell you that I'm a bit of an underling: I take orders from my bosses." This almost honest admission made me feel a little better: a slightly less blatant fraud, at any rate.

"Tell me," she said, "how would you go about tracing someone—like that boy from the war?"

"Are you going to hire me?"

"It would depend on your rates."

"Ah, you'd have to sort that out with my boss."

"Oh. But how would you set about it, anyway?"

"Well, I suppose it would be a question of interviewing people who might remember him, and then checking up in the records—parish registers, that sort of thing, and old newspaper reports." After a pause, I added, "It's not all glamour, guns and fast cars, you know."

"No," she said, "I never thought it was," and her maybe-not-so-innocent Bambi eyes looked me up and down from my espadrille to my faded T-shirt. "Anyway, I want to know some more about this Piers."

"Ah, well, as I said, my information on him is all strictly confidential. I'm afraid—"

"Oh, come on, I gave you the statue lead in the first place, didn't I?"

Would she buy a line that I'd only got talking to her to follow that lead up? Probably not. "Yes, but I'm afraid I'm bound by the promise I made to my client."

"Oh, don't be so mean."

I was going to have to pull out that grim-visaged stuff about it not being a game if she went on like this. I even opened my mouth to say something along these lines—but then realised I didn't feel confident enough about the grimness of my visage. All it would take to ruin that pose would be one giggle from her—I would immediately burst out laughing too. So, still without looking at her, I said simply, "Look, I'm sorry if I seem ungrateful, but I just can't let you in on it. That's all there is to it."

"So what do you want me to do? Close my eyes and count ten while you run off into the woods?"

"No, I'd just like you to make your own way back to the village while I try and track down this motorbike. Maybe you could cut through the woods if we come across a path."

"All right," she said and closed her mouth in a resentful thin line. Then, after a pause, she said again, "All right."

We walked on in silence for a few minutes or so during which I experimented a few grim looks in the direction of the trees and they all looked extremely unimpressed and she added an extra petulant flounce to her gait. Then she said, "I suppose that path goes down to the village. I'll take it. Bye, and I still think you're mean."

"Good-bye."

She set off down the path, which was obviously a shortcut to the village, avoiding the long looping bends of the road. I stood still and watched her walking away, and as on the previous night felt a sudden regret at being left alone. But I told myself that the attraction of her rear view was no good reason for unprofessional behaviour and I set off determinedly towards the next bend in the road. There was almost complete silence— just the birds and the faint buzz of traffic down in the valley.

Even though this road seemed to be totally unused, I decided it might be better to follow it from the protection of the trees. It would at least make me feel that bit more professional.

First I opened my shoulder bag and took a black beret from it. I hadn't worn it since Naples—since *those* days in Naples— and I discovered that the mere action of jamming it on my head, covering my rather too noticeable blond hair, was as bracing as a glass of grappa. I was glad that I was wearing a dark T-shirt instead of my more usual whitish one. I wondered whether I should smear my face with earth, but decided the beret was sufficient for the moment. I pushed it to as jaunty an angle as I could without revealing any hair and stepped into the cobwebby gloom. Action at last: my nerves were atingle, my spirits were afire, the beret was askew—and the game was afoot.

Fortunately there wasn't too much undergrowth, and I was thus able to make reasonable progress without having to thrash about and tear my clothes. My espadrilles padded with catlike gentleness on the dry forest floor, and I weaved through the trees with my ears and eyes pricked and cocked for the softest, slightest sound or sight.

After two or three bends in the road I found a break in the trees where a very rough path made into the woods, and I saw the undisguisable track of a motorbike in the dry-paste mixture of leaves and earth at the start of the path. A different kind of detective would no doubt have been able to identify the tyre-tread. I made my way along the path which led straight into the depths of the forest, along uneven ground. I guessed the driver must have dismounted. As I got deeper into the woods, the ground got mushier: clue number one.

And then after about fifty yards I saw the bike itself, leaning against a tree, the rider's helmet perched on the pillion as before. I looked all around, studying the near and far trees, the gently moving leaves and shifting shades, the vibrating cob-webs. . . . There was no greater movement than this. I approached the bike with infinite caution. . . .

"BOOO!"

It was like a gas explosion in the middle of my head and I must have leapt about a foot. I came to earth again eventually, though my heart took a little longer, and I saw Linda standing to one side of a tree behind the bike; she was smiling but had already gone red enough to look like a fire hazard in these woods. "Sorry, sorry, sorry," she said. "That was really silly."

"Yes."

"But I just couldn't resist it. When I saw you tiptoeing along like that . . . I'm sorry. You must think me very childish."

"Well—"

"But I was coming down a path over there," she said, pointing, "And I saw the tracks of the bike and so, well, I just had to follow them, and then I saw the bike itself—well, I just saw the helmet actually, it's rather noticeable—and I thought, well, if *you* don't find it, you might thank me for doing so. And so I came over to have a look at it. And then I saw you coming along like Chingachgook, and it was irresistible."

"Okay, okay." I was glad that I hadn't smeared my face with earth. It struck me that she had at least made it very easy for me to use the not-a-game line now. However, I merely said: "But maybe you'd better go on now, before he comes back."

"Yes, okay. Please say you forgive me, please."

"All right, I forgive you."

"Thanks. Love your beret." She gave me a luminous smile; there was something endearing about her. I could imagine falling for her in the right circumstances—like a sixth-form dormitory feast.

I watched her set off down the path. She turned and said, "I think he went thataway," and she pointed to her right.

"Why?"

"Um, well, I'll leave that for you to discover. That tree over there."

I refused to be tantalised. "Okay," I said, "I'll have a look. Bye."

"Bye. Good hunting." She walked off, whistling something.

First of all I studied the bike again—purely, I think, from a childish refusal to be seen rushing off at her instigation. It took me about fifteen seconds: it was still just a motorbike with a hot engine and a crash helmet. Then I set off to the tree she'd indicated. I saw at once what she meant: a pool of urine, not exactly still steaming, but still seeping oilily through the vegetation at the roots of the tree.

Well, it was a more definite clue than an old cigarette stub or sweet wrapper would have been. And it was less likely to be a carefully laid trick too, I felt. But it wasn't a clue I cared to study in too much depth—and I hastily shifted my all-too-absorbent espadrilles and set off in the direction thus indicated. It turned out to be a very vague indication. The rough path I was following became rougher at every step and every few yards or so it branched off into other rough paths, all of which offered to my eyes equal signs of having possibly been trampled on in the last twenty minutes—and all of which might not have been so for the last twenty years. The undergrowth just wasn't thick enough, and the ground wasn't mushy enough for my untrained eyes to discern any definite signs. And I could hardly hope for more giveaway piss-pools. So I kept walking in what seemed to me the straightest line possible.

The fact that the wood I was traversing was on the side of a fairly steep hill meant that no line was straight. I was often clambering rather than simply walking, and the slope was often broken by mini-cliffs and rocky outcrops; the tree roots sometimes seemed to be scrabbling and clutching at the air as much as at the soil, and some trees looked as if one overweight sparrow landing in their upper branches could send them crashing. But this all reassured me rather than otherwise. I had a pretty good idea of what I was looking for now, and rocks and cliffs were the most likely places for it.

After forty minutes or so I came out into the sunlight again. I was at the edge of an open field which sloped down to the valley. Another village lay below me, which I couldn't identify. San Giorgio Veronese was nowhere in sight.

There was nothing for it but to turn round and reenter the woods. I was now feeling quite cheerful, since I was confident that a good day's tramping (or tiptoeing) would reveal to me what I was now expecting to find. After all, this forest wasn't the Amazon jungle, nor even Sherwood. And I knew that I had to concentrate my attention on the rockier or steeper portions of it. As an indication of my seriousness I put my hand down into the earth, scooped up a dollop of crumbly paste and smeared my face liberally. After all, it was childish to be put off doing something vital by fear of looking childish. I rubbed the earth well into my skin and felt the more earnest and real a detective for it.

As I became more used to the woods, I got better at assessing which roots I could trust as handholds, which rocks would not go rolling under my feet, causing mini-landslides, and which were the mushy rather than crackly leaves underfoot. My childhood jungle skills were in fact beginning to return—and as they did I realised I was enjoying myself.

Though, of course, I quickly told myself, it wasn't a game—definitely not a game.

I made my way back across the woods a little further down the hill and came across no living creature larger than a pigeon. When I reached the road, I walked back up the hill to where I'd entered the wood previously. The motorbike was no longer there. I decided to continue my search of the woods nonetheless. I started exploring further up.

It must have been getting on for midday—nearly an hour and a quarter later—when I spotted something blue through the trees. I immediately dropped to the ground. And I just lay there, peering through the grass up against my eyes, the stones a few feet away, and the trees in the near, middle, and far distance: I waited and peered for thirty seconds, and then the blue shape moved; it was a denim shirt, like the one Luca had been wearing, and above it was the back of a head with dark hair—again like the hair Luca had been wearing. I began a slow wormlike crawl in his direction.

It was Luca, and he was sitting on the ground leaning against a large rock. The rock was part of a whole craggy mass that lay below a cliff of some twenty feet in height—the highest I'd seen in the woods so far. He was smoking and there was something straight and dark resting against his knees. I crawled another few feet, and recognised the object as a rifle. I stopped crawling.

I lay still for several minutes, my face pressed as close to the ground as possible. I became familiar with every crinkle in the earth's surface, and a whole colony of ants became familiar with my every crinkle. Still I didn't move: I just lay and watched.

So Luca hadn't gone off on the motorbike—which meant

someone else had. Which meant that Luca had come here and substituted somebody. (I felt I could rule out the possibility that a passerby had pinched it.) Which was to say that there had been a changing of the guard. Which meant that something or someone was being guarded here.

I had, I felt sure, found Piers. I lifted my head an inch or two (causing panic amidst the various multilegged things that had set up a dance floor there) and studied the rocks behind him. I could see the dark fissure of a cranny. His father's wartime address. I lowered my head again and waited.

TWELVE

· · · · · · ·

ABOUT FIVE MINUTES LATER (by which time the urge to join the lambada that was being performed on every square inch of my body, whether clothed or not, had become almost uncontrollable) I saw Luca look at his watch, then stand up and move to the cliff. He picked up something floppy and dark from a rock by the cave entrance and pulled it over his head: a balaclava helmet. Then he took a bag from beside the rock and entered. I heard him say, speaking this time in Italian rather than dialect: "Do you want something to eat?" His voice was muffled and echoey.

Another noise came from within the rocks; the stifled *Mmmm* of someone protesting through a gag. Then Luca must have untied his gag and a new voice said something I couldn't hear—a young man's voice.

"Bread and cheese and a can of beer," answered Luca.

He had left the gun outside.

My whole body tensed up: my hands pressed hard into the earth while my elbows crooked out sideways ready to lift me, my toes dug in more firmly, my every muscle tightened, and my eyes assessed the distance and the terrain—and then I thought about my espadrilles and their unreliable nature and what a lot of nasty roots there were, and at that point Luca came back out of the cave, picked the rifle up and went back in carrying it.

I flopped back down again.

Then I thought I could at least take advantage of the changed situation to get a bit closer. I rose to a crouching position, freed myself of as many insects as I could by a simple brushing movement (about half of them, the other more insidious half having gone "underground") and I made my way towards a large rock that lay about fifteen feet from the cave entrance. I could hear the voices still talking and the unknown voice—well, Piers's—was getting louder with petulance: "And how long do you think you can keep me like this?" Sir Alfred was right, I thought. There was a hint of Tuscan in his accent, particularly in the breathy Irish-sounding *c*'s.

"Like we said, as long as we need." Luca didn't allow his voice to rise; it remained a steady whine, just slightly muffled by the balaclava helmet. "Until you tell us what we want to know."

"And how many times do I have to say that I haven't got anything else to tell you?"

"We just want to know what you told Zeno. That's all."

"My God, how many times . . . How often do I have to say it? I didn't tell him anything. I *asked* him something."

"What?"

"Christ, I've told you: I asked him about a chapel above the castle. I'm interested in history."

"Yeah, well, we'll keep you until you start telling us something we believe."

"You must be mad. You can't hope to get away with it. This isn't Calabria."

"Nobody's looking for you. And if they are, we're far enough away."

It struck me that this was a bit of an exaggeration. But presumably Luca and his companions, whoever they were, had no intention of keeping him there for months, as Calabrian professionals might; they weren't after a ransom, after all. I guessed the kidnap had been an improvised business, which was reassuring from my point of view. It meant I was up against amateurs.

Just a pity I was one too—even if I had smeared my face.

And a pity they were amateurs with guns.

Piers said, "You're both bloody crazy."

Both. That was reassuring too. I wondered if they had a gun each.

There was silence from within the cave now. Then after a while Luca said, "Are you going to tell me now who that blond Englishman is?"

"I just spend all my time repeating things to you. I don't know. I don't know anybody in this area, blond or otherwise."

"You'd be advised to answer me, you know, because my mate is getting impatient—and I told you about what a nasty temper he's got. When he comes back he's going to be really displeased if I tell him you're still not talking. And when he's displeased he shows it. He does things that make me feel sick. I mean, really nasty things. Just thought I should tell you this." His voice never altered its boring, slightly whining tone: all this was said as if he had a personal grievance against Piers for his effect on his friend's temper.

"If you're trying to scare me, you can just piss off." Piers was clearly very scared.

I suddenly realised—it was my heartbeats that told me, I think—how close I'd got; true, the rock would screen me when Luca came out, but I'd be blocked there unless he suddenly went into a deep sleep.

"Just telling you. Remember he'll be taking over from me this evening. Just think it over. I've seen him do things with a cigarette lighter. Don't want to put you off your sandwich, but just bear it in mind, I advise you. And a pocketknife he uses, sometimes—with the blade heated up. When he gets angry, like I said. And you're going the way to make him angry. Just think it over. All you have to do is talk."

I decided I'd heard enough. I had to get away while Luca was inside the cave. So I backed away and then took a path that led up to the top of the cliff. I took note of the location of the place and made my way back to the road.

I didn't find a stream, and had to content myself with wiping my face on some spit-wet grass and leaves. The looks I received from passersby as I walked through the village suggested that grass and gob were never going to replace soap and water. I was going to have to return to the hotel.

When I entered it I trusted in the hall's funereal gloom to conceal me, but the expression on the hotel manager's face as he handed me the key seemed to indicate that in fact the shadows gave a greater and richer depth to my new son-of-the-soil look. I said, "I fell over walking in the hills."

"Oh, yes, sir?"

When I got to my room and looked in the mirror I realised that my explanation must have seemed a little inadequate. "I went for a swim in the pig-trough" might just about have carried conviction.

I looked around the room and saw that it had been searched—as I'd expected. That window was far from impregnable. Well, I could take that: all part of the job. I checked my belongings, and nothing seemed to have disappeared—not even my Walkman. The search wouldn't have told them much about myself, except that I was no Beau Brummel, and liked Italian opera and science fiction. My personal documents I had kept on myself.

I washed, changed my T-shirt, shook the remaining insects out of my hair, jeans, pants, armpits, and other nooks onto the floor where they scuttled away, terror-struck by the lack of cover. I expected to renew the pleasure of their acquaintance in bed that night.

I went along to the loo and checked that the novel was still there, with its precious contents. It was. Amateurs, amateurs, I said again—still trying to forget about the gun. I had another quick read of Giorgio Malberti's epistle. It gave me some interesting leads, but still left me asking a lot of questions. Well, maybe Piers would be able to answer them, once I'd sprung him.

But that would have to wait, I thought, until the night. In the meantime I would try and get another independent viewpoint on the village and its goings-on. I made my way to the church in the square. After all, I'd met the local squire, local barman, local historian, and assorted local loonies, so the local priest seemed a logical next step.

The church's interior was a cosy mish-mash of architectural styles, with baroque chapels lining a Renaissance aisle leading up to a Gothic apse housing a rococo altar. There was a little old lady (standard Victorian) lighting candles in a side chapel and a gloomy sacristan (late Perpendicular) dusting the plastic flowers in the Madonna's dress (Zeffirelliate-Kitsch).

I did my tourist bit for a few minutes, studying the paintings and the carvings prior to asking the sacristan if I could talk to the priest. Then Don Luigi himself came in from a side door and bustled over to the sacristan. He was a tiny figure with a great mop of white hair. He must have been well over eighty, but moved with a determined energy that seemed to communicate itself to the whole church. The candles glittered harder, the old lady muttered faster, and even the smile on the Madonna's face seemed a shade less vacuous. He went over to the sacristan and talked to him for a minute or so. The sacristan's dusting really began to disturb the dust. I was still thinking of a good opening line when Don Luigi whirled up to me and said, "A visitor?"

"Yes?"

"Where from?"

"England."

"Ah. Wonderful. I'm sorry I have no English. You understand me, do you? Excellent. Have you seen the Brusasorci paintings? Not his finest, in my opinion, though experts seem very appreciative. And the high altar? Rather over the top, some feel—more suited to a fountain, I've even heard it said—but I think it works, don't you? There is an undoubted life and energy in the figures, don't you think? And how about the St. George?"

"Oh, yes." I only now realised that the front of the altar was another representation of the saint and the dragon: this time a stylised version of the Carpaccio painting in Venice. "St. George seems very important here. Well, I suppose he's bound to be . . ."

"You've been to the museum? You have? Oh, excellent. Such a tragedy about the original statue. Have you seen the tiles in this chapel?" He pointed to blue floor tiles with white and grey carvings. "Another of our local glories, I feel: eighteenth century—you recognise the buildings depicted there? The square, the church, the villa. . . . This craftsman carried out these exquisite little masterpieces in churches up and down the valley. And this statue here—St. Jerome: no beauty, I admit, reminds me of the bishop rather, but undeniably vigorous, don't you think? But you were talking of St. George. You really should talk to our local expert on the subject—Professor Pigozzi."

"Well, actually I have spoken to him."

"You have? I see you're an enthusiast." This obviously pleased him.

I said, "Well, I'm doing research into the statue, and I was rather hoping that I might ask you a few questions about it—if it's not too much trouble."

"No trouble at all. I'm glad to meet an enthusiast; so few people seem to have heard of our treasure—or what was our treasure. Do come and take a glass of wine. I know the English are usually so fond of a drop of wine—well, and beer too. Not to mention whisky."

"That's very kind of you." Just moments later I was sitting in an oak-lined study with bishops frowning down at me between the bookcases. I couldn't actually recall how we had got there, though from the fact that I was winded I suppose we must have walked, not simply rematerialised. He had already opened a bottle of red wine. Maybe he'd had it under his hassock.

"So you've met Pigozzi, you say. Most learned man, if sometimes a little—well, a little uncompromising in his opinions."

"Not a great churchman, I suspect."

Don Luigi laughed. "You could say that. I think he's never forgiven us for stopping the burning of heretics. But a most learned man. He was a highly respected figure in the university before he retired."

"He believes the statue—the St. George statue—is still to be found."

"Oh, dear, that old story."

"You don't believe it then?"

"I don't think about it. I'm afraid this village has far too many other problems for me to start troubling myself with that." He handed me a glass and poured one out for himself.

"Yes, I've heard something about it. The Knights of St. George."

He looked very serious. "Racist nonsense. But dangerous nonsense. I've already announced my intention to organise a vigil for peace and tolerance on Friday. I think it quite likely I'll be announcing it on television soon. On the eight o'clock news, who knows. The village is coming rather into the public eye—and not in a way I like."

"Who do you think these people are?" I said.

"Oh, I'm sure they're nobody. Just local hooligans who've heard of the Knights of St. George and have decided to adopt the name to sound impressive."

"These knights really did exist then?"

He looked embarrassed. "Oh, you know how it is. Every little community in Italy had its secret society. It's the same with this valley." He stood up. "Follow me."

"Oh, right." Well, I suppose we'd been sitting down for nearly a whole minute.

He led me into the next room: more oak, more books, and more paintings. He pointed out a dark canvas in the corner of the room. I went over and studied it: another St. George painting, the figure of the saint this time clearly modelled on the statue—the same stumpy vigour and the same surly face. The dragon was writhing underneath his feet, more like a squashed garden worm than a firebreathing monster, so the Mauro bullying expression seemed particularly appropriate. In the background, where one might have expected a chained damsel, was a group of kneeling figures, whose seventeenth-century clothes and closely painted features made it obvious that they were actual portraits. They were all men, and despite their prayer-joined hands, seemed to be enjoying the live show.

"The Knights of St. George," he said. "This painting was given to the church last century by a local family, but I had it removed from its chapel. I have my doubts about the piety of these figures. It may be that in origin the society was formed to promote good works, but the rumours are that it degenerated into a mere petty local Mafia. It was revived by the Carbonari, I believe, but once again degenerated. No more was heard of it until very recently, when a local journalist claimed that Licio Gelli's Masonic Group had established contacts with the society. And I think someone tried to suggest a link with Gladio—" He looked at me quizzically, as if to see if I knew what he was referring to. I nodded and he went on: "But you know how it is in Italy: you can claim anything is linked with anything, and anybody with anybody, from the Pope downwards, and nobody can prove you wrong." He gave a gesture of distaste and ushered me back to the other room.

I sat down again. "I suppose you must remember when the statue got taken by the Germans."

"I'm not likely to forget it," he said. "I was parish priest already then."

"And the partisans' reaction."

"Yes. But you can't really want to hear about these things."

"No, I assure you. I'd be most interested."

"Well, if you say so. What exactly do you wish to know?"

"How it happened. I mean, how you all heard about it."

He didn't need any time for recollection; he went straight into the account. "Well, we none of us witnessed the partisans' attack. It happened at night. The Germans had occupied the local school as their headquarters. We heard an explosion and then gunfire. The next day the Germans told us what had happened. We were all terrified of course, because we'd heard of some of the terrible reprisals that had been taken elsewhere in the country: whole villages destroyed, or people taken out and shot at random. Fortunately the local commander was not of this brutal nature; he simply announced that the crime would not go unavenged and that they were already on the trail of the 'rebels.' " He was now obviously back in 1944. "And we realised that a whole platoon of German soldiers was in fact making its way up into the hills. For the rest of the day we could do nothing but wait—and then at around lunchtime—was it really very hot? I suppose it can't have been, not in April, but that's how I remember it—well, at lunchtime that boy came running into the square, pale but not crying. He told the whole story: he'd seen them set fire to the building—heard their screams. . . ." He shook his head. "Just a boy, you know, a boy. I find it difficult to forgive Giorgio that. But then, poor Giorgio too, of course."

"You mean Giorgio Malberti?"

"Yes. Giorgio should never have allowed him to get involved at that age. Admittedly the boy was very determined, not the sort to be put off a thing once he'd decided on it—rather like Giorgio himself, in fact—but he hero-worshipped Giorgio, and I'm sure if Giorgio had ordered him to stay at home he'd have done so."

"Who was he?" I said.

"Oh, he wasn't from here—Emilia Romagna or somewhere like that. I believe he had relatives or something here, I can't recall. I think he was called Johnny—or something foreign like that. At least that was what he called himself."

"And the relatives are no longer here?"

"No. Maybe they were in the next village in fact. I really can't recall. I just remember his thin little face—always deadly serious and determined: rather like Giorgio in character, in fact, as I say."

"Deadly serious?"

"Well, no—Giorgio was never that, certainly. I taught Giorgio, you know—or tried to. The Catechism." He shook his head with a trace of a smile, obviously recalling some of Giorgio's less serious moments. "But he was extremely determined—stubborn even. He'd persist in something even when it was clearly wrong. I remember hearing about a game of hide-and-seek when he was quite a young boy, and he wouldn't come out and show himself even when his mother was in floods of tears. Federico had to get him to give himself up in the end. Well, this little boy had the same stubborn streak—and rather unforgiving streak too."

"Then what happened?" I said. "After the boy had come and told everybody about the fire?"

"Well, people went up to see of course. The boy went to tell

Giorgio's mother and brother. The boy! I suppose it must sound very strange—but in war the strangest—the cruellest things come to seem quite normal."

"And then?"

"Well, then the Germans searched everywhere for possible 'traitors'—people who might have helped the partisans, that is. I think the Malberti family managed to get the boy out of the valley. Dear me, what sad stories we seem to be telling." He poured me another glass of wine. "Not that the present seems any more cheerful at the moment. Will you be staying long?"

"I'm not sure," I said. It was nice to be able to reply honestly to at least one question.

"I hope you'll come along to our vigil on Friday at least. Have you met our African friends?" It didn't sound just like a cliché from him. "I think it would be extremely effective if we could have a whole mixture of people there. So if you can come . . ."

"I'll do my best if I'm still in the area. How are the, er, African friends taking the business?"

"Calmly, so far. They say they have faith in Italian justice. I can only hope they will continue in this attitude."

"And that their faith is well placed."

"That does indeed remain to be seen."

THIRTEEN

· · · · · · · · ·

I THEN WENT ALONG TO THE BAR for a sandwich-lunch. I could hear the usual din from within, with its heady mixture of the barman's voice, the cardplayers' bellows, and the merry massacring mayhem of the video game, and I decided to sit outside again. I braved the decibels just to go in and order a salami sandwich and a glass of white wine, and to pick up the bar's copy of the local newspaper.

There was one tiny article on the inside pages about the killing, which said that leads were being followed up and lines of inquiry gone into more profoundly—i.e., they hadn't got a clue. There was nothing about the car-bombing: that had obviously happened too late at night.

I finished the sandwich and the wine and then gazed tranquilly around the square like the two old men at the nearby table. As my eyes roved, I spotted a motorbike parked close to the bar. I only had to look at it for three seconds to know that it was the one I'd examined up in the woods. Its owner (or part-owner) was presumably in the bar at that very moment. I guessed the noisy bunch around the video games were the most likely suspects. Well, I'd just have to hang around and see who mounted it.

But first I had to phone Gigi. He was expecting a call from me right now, I thought, looking at my watch. I could make it from the phone on the other side of the square and still keep the bike under my eyes.

I crossed over, got the number of the hotel from directory inquiries, and phoned. I was put through to Gigi immediately.

"Yeah, *pronto*," he said.

"Jan here."

"Oh, yeah. So how you doing then?"

"Well, I've got a lead I'm following up."

"Oh, yeah."

"And there's a line of inquiry I'm going into."

"Oh, yeah."

"A little more profoundly, you know. I may have some news tomorrow."

"Oh, great."

"You don't believe me, do you?"

"Just give us results, Jan. We don't need the bullshit."

"Right." The temptation was strong to drop the words, "Well, I've found him," but I didn't. He would then offer help in springing Piers, and while I knew I could do with help of some kind, I also knew that I could do without Gigi's help, which would almost certainly involve guns.

I stifled the little voice inside myself which said if ever I was being childish it was now, since Luca and his pal had guns— and real ones. My specialty was improvisation, after all—and what kind of improviser was I if I couldn't improvise my way around a little thing like that?

I said, "Any chance of my having a word with Sir Alf?"

"He's gone off sight-seeing."

"Ah. Not fretting by the phone."

"Well, he can fret and sightsee, can't he?"

"What about Rita?"

"She's in her room right now, I think. What do you want her for?"

"Just one or two little questions. You know—leads to follow up, etcetera."

"Yeah, yeah." He put the phone down.

I phoned again and got put through to Rita's room. She said, "Hello?" and at once I saw her, with her brightly painted lips close to the receiver, her long legs folded one over the other. . . .

I got a grip on myself and said briskly, "Hello, it's Jan here. Phoning from San Giorgio."

"Well?"

"Well, I think I've got a definite lead, and I'm pretty sure he's around here. And alive."

"If you're just saying this to comfort me I swear I'll kill you."

"I'm not that stupid. I can't be more definite at the moment, I'm afraid."

"Okay. I suppose I've just got to trust you."

Wow, I thought. That was a different tone from yesterday. Then she went on, "I've got no choice, have I?"

"Well, no. But I swear I'll deserve it."

"You'd better."

"Listen," I said. "Could I ask you one or two little questions?"

"What about?"

"You and Piers. For instance, whose idea was it to come to Verona?"

"I told you. We decided together."

"What—you both said Verona and then *snap?*"

"No. We were talking about places and we agreed Verona sounded nice."

"Yes. But who first said it?"

A moment's pause and then she said, "I suppose he did."

"And did he seem to have any reason?"

"Just said it seemed interesting. You know, Roman remains and churches and that."

"He's interested in that sort of thing then."

"Well, you know, you come to Italy you expect to see a bit of that stuff."

"Okay. Listen: did you ever see him looking at a folder—a blue folder with some photocopies in it?"

"When?"

"On this holiday."

"No. What is it?"

"Never mind. It's a possible lead. Can I ask you something about Sir Alfred?"

"You can ask."

"Do you think he'd ever heard of San Giorgio Veronese?"

There was another moment's pause. Then she said, "Funny you say that."

"Why?"

"Well, you see—look, this is just a kind of impression I got—probably doesn't mean anything." She paused again and I could imagine her frowning, with those bright lips pursed.

"Go on." These gaps weren't good for my fervid imagination.

"Yeah, well, I think he might have done. Heard of it, I mean. But look, it's just an impression, like I said. I don't know what makes me think it. I mean, I didn't think it at the time, when I rang him up. It was just later, thinking back on what he said and that. And I can't even remember anything definite that he said that made me think it. I mean, nothing like, 'Oh, yes, San Giorgio, up by San Bonifacio.' Nothing like that. Just—just something about the way he answered. But I could be quite wrong."

"I see. Any ideas on where he might have heard of it?"

Another pause. "Well, you know, Piers has always been curious about what his father did in the war."

"Aha." I think I really did say it.

She didn't notice but went straight on. "You see, his dad has always told him he couldn't talk about it. And that's what made him curious. You see, he was definitely in Italy, and not as a regular soldier. But he's never said where he was and what he was doing."

"But why didn't he just ask him?"

"Like I said, he won't say. And anyway you've got to understand the way things are between Piers and his dad."

"Tell me then." I didn't say that she could have told me all this the day before.

"Well, they don't talk much. And the thing is, Piers has always had this feeling that his dad doesn't take him seriously. You know: he's not going to make 'a serious career.'" She put the last three words in pompous quote marks.

"He isn't going to join the Civil Service."

"Right. I mean, Piers has had this kind of stuff from his dad ever since he didn't go to university, if you see what I mean. And then of course when he went off to drama school. . . . So anyway, Piers has always had somewhere the aim of, well, proving himself to his father. You know, always longing for the day when he could say, 'Look at me now.' And stick two fingers up at the Civil Service and all it stands for."

"So Piers may have gone off to prove his manhood in some way?"

"Could have. He doesn't need to prove it to me, mind you."

"No, but he does to his father."

"Could be."

"One other thing," I said. "What's Sir Alf's Italian like?"

"Sounds good to me. But then so does Chico Marx's."

"Look, I've got to ring off now. Bye." I cut the phone call short abruptly, hoping she'd think I'd been surrounded by surly heavies. In fact, I'd just seen a young man come out of the bar and head towards the motorbike. I recognized him vaguely; he hadn't been playing the video machines, but had been sitting on his own with a paper. Someone had addressed him as Mario. He was wearing loose grey trousers, a lank T-shirt, and was unshaven.

Well, I'd identified him. What now?

He started putting his helmet on.

A pretty crazy idea came to me. I couldn't follow him, so . . .

I set across the square in the direction of the castle, whistling loudly. I wished I had a spade with me, which would have given a definite look of purpose to my walk. I just had to make do with a studied briskness of pace. I carefully avoided looking at the motorbike, but he couldn't have failed to see me. There were no shop windows nor even car mirrors along the route I was taking, so I had no means of discovering whether I was being followed, but I hadn't heard the motorbike start up yet.

I started up the path towards the castle. After a minute or so I felt sure I could hear stealthy footsteps somewhere in the trees below me. I kept walking and wondered how much of the sweat now breaking from my every pore was due to the heat. I didn't even have a weapon, I realised—not even a stout stick. I studied every bush and tree that I passed as a possible supplier, but remembered that my priority was to give no indication that I suspected I was being followed. Breaking off branches and brandishing them apemanlike might arouse suspicion.

I reached the castle and continued up the path that led to the chapel above. I did my best to keep that purposeful rhythm in my stride, despite the sticky heat and a general desire to fold up and faint into the ferns. Whatever else, I had to stimulate the man's curiosity, so that he'd want to find out what I was up to rather than just clobber me. My ears remained on permanent alert and I heard occasional twig-snaps and leaf-rustles behind me which I felt sure weren't caused by rabbits.

When I saw the stumpy shape of the chapel ahead of me I quickened my pace yet further. I was opening the flap on my shoulder bag at the same time, and I pulled out Pigozzi's guide-book. I panted up the steps into the clearing, dashed to the door of the chapel, and heaved up the bolt that secured it. The door let out its catlike squeal as I opened it, and I tossed the book into the cool gloom. Then I left the door slightly ajar and slipped round the side of the chapel where I pressed myself against the wall—into the arms of St. George.

I stood dead still and listened hard. I heard the birds, the trees, my heartbeats. . . . And then a suppressed but nonetheless audible panting. I tried to push myself further into St. George's armour-clad embrace. I now heard stealthy footsteps approaching the clearing. They faltered and I could imagine the man scanning the area from the cover of the bushes. He stifled his panting completely. There wasn't a sound from him for a full half-minute, during which I'm sure St. George's heart started throbbing too. Then I heard feet padding across the clearing to the chapel. I even heard the rustle as a hand was put to the wooden door, and I imagined I could hear the swivel of his eyeballs as he peered suspiciously into the interior.

Now I prayed hard to St. George: if he could take on dragons he could do a little thing like make this man spot the book on the floor, wonder about it, step towards it . . .

The door squealed, and then his footsteps clicked on the chapel's stone floor. I slipped round the corner, grabbed the door by its ring-handle, pulled it sharply shut, and shot the bolt down. I don't think I've ever done anything so fast in my life. I just had one shadowy glimpse of him, in mid-stoop towards the book on the floor, but with his face jerking round towards me. The next instant the first "Ueh!" rent the air and then there was a crash against the door. I looked at the wood and then at the bolt and reckoned it would probably hold. But I didn't care to sit and listen to the oaths and threats and pummelling. I'd come back another time to study the stones in the area.

I went back down the path at a run.

I now had just one kidnapper to think of. For the moment at any rate. When that man got out of the chapel I'd probably do well to bear him in mind too. But one thing at a time. And now it was rescue time.

FOURTEEN

. . . .

HALF AN HOUR LATER I WAS walking back through the woods
on the other side of the village. My first idea had been to leave
the rescue until nightfall, but that was out of the question now.
I didn't imagine that Mario was likely to resign himself to a
quiet afternoon's perusal of the guidebook. One way or another he was going to get out of that chapel—and he was the
one who turned nasty ("and I mean really nasty") when he got
angry. For this reason I now had my full rucksack on my back
and the hold-all in one hand. I had paid my bill at the hotel and
was now making a vow to the Church's other great demoted
saint: Christopher. I was going to become a traveller as soon as
possible—to Timbuctoo or Trebizond, for preference.

It was possible, I thought, that I'd been a touch impulsive:
maybe that improvisatory instinct of mine needed backing by
occasional use of the brain cells as well. It was true that I'd put
one of the thugs out of action, but I'd made the whole rescue a
good deal more urgent by so doing; earlier I'd been thinking of
wandering the wood all afternoon in order to make myself
thoroughly familiar with their every path and pothole, but now
I had to come up with a plan for a lightning strike.

And even as I thought this I found myself slowing my pace.
And ten seconds later I came to a complete halt and took the
rucksack off my back. Its weight and size and colour scheme
gave me all the stealth and discretion of a heavy-metal rock

band in these woods. I found a convenient nook for it and the hold-all, and made some kind of pretence of concealing them in the undergrowth.

I started walking again, my shirt glued to my back, and I smeared my face with earth as I walked. It was nice to know that I had some wet wipes in my pocket, for after the rescue.

I kept walking and hoping that some plan for this rescue would come to mind. After all, it was only one man I was up against. And one gun . . .

I was already lamenting my foolishness in not calling in my brother—just because of some nitpicking scruple against us (the goodies) using guns. Entirely childish; after all, if things were prepared properly, no bullet need actually be fired. "Drop that rifle—you're covered"—that kind of setup.

Now I had to achieve that same result without actually being able to cover him. I was approaching the mini-cliff where the kidnap-cave was, and my pace was getting slower and stealthier than ever. Various ideas were going through my mind now: unfortunately they all involved items that I didn't actually possess, such as tear gas grenades and rope ladders. I decided to work from the other end, by seeing what I actually did have with me.

This stocktaking didn't take long (pen, notebook, penknife, wet wipes . . .) and brought no enlightenment.

I crawled on my belly towards the top of the cliff. I could hear Luca moving around below. I peered through the grass at the edge and saw him with a cigarette in his lips, idly walking up and down. His foetal features were abbreviated almost to zero by this foreshortened view. They were on tracking-scan, however, and the gun was on display and on hand. And all I was on was edge.

Well, it just needed one well-aimed rock, and he'd not be using that gun, I thought. Then I thought that the trouble with that was that I was about as good at aiming as I was at long-term planning—and I wouldn't be given a second try. Looking around my hiding place I could see one or two rocks which if levered over the edge would be guaranteed to cause maximum destruction within a radius of six feet from their centre, but that would make my objections to using guns merely aesthetic ones.

So I lay still and observed. Half a minute later he tossed the cigarette stub into the grass—which, with the September woods like expectant tinder, could have solved the whole question (including my long-term future) in spectacular fashion, but a second or two later he thought better of it and went and stamped it out properly. Then he picked up the gun and started training it on the nearby bushes. I almost expected to hear him muttering "Bang bang," and wondered how come he still hadn't smeared his face up.

Eventually he tired of this and propped the gun against a rock. I started thinking of plans that involved nothing more sophisticated than fishing rods and/or magnets—and then did my best to reconcile them with that depressing list I'd already formulated.

But, I suddenly thought, I did have more stuff in the rucksack. I lay still and ran through the contents mentally. The glimmerings of an idea began to form.

The next half hour saw me at my most sinuously Mohican, squirming, sliding, slithering, serpenting, and sidling through the trees in a fifty-foot radius from the cave. Any observer would have imagined I was engaged on some arts council project to give the woods a new look, since my main occupation was draping the trees and bushes with my dirty clothes. While doing so I picked up all suitable stones that I came across and put them in my shoulder bag. I took great care to remain out of sight at all times, though there was one moment when I guessed from the extra-tense hush that Luca had caught some odd noise and was standing still and listening hard. I did the same, though unfortunately the emergency had caught me in a most painful crouching position. Eventually the renewed sound of pacing feet indicated that he'd shrugged his suspicions off. I rose to my feet, rather surprised to find that I could do so.

Then I took my old Walkman and slotted in a cassette I discovered I'd taken from the Oxbridge Institute: Thompson and Martinet grammar drills. It was perfect for what I was planning, far more suitable than the other cassettes (mostly Verdi and Puccini) would have been.

I switched it on and placed it underneath a miniature carpet of ivy with the tiny headphones pointing upwards: a carefully articulated English voice started fizzing from the leaves: "Present Perfect Progressive: I have been drinking . . ." I pushed the volume up to maximum and slid away. When I'd got about twenty feet away, I stood still and listened: it was a just audible crackle—and each time my ears homed in on it, the voice stopped—for the student-listener to reply to the drill, of course. It could almost have been designed for its present use.

I made my way to a tree I'd already picked out and climbed into its lower branches and squatted there; I wasn't lonely—a hundred spiders had had the same idea, and I soon found myself hosting an enthusiastic welcoming committee. I did my best not to seem too standoffish, and kept as still as possible while they got to know me intimately.

I couldn't see Luca, or the cave, but I could hear his occasional bored footsteps. The little voice crackled on, drilling the local insect population in the complexities of English verb tenses. And eventually I heard what I'd hoped for—Luca's footsteps coming closer to the edge of the clearing. Then they stopped and there was complete silence from his direction again; the crackled started up again, and then was silent for five seconds. And then it started again. . . . Luca's attention was definitely caught now. I could imagine the fierce concentration on his tiny features as he tried to identify the noise and its direction.

Then he started picking his way through the trees. A few seconds later I caught a glimpse through the foliage of his denim shirt, about thirty feet away. He disappeared behind some more trees. Another few seconds passed and then I saw him clearly, his face panning round, clearly unable to home in on the cassette machine. At that moment I shouted in Italian, accentuating my natural Neapolitan accent almost to caricature: "Drop that gun, put your hands on your head, this is the Carabinieri."

It was as if he'd suddenly had a million volts shoved through his circuits: the slow swinging movement of his head was instantly speeded up about a thousand times and the rifle jerked wildly, jabbing into the air in a thousand directions. Then he dropped to the ground. He did not drop the gun, however.

Well, that was the end of that plan. I'd just have to ask him to go back while I thought up another one.

Then I realised that he hadn't located me. I threw one of the stones into the bushes to his left. His gun swung round and he fired. He had evidently seen one of my haute-couture bushes. I threw another stone, to his right. I wasn't intending to hit him; my only plan was to keep him confused—to prevent him from thinking too rationally. The random noises in the bushes and the sight of clothes here and there were all designed to make him panic. His gun swung again and fired again. I threw another stone and then shouted again: "Drop that gun or we'll fire. You are surrounded."

Unless he started wondering why we hadn't fired already, there was no reason for him not to believe it was the Carabinieri. He certainly would have no idea that the blond Englishman he'd been curious about in the village could speak with a perfect Neapolitan accent. And I hoped that his instinct would be just to get out.

He raised himself and then started running: I had left one area undecorated with articles from my wardrobe, and that was the direction he took, as I had hoped. There was one obvious path in that direction and it passed directly beneath my tree. I hadn't taken any definite decision as to whether I would just let him go or drop down on him as he passed. My Errol Flynn side of course urged me to come to grips with the varlet, but my Flashman side was for staying up there quietly with the spiders. I could feel my heart beating faster, almost in time to his footsteps, as his crouching, panic-stricken figure approached.

I don't know when I made the decision. Maybe some impatient spider pushed me. Anyway I dropped down and my feet landed in his neck and he went sprawling. So, of course, did I. But on top of him, and with all the advantages of not being quite so surprised as he was (though I hadn't expected him to be so hard to land on). One instant later I had grabbed hold of the gun and jerked it from his hand, which made hardly any resistance. Then I jumped to my feet and waved the rifle at him and said, "Get up."

He had twisted himself round to look up at me, and I would never have thought such tiny eyes could emanate quite so much hatred; I suppose it came concentrated. He didn't move. I repeated it and he must have caught the Neapolitan accent. He said, "Who are you?"

"That doesn't matter. Put your hands on your head and take me to that cave, and I warn you one false step and it'll be your last." It wasn't the first time I'd noticed how melodramatic situations bring out the clichés in me.

He got to his feet looking more sullen than ever; but he put his hands on his head, turned and started making towards the cave. I followed and took advantage of his back being towards me to study the gun and make sure I'd be able to fire it if the situation required. Well, I'd got the trigger sussed out, and the bullet more than likely came out of the other end. I took care to keep my finger off the trigger.

We crossed the clearing and I said loudly in English, "Piers Ainsley, I'm here to set you free."

I heard a sound of muffled puzzlement from within. I jabbed Luca in the back, urging him into the cave. It was dark and damp inside and I couldn't at once see Piers. Then I made him out—a huddled shape sitting up against the curving wall at the far end, about fifteen feet away. Luca had halted just a few steps into the cave. I said, "Untie him," and prodded him again with the rifle. Luca walked towards the huddled figure and I glanced around the cave.

There were some plastic shopping bags by the entrance, a large blue rucksack, a few loosely folded blankets, and a litter of beer cans, plastic mineral water bottles, half-eaten bread rolls and some strip-cartoon magazines. The ground was hard earth broken by knobby rocks which glistened slimily with the little light from the entrance. Blackened leaves hung around in damp piles against the rocks. It was impossible to make out the full extent of the cave, as there were fissures and crevices here and there that led into impenetrable blackness; I felt sure that five minutes in there alone would convince me of the existence of the devil. I hoped that Piers had little imagination, or enough jolly memories to keep him company.

Piers was leaning forwards now, while Luca fiddled at his wrists behind his back. Only now could I see sufficiently in the gloom to make out that he had a gag in his mouth. Luca turned to me and said, "I can't untie it—I'll need a knife."

"Oh, yeah—or would you prefer this gun?"

"I mean it, it's really tight. My mate tied it."

"I'll give you just twenty seconds to do it. Use your teeth if you like, but I'm not letting you have a knife."

"But—"

"Just get on with it."

I could now see Piers's eyes looking up at me—I hoped with admiration, or at least relief. It was difficult to make out his expression with just his eyes visible.

Luca returned to the wrists. I saw that the rope that tied them together hung down from a spiky rock protruding from the wall a foot or so above Piers's head. A little while later—more than twenty seconds, in fact—Piers swung his hands free and tore the gag from his mouth.

"Who are you?" he said.

"Never mind about that now. Let's get this bloke tied up." I waved the gun at Luca, who was still hovering over Piers.

"But are you English or Italian?"

"A bit of both." As if to prove it I switched back to Italian, addressing Luca. "Sit down just where he was sitting."

He didn't move. "My mate will be back soon."

"I know," I said, "and he gets angry. And when he gets angry, he gets very nasty. Well, I'm feeling pretty nasty now, and so I'm sure is Piers here."

Piers showed it by shoving the gag into his mouth and forcing him to sit down. He did it with a sudden savagery that took me aback, despite what I'd just said. I felt I could hardly criticise him however; he had, after all, been sitting there gagged and tied up for the last two days. He bent over and started tying Luca.

"So your mate will have the pleasure of untying you," I said.

"You piece of shit," Piers said in Italian like me, and he stood back and then suddenly kicked him in the side. Luca merely turned up those piggy eyes and fixed him with them.

"Come on," I said, a little uneasily. "Let's get away."

"Sorry," Piers said, turning to me. "I just—well, I just feel so angry." He pushed back some loose hair from his eyes and then turned and looked at me with a rather dazed expression on his face.

"Come on," I backed out, the rifle still trained on Luca. Piers took a few stiff steps, and then bent and massaged his legs with a groan. He moved to the entrance, picked up the blue rucksack and slung it onto his shoulders. I said, "Shall I . . ." but he waved one hand in refusal and then followed me out of the cave. He stood blinking in the leaf-filtered light.

"What time is it?" he said.

"About a quarter past three," I said. "Er, Thursday."

"Yes," he said. Then with a kind of irritation, "Yes, I'm not that far gone."

That wasn't evident from looking at him. Apart from his obviously unkempt appearance—matted hair, unshaven face, crumpled shirt and trousers—his eyes were strained, almost wild, and there was the hint of a twitch at the corner of his mouth. He bore only a coincidental resemblance to the careless young hearty in his father's photos. I said, "We can have explanations later. First let's get right away from this area. Are you up to walking?"

"I suppose so. But where the hell are we?"

"Don't worry. It's not too far to civilization. First I'd just like to pick up my clothes."

"Your what?"

"You'll see." I led the way to those bushes I'd adorned. I draped the clothes over my shoulder, so that I still had the gun free in my hand. I discovered one T-shirt with a bullet hole almost dead centre. I was glad I hadn't known that he could do that kind of thing when I was tossing stones at him. Piers followed me in a rather zombielike way, asking no further questions, just occasionally pushing the hair from his eyes with a ticlike gesture. Finally I picked up my Walkman, which was now explaining the use of the passive voice in English, switched it off and clipped it onto my belt. "Right, let's go."

He said, "You're sure you've got everything now?" There was just a hint of peevishness in the sarcasm here.

I told myself what a lot he'd been through. "Yes, yes. I'll explain the whole business in a moment. Let's go."

"Just tell me who you are. You seem to know who I am."

"I've come from your girlfriend." This seemed the easiest explanation for the moment—as well as being in line with his father's request not to mention him.

"Not my father?"

"What? Why should you think that?"

"He's usually behind most things."

"Oh. Well, I've met him . . ."

"I knew it. Anyway thanks."

"That's all right. My job."

"Oh, yeah? Well, that must be fun." He didn't sound impressed.

I told myself again that this man had had a very rough couple of days—and also that this was probably what I needed to keep my head a reasonable size. I said very sweetly and simply, "Shall we go?"

"After you."

I led the way along a path that led towards my bags. As we crossed a tiny clearing a voice yelled out: "Drop that gun!" and a shot rang out.

Piers dived for cover and I was left wildly swinging my rifle all round; the clothes all fell from my shoulder. I must have borne a very strong resemblance to Luca in similar circumstances about five minutes earlier. Then another shot hit a tree just behind me and I dropped the rifle onto the T-shirts and pullovers and raised my hands.

Out of the trees stepped Mario. He was holding a rifle similar to the one I'd dropped and he had a very nasty smile on his face. I suddenly found myself believing all the things that Luca had said about him. He swung the rifle in the direction of Piers, who was still cowering under his rucksack like a psychedelic tortoise, and he said to him in Italian, "Get up."

Piers rose with difficulty. He looked at me and said, "Well, thanks a million for the walk."

"Shut up," said Mario in Italian. Then to me: "Do you know how I got out?"

"Go on then, tell me."

"Your girlfriend let me out."

"Who?"

"Your girlfriend. The little one with the short blond hair."

Linda. "Oh. Nice of her." There didn't seem to be much else I could say to that. I raised a different subject. "What do you think you're going to get out of this? We've both seen your face and your friend Luca's. You can't hope to get away with it."

"That's a problem, isn't it?" he said, still smiling. "What do you think I'm going to do about it? What would your solution be?"

"Well, you can just say sorry and hope we'll be magnanimous enough to forget all about it."

"Oh, yes, of course. What a nice idea. What a nice idea. We'll have to think that over. Back at the cave—with my friend Luca. And I hope he's all right. If I find out he's not all right, I tell you I could get very angry and then your nice idea might not seem so nice to me." I recognised where Luca had picked up his line of talk. It sounded far more convincing from Mario, however—and I don't think that was just because I was at the wrong end of his gun. After a pause he suddenly burst out in a quiet fury: "This time we'll leave you in that cave with the entrance walled up. When they do find your bodies they'll wonder why your pricks have been cut off and shoved in your mouths. Get moving."

We both started moving back in the direction of the cave. We left the gun in the grass. This time I followed Piers and there was total despair in the curve of his back. It was lucky I hadn't tried to insist on his showing a little more gratitude.

Then as we crossed the clearing towards the cave entrance another voice broke the silence from behind us. "Drop that gun or I shoot you in the back. Don't turn round." It was a female voice speaking in English-accented Italian. I didn't immediately recognise it—mainly because it was so utterly unexpected.

Mario must have made a movement behind us because there was the sound of another shot. Then I heard the clatter of his rifle being dropped.

"Okay, Jan," the voice said in English, "turn round and pick up his gun."

"My God," I said as I turned, "how the hell—how the hell—"

Linda said, "Don't waste time. Pick up that gun." She was standing between two trees at the edge of the clearing with her legs slightly apart and was holding a large pistol with both hands. The stance looked entirely professional. They obviously taught things at finishing schools I had never suspected. She was wearing dark trousers and sweatshirt and had a dark scarf over her hair—and her face was smeared all over with mud.

I made my way past Mario, whose smile had turned into a desperate sneer, and I said, "There's still time to say sorry." It was cheap of me, but I couldn't repress it. I picked up his rifle.

"Now bash him with it," said Piers.

I found myself for one moment looking at Linda for instructions, but then I got a grip on myself and said to Mario, "Into the cave."

"We haven't got any more rope," said Piers. "We'll have to bash him."

"You want to be done for homicide?" I said. "We can use the blankets or something."

"Or we can give them a little talking to," said Linda.

"Oh, yes, of course," said Piers. "And smack their little botties."

"Don't be silly," said Linda. "I've got something to say to them which I'm sure they'll listen to."

"Go ahead," I said. I was completely out of my depth by now. I wondered if I could beg to be excused and just go off and collect my four thousand pounds.

She switched to Italian, which she spoke with the tiptoeing respect of those who find it just so beautifully musical. "Go on into the cave, as this signore told you to."

We all followed Mario—and I think we all of us (with the possible exception of Linda) felt our backs tingling as we wondered who was going to spring out with the next gun: Giorgio Malberti himself?

We entered the cave and Luca made *mm-mm* noises from the far end—whether of welcome or rage we couldn't tell.

"Go over and sit next to him," said Linda. She made it sound like some new party game. But when he hesitated she dug her gun hard into his back. He moved quickly and plonked himself next to Luca, whom he didn't once look at.

"Now," said Linda, "I just want to tell you both that we're not to going to get you into any trouble. We'll leave you free to go off back home. But we just want to warn you that you've been putting your nose into business that is bigger than you."

Mario laughed. "You think you can scare us like this, a little girl like you? And your two amateur friends?"

She answered mildly, "I can tell you that I'm no amateur. And I'm pretty sure you really don't know what all this is about."

Well, that made three of us. At least.

Piers looked at her and said in English, "You do know?"

"Yes."

"Who are you?"

"I'll tell you all that in a moment. Just now I'm trying to get through to these silly nits." Then she said in Italian again, "If you meddle any more in this business, I tell you you'll get your balls blown off."

I think we were all a little taken aback, and she looked at us and said in English, "Sorry, I think it's the only kind of language they understand." Her muddy cheeks glowed in the cave's gloom.

"We are so frightened," Mario said. "We are so terrified."

She was holding the gun with one hand. With her other she was rummaging in her shoulder bag. Suddenly a tinny voice started talking out of it: ". . . very angry and then your nice idea might not seem so nice to me. This time we'll leave you in that cave with the entrance walled up. When they do find your bodies they'll wonder why your pricks have been cut off and shoved in your mouths. Get moving." She clicked the recorder off. "Recognise that? Do you think the police will?"

He shrugged. "So we were having a bit of a joke together."

"Well, I don't know what terms you're on with the police. I think you'd have to be very good friends with them to make them believe that." And then she added, with a slight tone of apology, as if acknowledging an unfortunate but necessary lapse in taste, "And I do have friends at top level."

He was silent for a moment. "So why all this secrecy? Why are you going to let us go?"

"I told you: this is serious business—much more serious than you've ever been used to. We don't want small irrelevant people mixed up in it and confusing things. That is all."

"So who killed Zeno?" Mario said. "Who killed him? Tell me that."

She shrugged. "I can't say. But it was nothing to do with us."

I was getting very intrigued by all these we's and us's. Just who were we? I thought it better not to ask just at that moment, while she seemed to have the situation under such fine control.

"So," she went on, "we will leave you here, roughly tied up. Just so we have time to leave without feeling rushed. When you manage to free yourselves, I suggest you just go home and forget all about this. Because I will be handing over this tape to someone who will know how to make use of it if anything happens to any of us. All right?"

"You bastards," he said very quietly, and looking at all of us in turn. "I won't forget any of this. Nor will my mate."

"Well, really, you might as well try to," Linda said. "It'll do you no good to—to—" She looked at me and said, "How do you say 'brood' in Italian?"

"Just say 'think it over too much.' Unless you want to start clucking. But I don't think there's much point in reasoning things over like that. Let's just clear out."

"Yes, I suppose so. Shall we take that chap's gag out so they can at least chat?"

"And wrap them up warmly and give them a goodnight kiss," said Piers. "Christ. I still say bash them."

"Now, now," said Linda. "I know you've had a hard time of it but don't—don't—"

"Don't brood," I said. I moved towards Luca to take the gag out but was stopped by Mario.

"Spare me that at least," he said. "The bastard'll only moan."

"All right," I said. "As you like."

Linda said to Piers, "Would you mind holding this a moment?" and she gave him her gun. "But do be careful. Triggers are funny little things, you know." She moved towards the two men, rummaging again in her bag. "Now I know I should have some somewhere. . . . Where, oh where . . . Ah, here it is." She drew out a length of cord, neatly looped round with a plastic-coated wire. "Okay, hands behind your back. And no breathing in."

She trussed him expertly and then turned and looked at Luca's bonds. "Hmm," she said, "I think I can do a little better than that." Half a minute later she had tied Luca more securely than we had managed to do. She said to them both, "Now I'm quite sure that two strong men like you will be able to get out of those ropes before too long, so I won't make any provisions for your rescue. And please remember just to keep your nose out of things. Trust in the police to clear up your friend's murder for a start."

Neither of them made any answer. But if they'd applied the looks they were giving her to their ropes, they'd have been free already.

"Okay," said Linda, looking round at Piers and me, "shall we go?"

We nodded and she beckoned us to go out before her. Piers didn't ask if he could have a last kick. Once outside I said, "I'll just go and get those things of mine." It was one way of avoiding asking her what we did next. I made my way over to the little clearing and picked up the rifle. I handed it to Piers. "Here, you must be feeling out of things."

"You'll have to dump those somewhere," said Linda. "We can't go strolling into town with them."

"They're only hunting rifles," I said, picking up all my clothes again.

"Right. And no one is ever going to think you're a hunter."

"And where did you get that pistol?" I asked. She'd tucked it away now in her shoulder bag.

"It's a .357 Magnum. Standard MI6-issue for agents in the field."

"You're a— My God." I stared at her, as did Piers.

"Well, what good's a secret agent who everyone immediately recognises as one?" she said with a smile.

"Ah," I said. "Yes. Yes, there could be something in that."

"I want someone to tell me just who the hell you both are and what's going on," said Piers.

"You took the words out of my mouth," I said. "I just hope one of us knows a bit more than I do. But shall we first get away from here?"

"I've got a car at the top end of the village," said Linda.

"Not in your bag there?" I said.

She ignored this. "If you like I can go and get it, while you two with the rucksacks just make your way to the road, and I'll pick you up there."

"Fine by me," I said. It would give me a chance to have a word with Piers on my own.

Piers just gave a weary nod and Linda said, "Right, see you later, chaps," and set off through the trees. She still looked more like Monica of the Fifth than Modesty Blaise.

FIFTEEN

· · · · · · ·

WE REACHED THE ROAD A QUARTER of an hour later. I suggested staying in among the trees until the car came into sight. We still hadn't dumped the guns: I couldn't speak for Piers, but I know that I didn't like the thought of leaving them anywhere within a five-mile radius of those two thugs, however expertly trussed they were with MI6-issue nylon cord.

We took our rucksacks off and both flapped our shirts a little in the nonexistent breeze. I pulled the packet of wet wipes from my pocket and started cleaning my face. It was a bit like trying to muck out the city sewers with a toothbrush. I asked if he wanted one, but he shrugged a no. Presumably he felt there was no point in trifling with the surface like that. After a while he said, "You haven't got a cigarette, have you?"

"Sorry," I said.

"Those bastards smoked my last."

"Ah. No wonder you felt angry."

His face twitched; it may have been an acknowledgement of a joke, or it may have been just a twitch. He said, "So, anyway who are you?"

"I told you. Sent by Rita." I paused and then added, "And a little bit by your father."

"And what did he tell you?"

"To find you."

"And keep things quiet, right?"

"More or less. Do you want things made noisy?"

"I don't give a damn. I just don't care anymore." He sat down against his rucksack, but he looked far from relaxed. He said, "And why the hell did he get MI5 onto me as well?" He was asking the trees as much as me.

"That is a question. Just who is your father?"

"I don't know. I don't bloody know."

"Ah." It looked as if this explanation was going to take longer than I thought.

After a while Piers went on, "That's partly why I came here. To find out."

It looked as if I wasn't the only one with a mild identity crisis.

"But who are you?" he said, turning to me.

I debated shaking my head sorrowfully and saying, "Ah, would that I knew," but decided it might be better to hurry things along a little. "Well, I'm a kind of private detective."

He didn't laugh, which surprised me a little—and then I got irritated with myself for being surprised: hadn't I rescued him after all? (With a little help from MI6.) I went on, "Rita got onto your father when you disappeared and he got onto my brother who has an agency and he got onto me, as I was in the area. And that's it. I got onto the tail of those two thugs and kept them under watch, and so I got onto where you were being kept. And the rest you more or less saw for yourself."

"Uh-huh."

Maybe someone had warned him against overenthusiasm in early youth.

He thought for a moment, then said, "And what did Rita think of it all?"

"Well, she was worried, of course."

"Oh, yeah." It seemed this hadn't crossed his mind. "Well, I suppose I'd better let her know I'm all right."

"You could do that, yes."

"Christ, it's complicated. What did happen to that Zeno guy?"

"He got shot through the neck."

"Yes, but who by?"

"Well, I'm just glad to know that it wasn't you. It *wasn't,* was it?"

He stared hard at me, as if to see whether I was joking or not. Then he said, "You've got a bloody nerve, haven't you?"

"Well, you can understand me being curious, can't you?"

"How much are you getting paid for all this?"

"Four thousand pounds. Okay, I'm sorry if that last question was offensive; at least you can tell me who this Zeno was."

"He's just a guy I met. That's all." Then he whistled. "Four thousand pounds."

"Nice to know you're appreciated, right?"

"I suppose that's how much it costs to keep things under the carpet."

"Well, I've not disturbed anything under it yet. But that's because I haven't been able to get a peek. I've got no idea what you've been up to—or your father—and I'm getting a little curious. I mean, what am I going to say if they arrest *me* for the murder of this Zeno?"

"You flash your private investigator card presumably and tell them to get in touch with the Ainsley family. Once you've cashed your cheque, of course."

I sighed. I could see that the long heart-to-heart talk that would explain all was a long way off yet. I said, "Your father was here in the war, wasn't he?"

"So you do know something about it. Did he tell you that?"

"No. He didn't even let on that he'd heard of San Giorgio Veronese."

"That sounds like him. Never admit anything until it's impossible to deny it."

"It sounds like the whole of the Civil Service to me. So what was he doing in the war? Was he in Special Ops?"

"I told you, I don't know. That's what I came to find out."

"And you brought with you a goodbye letter from a partisan, a note about a chapel and a castle, and a story about a priceless statue of St. George, right?"

For the first time he showed surprise; his face jerked towards me for one second, and he scrutinised me with the beginnings of curiosity. And then he resumed his look of fatigued disinterest. "Bravo. You found that stuff on top of the wardrobe then."

So that's where he'd kept it: not quite James Bond. "You can have them back," I said, "when I unpack."

He acknowledged this with a nod and went on, "But I'd never heard of that statue until I got here. I didn't come looking for treasure."

"What for then? Scandal?"

"Just the truth."

"And did you find any?" I asked.

"You saw what I found. A bloody cave in the woods with two illiterate thugs."

"Zeno's brother and friend."

"That who they were?"

"So who did tell you about the statue?"

"Zeno, of course."

Here we go round the mulberry bush. "And who's Zeno?"

"That must be the car," he said.

He was right. A blue car was making its way slowly up the hill, and behind the wheel we could see Linda, her eyes carefully scanning the roadside. Her face shone a fresh pink. I got to my feet and stepped out of the trees and she pulled up. It looked a fairly expensive car (I never notice the make of cars, I'm afraid), and I suppose had been hired with MI6 funds. Or perhaps it was an MI6 car, complete with missile launchers and laser-gun attachments.

"Hi," she said. "Get in. You haven't still got those guns, have you? Oh, I suppose we can ditch them somewhere along the road. Put them in the boot with the bags."

We did as she said. Piers then got in the front without raising a single questioning eyebrow in my direction and so I got in the back, making room for myself among the maps, coats, Anita Brookner novels, and cuddly toys (a teddy bear and a panda). "Sorry about the mess," she said with a slightly self-conscious laugh. "Everything gets chucked there."

I said, "How would you tell if someone had slipped a bugging device in here?"

"Oh," she said as we drove off, "I'm not that important. Nobody would want to bug me. Oh, by the way, sorry about the reappearance of that second chap. I had to free him from that chapel, after following you up there. I waited for a while before I let him out so that you'd have time to do whatever you were going to do."

"You were following me. . . ." I said stupidly. Then I pulled myself together. "Er, why did you have to let him out?"

"Well, I couldn't think how else I'd find out where, em . . ." She laughed a little self-consciously, and went on; "Where the action was in the woods. I let him out and followed him. I could have followed you, I suppose you'll say, but I thought you might be on your guard."

This was probably a belated attempt to pander to my ego. Well, it could do with it.

She went on, "And I guessed he'd be so enraged that he'd go straight there without wasting time checking up if he was being followed. And I'd already spiked his bike, so he'd have to walk. But sorry, as I say. It must have given you a nasty moment."

"Yes," I said. I thought of something. "Er, just suppose you'd lost him?"

"Oh, I wouldn't have let myself do that," she said, without even thinking about it. "Anyway, have you two had a good chat? Sorted things out?"

"He's told me how much he's getting for the job," Piers said.

"And do you have to split that with your brother?" she said over her shoulder to me.

"You what?"

"With Luigi."

"Okay," I said, "now tell me my shoe size and blood group—but then please tell me who you are and what you're doing."

"Well, I told you I'm from MI6." She laughed a little. "It always sounds so silly, I know, announcing it like that." And she put on what was presumably intended as a caricature upper-class-twit voice, but which merely sounded like a logical extension of her usual vowel sounds: " 'Hello, Carruthers heah from MI6.' It makes you think of so many awful films, but we're really only a branch of the Civil Service, and we're quite as boring for most of the time."

I wondered if she was deliberately parodying the way I'd been so self-deprecating about the glamour of a private detective's life. I suddenly thought that she'd probably known all along who I was—an out-of-work duck salesman. I found myself clutching at the toy panda for comfort.

She went on: "In the service we've long been curious about certain possible links between some retired agents of ours and some subversive right-wing groups in Italy."

Piers broke in: "Are you saying that my father—"

"That is one possibility we've been looking into. And you yourself had suspicions of him, didn't you?"

"I just wanted to know what he'd done in the war."

"And so did we. Because we think it was then that the links, if any, were established. You presumably know that in 1943 your father was sent on a mission to this area for SOE, right?"

"I worked that out. But he's never said anything about it."

"Well, of course after the war he continued working for us for some years"—she made it sound as if she'd been personally supervising him—"and the instructions are that you talk about nothing to anyone, no matter how long ago it happened. But it's true that war experiences are considered rather differently, and we accept a little, em—"

"Bragging," I suggested.

"Well, a little gentle reminiscing."

"I suppose MI6 realised that Mussolini wasn't so much of a threat," I said, feebly attempting to reassert myself.

"What was he doing here in the war?" Piers broke in.

"He was sent here in 1943 to establish links with the partisans. He knew the area, as he'd spent holidays here as a child, and he spoke good Italian so he seemed a perfect choice. He even knew the partisan leader, Giorgio Malberti, personally."

"Ah," I said, "I remember the old count said that he'd learnt his English from an English family that had a house in the area. Would that have been your father then?"

"Probably," said Piers. "I know that they did come and stay somewhere in the Veneto, but he's never told us where. He's never been a great one for childhood reminiscences, and he didn't have any other relatives I could ask."

Linda went on. "As far as we know he accomplished his mission to the best of his abilities. After Malberti's death, he crossed over to the next valley and joined a band of partisans there, and worked alongside them until the end of the war."

We were winding up the hill, which entailed some pretty vigorous work with the steering wheel, but she didn't allow this to interfere with her flow of talk. Official business was official business, after all.

"And so?" said Piers.

"Well, when your father left the service—in the seventies—we kept tabs on him, just as we do all old service members."

"In case they start getting too reminiscent?" I said.

"That kind of thing," she said. "And we got some evidence of his keeping up links with San Giorgio—despite the fact that he never visited the area."

"What sort of links?" Piers said.

"Occasional letters and phone calls."

"You mean you were watching his post?" he said.

"They are MI6, Piers," I said. "That's their job. Watching themselves. Especially now they don't have to watch the Ruskies." After making these cheap jibes I felt as unreasserted as ever. I went back to the panda.

"Now, now," said Linda. "It may seem silly to outsiders, but I can assure you we know what we're up to."

"I thought the point was to know what the other side was up to," said Piers between his teeth.

She ignored this and went on, "So anyway this made us a little curious and we decided to keep the tabs on him. We then heard about that little affair with your father's desk—"

"Christ!" Piers said. He was obviously really shaken. "You've got our bloody house bugged then."

"No, no, nothing so drastic. We heard about it through a friend of your mother's. A lady who's been keeping a discreet watch on your family affairs. . . ."

"Who's that?"

"Oh, just a friend of your mother's."

"Not Mrs. O'Hanrahan."

"Well, I really shouldn't say . . ."

"The old cow. The old bitch."

"Now, now, she's quite genuinely fond of your mother, but at the same time she's been doing her duty to the service in—"

"When I think of those bloody coffee mornings—Christ, my mother tells her everything. . . ."

"Sorry, what is this desk affair?" I said.

Piers answered, almost through clenched teeth: "Since the whole of bloody MI6 know about it, which probably means Saddem Hussein and Gadaffi too, I don't see why not. It's where it all started for me."

"Oh, really?" Linda said.

"Yes. I mean I may have been vaguely curious about Daddy's past before that, but not enough to start me—em— well, investigating." He looked out of the window. "Where are we going?"

"Well, I thought back to Verona," she said. "I thought I'd take this road into the next valley and then we'd go down and hit the *strada provinciale* further along. Is that all right?"

We both agreed. I think we'd have said yes if she'd said she was taking us to Baghdad, just so long as we didn't have to do anything strenuous like making a decision. Piers went on: "But anyway one day a few months back I needed an envelope and I went into my father's study and opened his desk. He'd never said that we weren't to, it was just a kind of unwritten rule that we asked his permission before going in there. But I really needed this envelope, I was writing to someone who might back an idea I had for a show, well, never mind, nothing came of it even though it really was quite an idea, so I went in there and looked through his desk. And there was this drawer at the back that I opened and I saw all this really old paper, with stuff written in Italian, and I got curious and just took a couple of sheets out and at that moment Daddy came in and he laid into me in a way he'd never done before. I mean, shouting and swearing and getting really worked up, and Mummy heard and she came and asked what was going on: I mean, it really was one hell of a scene. Jesus, like I'd been rifling through his pockets or something. Then he calmed down and said he was sorry for flying off the handle like that and he'd had a tough day and was tired and I wasn't to worry. And my guess was that he just wanted to stop me getting too curious about the stuff in that drawer."

"So why didn't you just ask him about it?" I said.

"You don't know my father. He won't tell you the time unless you ask him in writing beforehand. So anyway the result was that I *did* get curious about that drawer. I mean, not sort of dying of curiosity, just—well, just curious. And one morning when I knew he was out for the whole day I sneaked in again to have a look. Of course I found he'd locked it, and it took me half an hour to find a way of opening it which wasn't too obvious. Well, the stuff in it didn't mean too much to me, but I guessed it was all documentation from his time in the war, and I took some of the papers and photocopied them, thinking that if I ever had time in Italy I might chase them up, see what they were about. Then I put it all back; there was nothing to show that I'd forced the lock, I thought, unless he looked really hard."

"And then you came on holiday," I said.

"Yes." He seemed to have reconciled himself to the task of telling all. I got the impression that he even found it useful as a way of keeping himself calm. He was a natural raconteur, and his voice slipped it into occasional parodic tones whenever he brought anyone else into the story. He might even make it as an actor, I thought. He went on, "In fact when I got out to the villa, I forgot all about it. I mean, it was just too hot, and I was quite happy to stay there. But then Rita got the travel itch, I mean she really doesn't know how to relax, that girl, so when she said, 'Can't we go somewhere else?' "—he exaggerated the

Liverpudlian inflection, but not absurdly so—"I thought, well, why not, and I suggested Verona. Then when we got to Verona, I said I wanted a day on my own and I came out to San Giorgio, which was the place mentioned in these documents."

"And you met Zeno," I said.

"Yes. By chance. He must have seen me pottering around the place and got curious." He smiled. "Well, actually at first I think he just saw me as a possible client, because he tried to sell me some marijuana, but then we got into conversation and he asked what I was up to. And I thought, well, a bit of information from a local could come in useful, so I told him I was trying to trace my father's footsteps in the war, only I made it sound like my father was dead. I showed him these documents, but I didn't let him keep them as he wanted. He told me the story about the statue, which it seems everyone in the place is brought up on—do you know what I'm talking about?"

"Yes," we both said.

"Anyway, he thought it might be connected with my papers. He told me not to tell anyone and to come back the next day and meet him up at the castle—it was getting late, you see, and I had to get back to Verona before Rita started worrying."

"And you trusted this guy?" I said.

"Well, he was a bit creepy, but he seemed to know what he was talking about. And I wasn't paying him anything after all. So the next day I came up with Rita and we met him at the castle and he started telling me about a chapel further up the hill. Rita got a bit bored and said 'See ya' and went off, and Zeno and I went up the hill together. Only we didn't find anything, though we looked for ages. It must have been around seven when we gave up. Zeno said he had to get back to dinner and I went back to the hotel to find Rita. But when I got there I discovered she'd upped and offed, and I thought, well, what the hell, that's her look-out. The next day I went back up to the chapel on my own and had another look around and then on the way down—" Here his voice suddenly became jumpy, and it struck me what an amazing job he'd done in keeping it under control so far. He swallowed a couple of times and looked out at the cherry-tree covered hills. Then he went on, "I got jumped by these two guys in balaclava helmets. They just came at me in the lane below the castle and they stuck a gun in my side and put a blindfold on me and made me get into a car and lie on the floor. I was terrified, I can tell you. And then after ten minutes or so they got me out and made me walk for miles through the woods, still with this blindfold on. Then when we got to the cave they let me take it off, and they told me they were friends of Zeno's, who'd been killed, and they wanted to know what I'd been up to with him. It seems he'd told them something about these papers I'd got, but really vaguely; he was kind of bragging that he was onto something big, but without saying what. They wanted the papers. It seems one of them even put a false beard on or something to go and get my luggage from the hotel." He fell silent.

I looked at Linda in the mirror, trying to see if any of this was new to her, but she seemed to be just concentrating on the traffic now that we'd joined the main road in the next valley, and there was no way of telling what she was thinking. But then she'd fooled me like that all along, so that was no surprise. I tickled the panda's ears idly and wondered how much of the schoolgirlishness was an act and how much was genuine: was this panda in fact a radio transmitter?

Then I tried to restore some of my self-confidence by telling myself that probably you really did have to be childish to get anywhere in MI6—after all, it was the Great Game.

It didn't work: it just brought home to me that what I'd been involved in was the Little Game—or maybe even the Infant Game.

Piers broke the silence. "Those two bastards," he said, and his voice was shaking again.

I remembered that sickening moment when I'd seen the faceless thug looming over me in my bedroom the previous night and found I was squeezing the panda. Piers had had two days of those faceless thugs looming over him while he was tied up in a cave which had looked like a setting for a Dario Argento film. A little tremor in the voice was comprehensible, I felt. I'd be jellified from brain to bowel. Maybe I should offer him the teddy bear.

"And you didn't tell them where the papers were?" I said.

"No," he said, "why should I?" He sounded truculent all of a sudden, as if I were accusing him of unfairness.

"Well, I know I'd have handed them everything from my shoelaces to my pension book to get out of there," I said.

"Oh, me too," said Linda with a cosy shiver. "I'm a terrible coward."

"Well," he said, "I knew someone had to come along and rescue me sooner or later. I mean, this is Italy, isn't it—not Beirut?"

"Good for you," said Linda. "So they didn't learn anything."

"No," he said.

"Linda," I said.

"Yes?"

"That is your name?"

"Oh, yes. Why not?"

"I suppose I must just be a distrustful bastard. No, what I really want to ask is, are you truly interested in this statue or not?"

"Oh, it's a fascinating story, don't you think?"

"That's not what I'm asking you. Are you here for the statue or not?"

"Oh, of course not."

"Ah."

"I came here when I got a report from an agent in Tuscany that Sir Alfred's son, contrary to usual practice, had left the villa there to come up to Verona. So I flew out—on a hunch more than anything else—and anticipated things by going straight out to San Giorgio. I'd already mugged up the statue as a useful cover story if ever I did have to poke around there. It would even give me the chance to ask questions about the war."

I should have guessed that her real interest wasn't antiquarian, I suppose, from the fact that she'd clearly never spoken to either Pigozzi or Don Luigi about the statue. I also thought back to her sudden "chance appearance" up at the castle the previous evening; presumably she'd got curious about me when she saw me chatting away to Signor Menegallo.

Piers said, "You mean you were watching me even down at the villa?"

"Oh, especially there. Any links of any member of the family with Italy had to be checked. But it was only a question of occasional spot checks; you weren't under continual surveillance." She laughed. "We really haven't the resources for that."

"So what did you think I was up to?" Piers said rather sulkily.

"Well, I thought it might have something to do with what you'd discovered in that desk. We hadn't yet found a way to have a look at that desk ourselves...."

"Christ," said Piers, "I should hope not. Look, just what are you accusing my father of?"

"We're not accusing him of anything. We merely want to know why he keeps in touch with Count Malberti, who has links with a subversive organisation here in Italy."

"What's this organisation?" I asked.

"Oh, it's some kind of Masonic lodge, some of whose members are connected with various terrorist organisations."

"So you follow Piers because he's the son of a man who has links with a man who has links with an organisation that has members who have links with organisations that have links with terrorists," I said.

"We have to follow things up," she said. "That's our job."

"So what do you think Sir Alfred is up to?" I said. "In concrete fact."

"What do you mean, up to?" she said.

"I mean, is he out to assassinate the Pope? Kidnap the President? Blow up the Ponte Vecchio? Reorganise Gladio? Or does he just like dressing up in hooded nighties and giving funny handshakes?"

"Well, that's what we're going to ask him now, isn't it?" said Piers, biting the words out.

"Oh, em, is it?" said Linda. This was obviously an approach she hadn't thought of. Far too straightforward.

SIXTEEN

· · · · · · ·

WE DIDN'T HAVE MUCH MORE CONVERSATION on the way back because Piers fell into an edgy silence, which he broke only to say how dirty he felt. Linda stopped twice on the way: once to dump the guns in a suitably remote field, and then at a bar so she could go and phone "her superior" to let him know her progress. I wondered about this superior and who or where he'd be: a pin-striped bureaucrat at a leather-covered desk in Whitehall? or a cat-stroking aesthete sipping brandy in the back room of a Veronese riverside bar? Linda wouldn't say, smiling and explaining that some official secrets had to remain secrets.

Piers knocked back his grappa in one swig and then turned plum-coloured trying not to cough or choke. I think that was one theatrical gesture he wouldn't be repeating. After a second or two he said, rather unconvincingly, "That's better."

I thought this might be an opportunity to get him talking again and said, "What did you think you were going to find out about your father?"

"Christ, I don't know. Illegitimate children or long-lost wills or some such Victorian crap."

"Ah."

"I suppose I just didn't think, really. That's what my father would say anyway."

"He reckons you're disorganised, does he?"

"He just says I never think. I suppose he's right. I do things and see what happens next."

"Well, yes, I can see that must lead to awkwardness sometimes."

"At least it's not boring."

It struck me that this was a parody—but only a slight one—of my own attitude to life. And God it sounded fatuous.

I ordered another drink to cheer myself up. I told myself that I'd use the reward money to found the basis of a sensible career.

"Okay," said Linda returning from the phone, "everyone ready to go?"

"Yes, I suppose so," I said.

"All right," said Piers with a shrug.

We let Linda pay. MI6 were probably generous with expenses. Then I followed them to the car, working out how many ducks I'd be able to make from four thousand pounds' worth of string and cardboard.

"I'll ring his room," said the receptionist, looking even more bored than he had done the previous afternoon. Well, I suppose the prospect of getting through to Sir Alfred on the phone wasn't going to add zip to anyone's day. But Sir Alfred seemed to be the only one in. Both Gigi's and Rita's room keys were hanging up behind the desk.

After half a minute or so the receptionist said, "He's not answering. Perhaps he's in the bathroom or asleep." And now are you going to push off and leave me to my sports paper? his eyebrows said.

"All right," said Piers, "I'll go up to my room anyway."

"Your room, signore?"

"Yes, you remember—I was with Rita Palgrave in Room twenty-one. She's still there, isn't she?"

He looked at Piers and then shrugged, which either meant he remembered and supposed it was all right, or didn't remember and didn't care. Either way he gave him the key.

Linda said to me, "Shall we go and have a drink while he washes and changes?"

"Yes. We could go to one of the bars in the square—and I could tell you a story about it too."

Piers picked up his bag again and headed for the stairs. Halfway there he turned round and said, "Oh, er, thanks," and gave us a quick nervous smile.

"Don't mention it," I said—a bit presumptuously perhaps: maybe he was just thanking Linda for the lift.

I took her to the bar I'd sat at just two days earlier. Piazza Erbe hadn't changed much: the same throngs of people—the Italians flashing their rich tans and rich apparel and the northerners their peeling faces and appalling apparel. We ordered glasses of white wine and then I told her about my experience at this very table. She laughed.

"Typical MI6," she said.

"Oh, yes?"

"Yes. It's almost a standard part of recruitment procedure with us. Put a potential candidate in a tough situation without any explanation and observe his reactions. If he doesn't show the right initiative we proceed no further. In that case, he usually never finds out what it was all about."

"And what does the *right* initiative mean? Not going to the police about it?"

"Well, yes. We like to see a certain, em, spirit of—"

"Lawlessness."

"Well, a certain independence. And curiosity."

"I see. You've got to be ready to steam open other people's letters."

"That among other things. And don't look so priggish. You're obviously the right material yourself."

I perked up a little at this—and then of course perked down again at the thought that it took such a dubious compliment to restore my self-confidence. And the further thought that the compliment wouldn't even get me a job reduced my confidence to its usual rubble. I said, "So Sir Alf was pretty big in the service, was he?"

"I really can't tell you these things, you know. As it is you've already heard a lot of things you shouldn't have."

"I see. I know too much. So what happens to me? A clever suicide? A brainwashing?"

"You do have some pretty melodramatic ideas about us, don't you? Or maybe you're just joking."

"Well, I hope I am." It seemed that the only level I could meet her on now was that of banter: I couldn't hope to meet her on a professional one certainly—and banter made it seem as if I had no wish to. I had a definite regret for the loss of that pinkly innocent young enthusiast—and it was no comfort to tell myself that my regret was merely due to a lost feeling of male superiority. I said, "So what am I supposed to do now? Just bow my way off the scene?"

"Well, you've done what you were paid to do, haven't you?"

I frowned. "Look, could you please tell me how you know about me and my brother?"

"Well, we knew Sir Alfred had been in touch with a certain Luigi Esposito in England, and we looked into Luigi's background and came up with a mysterious half-brother, living in Italy at the moment. A bit of a wanderer who had perhaps been involved in some way with preventing a royal assassination in Naples."

My jaw dropped—and my glass of wine almost followed. A second or two later I managed to lever the jaw back up, force a restorative sip of wine into it, and then get my bantering act together again. I said, "Well, you certainly do your homework then. How come I haven't been asked to join you already?"

"Well, I can always put your name forwards. But, em . . ."

"Don't call you, you'll call me. And anyway you aren't in the phone book." And I haven't got the right accent. Or relatives.

On cue Gigi came into sight—burst into sight rather, slamming against the retina like a kaleidoscopic cannonball. Azure jacket and yellow shirt, snow-white trousers and orange shoes. The only private detective in the world to model himself sartorially on a beach umbrella. The full strength of his assault on the optical nerves can be judged by the fact that I didn't notice Rita next to him until a full two seconds later. What she had on show was mostly legs: she was wearing shorts that were just a centimetre removed from being part of a bikini.

They were walking across the square in the direction of the hotel; Gigi was talking and Rita was listening. Everybody else in the square except for the Roman statue was looking. I called out, "Hey, Gigi, Rita!" loudly enough to get the attention of everybody, including the statue. I could feel my companion trying to make her way into the Roman foundations of the square by nuclear meltdown.

Gigi and Rita walked towards our table. I stood up and greeted them, deciding reluctantly that our client-detective relationship didn't allow for kissing. Not even in Italy. Gigi said, "Jan, what's wiv you then? What are you doing here?"

"Just having a celebratory drink," I said.

"What?" Rita pounced on these words, and her lips remained slightly open after pronouncing this one word. I did my best not to think of that missed kiss.

I said, with all the casualness I could muster, "Piers is in there having a shower." I nodded towards the hotel.

"What? Where? How?"

"Have a drink and I'll explain," I said, resuming my seat.

They sat down and I introduced Linda, saying that I'd met her at the village, and Rita said, "Yes, yes, yes," and hardly even looked at her, obviously not remembering having seen her before. Gigi nodded familiarly and said, "Ciao"; he likes people to appreciate his bilingualism straightaway. Linda said a shy "How do you do" to them both. Gigi looked at me and gave a jerk of the head towards Linda and said, "Er . . ." I said, "Don't worry, she's in on this. But she can be trusted," while Linda glowed away bashfully.

Then, when drinks had been ordered, I gave a quick rundown of the story so far, not mentioning Linda's role in it: she pushed her foot into my shin as I approached the moment of her gun-swinging intervention, and I guessed she wasn't just wanting to play fond footsie. Rita sat opposite me, gazing at me and once again forgetting to put those lips together, which was pretty distracting, and Gigi sat next to her and nodded in a big-brotherly approving way as I recounted my adventures. I had thought it would be difficult to keep a note of smugness out of my voice, but Linda helped me out there—just by being present and being who she was—Agent Double Oh Gosh, the Professional. I didn't go into Piers's existential crises, merely saying that he had gone to the village to find out something about his father and the best thing we could do now was ask his father about it, a procedure which, if it had been tried earlier, would have saved a lot of time, not to mention bullets, nerves, and wet wipes.

"So he's in there now cleaning up," I concluded, "and I wish I could too."

"So who's she?" Gigi said, jerking his thumb at Linda.

"Oh, er, she's—she was in the hotel as well. Er, she—"

"Well, I work in Sir Alfred's old office," she said, and smiled shyly. "I helped January out."

"Why?" said Rita. "What have you got to do with it?" There was definite resentment in her tone. It presumably wasn't on my account; I suppose she didn't like the thought of yet further complications for Piers.

"Well, it's all rather confused, you know," Linda said. "We really will all have to have a good talk with Sir Alfred."

"Yeah, well, family first," Gigi said. I'd never known him to express such sentiments before. Come to think of it, I'd hardly ever heard him express any sentiments before.

"I'm going to see Piers," Rita said, rising from her chair. She hadn't even touched her drink.

"Shall we all go then?" asked Linda brightly.

And it was my turn to hack her shin. She turned and looked at me and then said, "Ah, yes, I see." And she blushed.

We watched Rita make her way across the square (we weren't alone in so doing). Then Gigi turned to me and said, "You were supposed to do it all on your own."

"You know, I had a sneaky feeling you weren't going to start singing 'for he's a jolly good fellow.' "

"So you were right, weren't you?"

Linda spoke up: "I think I ought to tell you that I forced myself on your brother, not the other way round."

"Oh, yeah?"

"You might as well know I'm from MI6," she said. Then we

had the whole routine of "Yes, I know it sounds silly, but honest I am . . ." together with the Terry Thomas imitation and the subsequent silvery laugh. "We were worried about Piers's disappearance too."

"And she won't be wanting a cut of the reward, if that's what you're worried about." I turned to her. "Er, you won't, will you?"

"Strictly forbidden." She sounded rather shocked.

"Yeah, well, it's just the principle, innit," Gigi said. "I mean, of course you got to ask people fings in this business, but you don't go dragging them round after you."

"Gigi dropped out from his evening course in etiquette," I explained to Linda. "But he's got a heart of gold there somewhere. So we all tell ourselves in the family anyway."

"Oh, I'm sure of it," she said, smiling through the flames. She even sounded as if she believed it. Then she said, "But really I think we should go and have a word with Sir Alfred. I mean, we can leave Piers and, um, his friend to—to meet up again, but I really do want to see Sir Alfred as soon as possible."

"He's in, then, is he?" Gigi said.

"His key's hanging up," I said, "but he didn't answer the phone. Must have been in the bathroom or something."

"He's in a funny mood, mind," he said. "Ever since someone rang him this morning. Gone all sort of broody. Let's go then."

"I'll pay here," I said.

Gigi looked at me and said, "Careful, you haven't had that four fousand yet."

I smiled and called the waiter.

I was going to remember that smile of mine later. And not with a smile.

When we approached the hotel desk again, the man was reading his sports paper and looking just a little brighter. Either he'd had good news about his favourite team or he'd been watching Rita's rear end disappear across the hall. Then he looked up and saw us, and we were obviously not in the same league as what he'd been dwelling on. Gigi said, *"Ciao, Piero, quattordici.*" He gave Gigi the key and said to us, "Il signore Ainsley is still in his room. Do you want me to try again?"

"Yes, please."

He dialed the room number, and we all waited, including Gigi. "Still no answer," he said after a while.

"Let's go up and knock on the door," said Gigi. He said to the receptionist, *"Va bene, no?"* and the receptionist had already gone back to the paper.

So we went up in the lift to the third floor. We were all silent, though the lift wasn't; its arthritis hadn't improved since I last used it. It wheezed to a painful halt and we tugged its metal concertina doors and walked towards Room 32. Gigi knocked. No answer. He gave another knock. "Must be out," he said, trying the door, which did not open.

"You mean he went out with the key in his pocket?" I said.

Linda said, "A key like that?" She was pointing at the one Gigi had in his hand; the key was attached to a heavy cylinder of wood, which bore the number painted on it in white.

I said, "Well, *I* could, but then I put everything into my pockets, but Sir Alfred . . ." I remembered that careful little man, who probably registered in triplicate every object in his possession.

"So what are you saying?" Gigi said.

"Just that we ought to get that door opened," Linda said. She was speaking in her usual breathily shy way, but she was obviously quite decided.

"I'll go and get Piero then," he said.

"Yes."

He went back down in the lift and Linda and I stood there, staring at that door and waiting. Eventually I said, "So you haven't got a set of skeleton keys in that bag."

"I probably could open it. But I don't want to cause any trouble with the bureaucrats, you know."

We heard the lift coming back up. Gigi came out, followed by Piero, who didn't look too pleased. He'd got his sports paper under his arm, as a sort of reproach. He put a key into the lock and said, "The key's in there on the other side." He poked and prodded for a few seconds and then we heard the dull clink of the key falling to the floor inside the room. He turned the key and opened the door.

"Oh, Cristo," he said, and didn't move.

We pushed and peered. Sir Alfred was facing us and was as quiet as ever, but not in appearance: his eyes were wild and staring, his face and tongue a mottled aubergine in hue; his grey clothes were correct in every detail except one, but that one detail was what caught the eye: he wore two ties and one, made of rope, hung straight up instead of down, and had snapped his head to one side, like a broken matchstick. His shoes swung with a gentle circling movement a foot or so above the floor they were never going to tread again: they were, of course, perfectly polished.

SEVENTEEN

· · · · · · · · · · ·

PIERO SEEMED PREPARED JUST TO STAY in the doorway saying, "Oh, Cristo," but the rest of us pushed past him. Gigi and I went up to the body in a purposeful fashion, but when we came within kicking distance of the feet stopped helplessly and looked at one another.

"Well, there's no point in trying to bring him round," said Gigi.

"No," I said. It wasn't the first corpse I'd ever seen, but it was the deadest one.

Piero eventually finished his prayers and came up to us. "Signori, you mustn't touch anything. Nor you, Signorina," he said to Linda, who was scouting round the table by the wall. She looked round and said, "Sorry, I was looking for a note."

"That's for the police," said Piero, and this last word plunged him into yet blacker depths of depression. He evidently foresaw a lot of tiresome time away from his football reports.

"Find anything?" said Gigi, ignoring Piero.

"No," she said.

We all ignored Piero then and looked around for a note. It didn't take us long to conclude that there wasn't one. The room was far from cluttered: there were no decorative trinkets on any of the surfaces, and Sir Alfred's possessions were all neatly arrayed: his clothes were obviously in the wardrobe, his washing things arranged in military file on the shelf above the basin, and his two or three books and copies of *The Times* in neat piles on the table. His body was the only unsymmetrical object in the room. Even the chair he'd stepped off was parallel to the wall.

Linda was now studying the body. "He must have gone out deliberately to buy that rope," she said. "It's not the sort of thing one keeps in one's pocket."

She probably had a length of the stuff in her bag for all eventualities, but I agreed with her. "No. I suppose the beam suggested it. So what now?"

"Well, as this chap says, it's now up to the police."

"Um, and what about Piers?" I said.

"Oh, yes," she said. "Someone will have to tell him. But look, I think I'd better slip away. My presence is only going to complicate things."

"Oh, great," I said. "Shall we all do that?"

"Well, no, I don't really think that would be on, you know."

"Yes, I do know. That was Heavy Irony."

"Ah. But you do see my point. I really have no standing here, whereas you can at least say you're a friend of the son."

Gigi said, "Well, go on then if you're going. No one's stopping you." I think Linda hadn't made a big hit with Gigi.

She gave us a final shy smile and slipped out of the room. Piero said, "Signorina," but not in a very convinced way, and she didn't answer.

The next hour or so was hell. It was somehow decided that I was the one who should break the news to Piers and Rita, and this wasn't made any easier by the fact that the two of them had obviously made up all their differences and answered my knock at their door with some degree of cheer. Piers's first words to me, before I'd said anything, were, "I've decided that I can't give a toss about my father." Unfortunately I didn't feel that I could take this quite literally. I broke the news baldly, seeing no point in trying to put any sort of euphemistic wig over it. They both stared, and then Piers said, "Daddy?" It could have been either an expression of disbelief or, well, a cry for Daddy. I just nodded and said, "I'm sorry."

"Daddy?" he said again. "Killed himself?"

"There's no doubt about that," I said. "The room was locked on the inside."

"But—but why?"

I don't suppose I was really expected to answer this. I gave a shrug which I hoped looked helpless rather than careless. I certainly wasn't feeling careless.

Rita said, "Had we better come up?"

"Up to you," I said. "Don't if you don't want to."

"No, Christ, I've got to see," said Piers. He was shaven and cleanly dressed now, but he looked even more fazed than he had done coming out of that cave.

We all made our way up the stairs in silence. I broke it only to say, "Um, be prepared, he's not—" and stopped before saying anything so silly as "not a pretty sight." Anyway, they understood.

They saw the body, made no comments, and returned to their room, Rita becoming suddenly very tender and protective, putting her arm round Piers and guiding him along. I had the feeling that she'd probably done this kind of motherly escort act on other occasions—like out of the pub or after a party. Gigi watched them with that indulgence I'd noticed before—doubly curious now that there was no money to be got out of the case. Maybe he was just getting sentimental in his middle age.

I asked Gigi if we had to wait for the police in the same room as the body, and he looked a bit surprised at my fastidiousness but took me along to his room, which was next door. The furniture was similarly drab, but odd articles of Gigi's clothing did their festive best to kick one in the eye. By his bed there was a pile of Italian Tex Willer comics, just about the only things he ever reads. He took a couple of beers from the fridge and gave me one and said, "Well, I suppose we can kiss our reward good-bye."

"Yes," I said. I couldn't pretend that this hadn't crossed my mind. "I don't really feel like asking Piers for it."

"Not now anyway. Later it might be possible to get something out of him. I mean, you did save his life, didn't you? Or at

least he can't prove you didn't. He'll have to show some gratitude."

"He hasn't shown any signs of it yet. Still, he's probably
under shock. And now this. . . ."

"Yeah. Who'd've fought it? Seemed a bloke who really had
his head screwed on."

"Yes." I tried not to think of the way the body next door
looked as if the head had been half screwed off. "Did he show
any signs of depression or anything?"

"Well, like I told you, he went all broody after that phone
call this morning."

"Oh, yes. Who was it?"

"I don't know. We were having a drink, round midday, in
his room and the phone rang, and he said, "Oh, yes,' and then
just looked at me and said, 'Would you mind . . .' Well, I can
take a hint, so I upped and offed."

"And you didn't hear him say anything?"

"No. Just 'oh, yes'."

"In English."

"Yeah. But that doesn't mean much really. I mean I might
say 'Oh, yes,' first fing, if Ornella Muti called me." He sipped
his drink thoughtfully. "In fact, I'd definitely say it if she did."

This didn't strike me as particularly to the point. "And afterwards?"

"Afterwards he come into my room and just said he was
going for a walk and he was all broody, like I said."

"Broody."

"Yeah. You know, like he had somefing on his mind."

"And not just his son's disappearance."

"Yeah. And then I didn't see him again—not until—well,
just now. So I suppose you could say that, yeah, he was acting
a bit strange like. But it didn't cross my mind he'd do anyfing
like that." He jerked his thumb at the separating wall and made
a little strangled noise in his throat, which didn't strike me as
actually necessary.

"So do you think he'd heard some kind of news or something?"

"I don't know. And seeing as he didn't leave a message, we're probably never going to know."

"So what are we going to say to the police?"

"Oh, just the usual stuff. Overwork, depression, come here to try and cool off, but it didn't work. They won't give a damn. Just so long as it's definitely suicide."

"And it is, isn't it?"

"Oh, come on, Jan. You finking of some ritual killing like that bloke strung up on Blackfriars Bridge? How do you get round that locked door?"

"I'm sure any detective writer could give you twenty ways round—or through or over. But no, I'm not really thinking anything. Not if you say he was acting oddly anyway." But after a thoughtful sip of beer I said, "It's just curious he didn't leave a note. Out of character, I'd have thought."

"You reckon before stringing himself up he's got to act just like he was in his office: 'Take a note, Miss Wobblebum. To whom it may concern I've decided to do meself in, please excuse any inconvenience or blood, Yours sincerely, Sir Alfred Ainsley, MBE and Order of the Noose.' "

"Well, I'd have thought he'd be tidier."

"Well, he didn't cut his froat, did he? Or jump out the window. You fink he should have buried himself as well?"

We were summoned to talk to the police at this point. Sir Alfred was swinging in a rather sickening fashion, after being disturbed by the sergeant's examination, and I found this made it difficult to concentrate on what I was being asked. Fortunately, after a few preliminary questions about who found the body and how, the sergeant, a man with a thick moustache and thicker Neapolitan accent, decided to continue the enquiry in Gigi's room. As Gigi had foretold, they proved perfectly happy to treat it as a straightforward suicide, and the sergeant nodded as Gigi kicked off with the story of Sir Alfred's depression. He was supported by Piers and by Rita, who had thoughtfully changed into a dress that covered rather more of her, even if its close adherence to what it covered meant that it was hardly any less revealing or distracting. At any rate the sergeant and his *agente* seemed to pay great attention to her nods of agreement, which was all she could contribute to the enquiry since it was conducted in Italian.

We all had our documents checked. I gave my address as the Pensione Margherita, which was where I'd been staying until the previous night. We were told we might be summoned to appear in court and they told us the body would be removed for an autopsy, but there would be no problem then in arranging for it to be shipped back to Britain. Piers said, "I think he might have wanted to be buried over here." He was still fairly fazed and he said this without much conviction. Neither he nor Rita had asked what had happened to Linda and I didn't mention her.

After the police had gone, together with the body and a reporter (I'd managed to warn everyone not to let it slip out that the dead man was a "Sir," which would have guaranteed photos in all the national papers and headlines of the kind: "MISTERIOSA MORTE DI UN BARONETTO INGLESE"), Piers and Rita sat there, both of them still looking dazed. Nobody said anything for a while, then Piers said, "I'm going to have to phone my mother." There was a slightly pleading note in his voice, as if he was hoping someone would do it for him.

Rita said, "Wait till you feel calmer."

That, I thought, would mean waiting a very long time. We all fell into silence again. After a few seconds Gigi coughed—a tactful, sober, but unmistakeably hinting cough, which reminded us that this was his room, and that if nobody else had anything better to do than sit in silence, he did. At any rate that's how I interpreted it, but maybe I was just being hypersensitive. I stood up. Piers and Rita still didn't move. They were sitting in chairs next to each other and she was holding his hand; he looked as if he'd just switch off if he didn't continue to receive that tactile charge from her. I said, "Okay, I think, er, I, er . . ."

It wasn't one of my most eloquent speeches, and I suppose it wasn't surprising Piers and Rita didn't take any notice. I moved to the door. Gigi came after me, his face registering resignation at the idea of them sitting on there until midnight. I said in an undertone to him just outside the door, "Be nice."

"Yeah, yeah. Where are you going?"

"Back to the Margherita, I suppose. After that . . ." I tried to make the dots imply that the world was my oyster, rather than that I didn't have the faintest idea.

"Need any money?"

"Well, if you've got four thousand pounds. No, don't worry. I've still got some of what you gave me."

"Here, have another couple of these. That's the rest of the advance he paid me." He gave me another two hundred thousand lire, and I made no noises of polite refusal. After all, if I didn't get it off him, I'd be busking on the street corner.

"Thanks," I said, pocketing it.

"See you."

Half an hour later I was sitting back in my old room, feeling more than usually pointless. Maybe my only function in life was to fill up the rooms in cheap *pensioni* that nobody else wanted. The hotel owner and his wife had accepted me with a kind of gloomy satisfaction. To complete this process of fatalistic regression it only remained for me to ring up Simon and grovel to get my job back.

I lay on the bed and listened to *La Bohème* on my Walkman. For sheer solipsistic wallowing, there is nothing to beat lying alone in a cheap bedroom at the top of an empty hotel listening to Puccini on headphones. Even the weather decided to give a hand, and just as Mimi came in out of the cold, a storm broke outside and the windows wept. Well, that saved me the trouble. Maybe if I opened them, I might even get consumption too.

Then just as she let out her first cough there came a knock at the door. I slipped the headphones off and went and opened up. Well, it wasn't Mimi: the hotel signora stood there, all fifteen stone of her, and behind her the equally unconsumptive, if more attractive, Rita.

"Lady to see you," said the signora. She gave me a long hard look, to remind me that mine was a single room, and then waddled off.

"Hi," I said to Rita. "Come in and dry your hair."

"Thanks." There was nothing bedraggled about her wetness: it was all a sexy shine and glisten, as if the storm's only purpose had been to make her clothes resemble cling-film. She picked up the towel from by the sink.

"Sorry," I said as she rubbed her hair with it. "I think it's made from old army rucksacks."

"Never mind," she said with a smile. "It's dry at least. The storm really caught me out. I was halfway here when it broke."

"Ah. How's Piers?"

"He's just lying down for the moment. I told him I was coming here and he agreed."

"Oh." Maybe she'd brought a cheque, I tried to stop myself thinking. "Good. Um, what brings you here?"

"Your brother gave me the address. I don't think he agrees with me coming here."

"Really."

"We want you to keep investigating." A great crash of thunder. Someone up there was as amazed as me.

"You what?"

"Keep looking into this business."

I choked back an unbelieving "Me?!" and got out a nonchalant "Oh" instead. Then I said, "Well, that's very, er, gratifying. What exactly do you want me to look into?"

"Piers is convinced his father wouldn't have committed suicide without explaining it. So he wants you to try and find out what really happened."

"He does, does he?" I looked at her as she continued to rub her hair vigorously. "A moment ago you said 'we.' "

"Yeah. That's right." She went and sat on the bed and stared straight at me. "It's Piers who said it first, but I go along with it. You're obviously not the wally I took you for at first."

"Thank you," I said. I tried to make my tone dry, but she was too wet herself to notice.

"I mean," she went on, "I don't know whether I'd do anything about it for choice myself, but Piers is in a terrible state. You know: wondering just what he's stirred up, thinking that maybe it's all his fault; really scared, in fact. It's only natural.

And I can see that he's not going to get over it unless he does something about it—like try and find out what really happened. Well, he can't do that himself. He's got all the bureaucratic hassle to think of. So first we went to your brother."

"Ah," I said.

"And he didn't want anything to do with it. Said to let sleeping dogs lie and all that."

"I see."

"Is that what you think?" she said.

"No. If you really want to know, I've got a nasty feeling this dog isn't going to stay lying. And the better we know what's been going on, the less risk we run of getting bitten in the bum."

"Yeah?"

"Yeah." I realised I was already feeling more cheerful. I couldn't decide whether it was because I was an untiring seeker of justice or just a nosey bastard.

"We'll pay you, of course," she said.

"Thanks." Maybe that was the real reason.

"So that's agreed then. Thanks. I'm sorry if I seemed a bit snotty when I first met you. And thanks for finding Piers."

"Don't mention it." Just give me the money.

"That Jussi Björling?" she said.

I realised the opera was still crackling out of the headphones on the pillow. "That's right," I said in surprise. "That's pretty clever, at that distance."

"Yeah, well, I told you I'm not all eccles cakes and chip butties." She gave me a big smile and turned to the door. She gave her hair a quick pat back into shape and said, "Come and fix things up with Piers later, will you?"

"I will."

"See you." She paused at the door. "And you'll do your best, won't you? 'Cos you know something? Sir Alf wasn't such a bad bastard after all." Then she slipped out into the storm again. I could only hope that the lightning was shortsighted.

EIGHTEEN

· · · · · · · · ·

I GAVE IT A DAY BEFORE RETURNING to San Giorgio Veronese. It meant I could finish the opera, see the storm out, have another chat with Piers and Rita, sit and think over things, get some rest, and see what the papers said the next day. The only truly investigatorial thing I did was to ask the man at the desk in the Piazza Erbe hotel if he had any idea who had phoned Sir Alfred the previous morning. He said he didn't and, despite having put the call through to the room, wouldn't venture a guess on the sex, age, or nationality of the caller.

The car bombing made the front page of quite a few national papers, along with Don Luigi's call for a vigil for peace and tolerance in the village's main square. A second-rank rock singer of the area had promised his support, and there was talk of busloads of schoolchildren and students preparing to go along. One revelation by the police was given prominence in all the papers: the car had not been petrol bombed, as had first been assumed. Plastic explosive had been used. As the *Corriere della Sera* put it: "This fact puts the so-called Knights of St. George on a far more worrying plane. Petrol bombs, however destructive in effect, are at least the weapons of amateurs. Access to plastic explosive suggests something far more professional and disturbing."

The question of where the explosive had come from gave rise to a good deal of speculation in all the papers. The fact that this episode came so soon after the discovery of the Milan arms horde (still unclaimed) gave further fuel to the discussion. Several of the papers pointed out that when Gladio was officially wound up in 1990, there had been rumours that the authorities had been unable to track down one or two arms stores belonging to it in the Verona area. The degree of credit that was given to this story depended of course (like everything in Italy) on the political affiliation of the newspaper. I read them all and hoped fervently that the blander (Christian-Democrat) versions were correct—trying to forget that believing them meant believing that nothing in Italy could ever be sweeter and lovelier than the way it was today.

The English suicide was a tiny item in the inside pages and no connection was made with events elsewhere in the area. (Which was far from inevitable: some of the darker-minded papers had tied the car bombing to every criminal outrage in the country from the Borgia poisonings onwards.)

I spent some time trying to track Gigi down, just to see if he knew anything more about Sir Alfred which might give me a line—and of course to get a brotherly blessing for my new enterprise. I eventually found him in the bar he'd taken me to the other day, and he proved strangely reluctant to talk. I got the impression that he'd undertaken some new enterprise of his own in the city and was just being instinctively cagey. I told myself that I'd check the Scaligeri tombs were still there the next time I visited Verona, and I wished him all the best. His last words to me were to tread very carefully because "the last fing we want is anyone tying us to anuvver stiff—particularly a stiff wiv bullet holes in its neck."

I arrived by bus in the Piazza Malberti just after lunch, and a platform was being erected in front of the statue. The motorcyclists around the monument were having to rev their engines with truly committed ferocity to make themselves heard over the clatter of scaffolding and hammering. There were a couple of Carabinieri, toting machine guns, some old men looking on with the same indifference that they looked on at the empty square all day, and a few young people in jeans and T-shirts putting up posters and oozing earnest goodwill. Nobody looked at me. I sloped off quickly before they got me singing Tracy Chapman songs.

I booked myself in at the Las Vegas and was welcomed by the manager with a Back-from-the-Dead smile. He gave me the same mortuary chamber as before and I told myself that I'd have been disappointed if he hadn't.

Then I set off to renew some more acquaintances. First call was Casa Menegallo. The door was answered by the old man who accepted my burbling apologies for disturbing him yet again, and told me that his son was at the other village bar, down by the bus depot.

This proved to be a smaller, shadier, and quieter version of the piazza bar. The barman was smaller and shadier too, and he poured my coffee out as if he were expecting a drugs raid at any moment. I looked around the place. There were just a few old men drinking wine and the noise of card playing from an inner room. I looked round the door into this room. There were two tables, one surrounded by cardplayers and the other with Mario and Luca drinking—of all things—Coca-Cola. I just had time to wonder if the atmosphere of shadiness was in fact all emanating from them, before they caught sight of me. Luca's mouth became briefly visible as a surprised O, and Mario's face screwed up with a sudden revulsion. The card players, after a brief glance, had returned to their game, so I was able to stroll up to Luca and Mario's table and sit down quite casually.

"*Ciao, ragazzi,*" I said.

"You bastard," said Mario. "What the hell do you want?"

I decided that exaggerated nonchalance was perhaps in bad taste—as well as being difficult to keep up. I came straight to the point: "Some information." I didn't bother about disguising my fluent Italian, nor my Neapolitan accent. They'd already heard it after all.

"*Vaffanculo,*" said Mario.

"Look," I said, "as you know I could make big trouble for you about what happened yesterday, but at the moment I've no intention of doing so. Now I'm not suggesting we shake hands and forget all about it. All I'm asking is that you answer one or two little questions, then you can go straight back to cursing me and my parents and my dead relatives. Okay?" I glanced at the other table. They were taking no notice of us.

"*Vaffanculo,*" said Luca, obviously not wanting to be out of things.

"Why should we tell you anything?" said Mario.

"Because, as you know, I could make trouble for you if you don't."

"We're so scared," said Mario.

"*Vaffanculo,*" said Luca, who wasn't one to let go of a good line when it came his way.

"You must have seen that there's a good deal of attention on this village at the moment," I said. "Journalists, policemen, and the like. There'll be a lot of interest in a story about a kidnapping. Particularly one carried out by the brother of a recent murder victim. Just the kind of thing people like. I expect there'll be television cameras along later. They'll love it."

"Go on then," sneered Mario. "Tell them. And tell them who you are too."

"Why shouldn't I?" I said. "I've no objections. A friend sent me to look for Piers Ainsley."

"So why didn't you go to the police?"

This was, of course, a question I had hoped he wouldn't ask. I thought I might as well try a little truth. "Because my friend wasn't quite sure what Piers had been up to in this village."

"Look, *stronzo,*" said Mario, "for all we know this Piers might have killed Zeno himself."

"No, he didn't—and I'm sure you know that."

"So who did?"

"Exactly: that's what I want your help in finding out."

"Leave it to the police was what your girlfriend told us."

Another tough one. "Look, you want to know what happened to Zeno, so do I. The police don't give a damn, because as far as they're concerned Zeno was just another troublemaker who's better off dead."

"Vaffanculo," said Luca. Well, I suppose that's one way of expressing fraternal grief.

"And why do you want to know what happened to him?" said Mario. "What's it to you?"

"Not for Zeno's sake. I just want to know what Piers got involved in."

"Listen, you're talking to Zeno's brother and a friend of his," Mario said. "He got shot through the neck by some bastard and you come here bothering us with your shitty little questions about your English boyfriend. Any moment now I'm going to break this bottle on your neck." He had reverted to that tone of concentrated viciousness he'd used when we were at the wrong end of his gun. True, I wasn't at the wrong end of a gun this time, but I didn't feel confident that calm reasoning was a sufficient counterweapon. Luca too was looking extra mean: that is to say, his eyes and mouth were microdots of compressed hate.

"Now look," I said placatingly, "there's no need to get upset. I'm not here to intrude on your grief or your anger or whatever. Just tell me what Zeno told you about Piers. And I'll tell you where your guns are, if you like." This last was a sudden inspiration. After all, I told myself, they were only hunting rifles, and probably they were perfectly entitled to have them. (Legally, I mean.) And I'd try and make sure I was some distance from the village by the time they got their hands on them.

"You thieving bastard," began Mario. But I could see that this had caught his interest.

Luca looked as if he were about to say *"Vaffanculo,"* but then thought better of it. He'd probably not been able to get to sleep without his gun.

"Is that a deal?" I said. "Let's face it: you know that you're never really going to get your hands on that statue. That was just a crazy dream of Zeno's."

They both pretended not to be caught off-guard by this reference to the statue. Mario said, "You'll tell us where those guns are, or I'll break your bloody neck." But it was mere token thuggery.

"What did Zeno tell you that made you kidnap Piers?"

Luca let out a last whining *"Vaffanculo,"* and then Mario said, "He just said there was this English cretin with some papers from the war that might lead to the statue. And he said he was going to lead him off the track so he could have a look for himself."

"Off the track?"

"Yes."

"What did he mean by that?"

Mario shrugged. He wasn't going to go as far as interpret things for me.

I said, "And did he tell you where he was going to look?"

"No. Why do you think we wanted to get the papers for ourselves?" This reminded him of something. "I still owe you for that crack on my head in the hotel, *stronzo.*"

"Well, you got me with that knife, didn't you? I'd say we were all square. Just tell me one thing: was Zeno anything to do with these *Cavalieri di San Giorgio?*"

"That crap?" said Mario. "No."

"No," said Luca.

I don't think there was any moral revulsion at the idea: it was mere disinterest. It sounded convincing enough to me.

"Okay," I said. I gave them instructions on how to find their guns and then said, "I don't suppose I can persuade you to come along to the piazza and join hands with me in brotherhood? No? Well, just an idea. Be seeing you. Ciao."

They glowered for a moment and then Luca said brightly, *"Vaffanculo."*

NINETEEN

· · · · · · · ·

I MADE MY WAY BACK TO THE SQUARE. The platform was now almost complete. An amplification system was being tested, with a young man saying "Uno due tre" into a microphone; the words resounded around the square with a backing of consumptive coughing, scorched-cat screeches, and scratched blackboards. The motorbikes were like nervous "ahems" in the midst of this titanic clatter. Workmen in overalls were standing around laconically, while the young people bustled around earnestly and eagerly and excessively.

Where the activity was most intense, I saw Don Luigi in the middle, like a miniature black whirlwind, weaving and bending and urging, imparting orders and instructions and energy. People approached him tentatively and then redeparted, their bustling suddenly serious bustling. I decided to watch it from the haven of the bar, which seemed far enough to be safe from any scattered sparks of Don Luigi's energy.

I went in and ordered another coffee. The barman seemed a little subdued today. All this industry in the defence of people whose presence was enough to cause nocturnal explosions must have struck him as misdirected, and yet he could hardly start voicing his opinions since these misdirected defenders were likely to be his biggest customers that day. He was thus limiting himself to occasional complaints about the noise: "Can't even hear ourselves talk, can we?" he said. "They call that freedom of expression?"

"Well, you must admit . . ." began a mild cappuccino, emboldened by the new spirit of the piazza.

"Can't hear you," he said immediately and crushingly.

I took my coffee outside to watch things. As I sat down I realised someone had followed me from the bar—someone I wouldn't have chosen as a morning coffee partner. "Hello," said Mauro. He wasn't alone. There was another thug beside him: not quite as hulking as Mauro, but no lissome reed either. He had a shaven head and squashed blubbery features which reminded me of stocking-masked bank robbers.

"Oh, hello."

"Still here then?"

"That's right."

"Listen," he said.

"Yes."

"Listen."

"I'm listening." There was even a slight reduction in the decibel level of the piazza, as the microphone had just given a *phut* and gone dead.

"We're not going to make any trouble for you today," he said. "Nor for these stinking Reds and Greens." He waved his massive hand around the square. They weren't that picturesque, unfortunately: denim blue predominated. "But don't hang round here too long. It wouldn't be healthy." He turned to his friend. "Would it, Carlo?"

Carlo's features made a blurred gesture at a sneer of agreement.

I said, "Right. Point taken. You're not going to sing along tonight then?"

Mauro made a dredging noise in his throat—not unsimilar to some of the microphone's more tortured moments—and then spat an oily blob of phlegm into the road. Once more I took the point.

They both turned away, then Mauro made a rather stagey turn. "Just one other thing," he said.

"Yes?"

"Don't go crying to anyone with your stories about me—because I'll know what to do about it if you do."

"Oh."

Then they left me and swaggered across the square, expressing their contempt for what was going on there with a few more carefully directed globs of phlegm. But it struck me that, for all his gobbing bravado, Mauro's main aim in addressing me had been to tell me to keep quiet. These Knights of St. George were probably by no means as conspiratorially terrifying a phenomenon as some people were choosing to think.

So I chose to hope.

I finished my cappuccino, still idly watching those busily working. The bikers I saw had finally accepted defeat and left the place. Maybe they knew of some really unspoilt village further up the valley.

I suddenly realised the black whirlwind had left the other side of the square and was heading my way—or towards the bar at least. I sat firm. He came tearing through the tables, put his hand to the door, then spotted me. A quick hassock-swirling swerve and he was by my side. I stood up.

"So you were able to stay," he said. "I'm so glad. So glad. It's most encouraging, the response . . ."

"Yes, it is. Can I offer you a coffee . . . ?"

"A glass of wine, yes, indeed, thank you." And he put his head in through the door. *"Do rossi, Bepi."*

And even the barman was energised. It only took him two minutes to appear at our table with the two drinks.

Don Luigi downed his in a couple of busy gulps, then turned to me and said, "How is your research progressing?"

"My . . . ? Oh, the statue?"

"Yes."

Next time I took on a case, I vowed to myself, I'd make sure I kept a proper record of my various disguises. "Well," I said, "not too badly. Mind you, my research is entirely amateur."

"You're not the first to be intrigued, of course," he said with a smile.

"No, I suppose not. Tell me, have you got time to answer a few more questions?"

"Well, if they're not too long—and not too theological."

"Oh, no. It's to do with Giorgio Malberti again."

"Oh, yes? And why him?"

"Well, I'm sure the clue to what happened to the statue lies with him."

He shook his head. "Well, if that's the way your research is tending, don't expect quick results. So what do you want to know?"

"Well, was he at all religious?"

He didn't burst out laughing. He frowned. "That's not so stupid a question as some people might think. Certainly he was no Mass-goer—and certainly his mother despaired of him."

"Despaired?" I said.

"Well, perhaps not despaired. But she was definitely saddened by many of his choices. The Malberti family have had a history of alternation, you might almost say: pious generation succeeded by extremely impious one throughout the ages."

"You mean his father was pious then?"

"Ah, no, he was no great saint either, but he married an extremely devout lady, and as he died when Giorgio was only about five, it was the mother who brought them up—and I suppose it was against her that Giorgio rebelled. She tried everything: she even sent him for periods to her own family, hoping they might calm him. She had a brother who was a priest and a sister who was a nun, but in the end they just refused to have anything more to do with him. It was the wrong way to treat someone like Giorgio. He needed more understanding. Still . . ."

"But was he antireligious?"

"No, definitely not. NO! OVER THERE!" These last few words were a sudden shout, in the direction of the square, where a few bearded men and a woman in a huge dress were putting up a large banner with a message of peace. He semaphored new instructions to them, then sat down and immediately resumed: "Why would he have rescued that statue otherwise?"

"Well, yes. That's what I'm trying to understand. But I do remember hearing something about his impiously playing with holy relics, and I wondered . . ."

Don Luigi looked at me in puzzlement. "Where . . . ? Well, you must have been asking a lot of questions."

"Well . . ." I said, trying to make my awkwardness sound merely like the modesty of the diligent researcher.

"I heard that story," he said. "But I think it was mere foolery. In the eighteenth century there was an extremely pious Contessa Malberti who devoted herself almost maniacally to the collecting of saints' relics. And it was these relics that young Giorgio was discovered to be using as part of his cannibal or Red Indian disguise. There may have been an intention to shock, but it was hardly Satanism, I feel."

This suddenly connected with something in my mind—with something I'd seen in the museum. I saw it quite clearly even now in my mind's eye and I almost burbled out a question. A very simple question. But I paused. . . . No, a little discretion might be best. I was already forming a plan, and if anything were to go wrong with it, certain questions would be remembered.

I changed the subject. "I've also heard rumours of an Englishman in this area during the war. A secret agent or something, I suppose."

"You've heard a great deal, young man. You couldn't give me any tips for the football pools this weekend? No? Oh, well . . . Rumours about Englishmen. . . . Well, of course, wartime lends itself to rumours. Not that peacetime is any less productive in Italy. You've heard of the Gladio arms store? The Knights of St. George? From some of the papers you would imagine that this village was never happy if it wasn't hosting a P2 reunion or Neo-Nazi get-together. But you were saying . . . An Englishman. Well, I can't pretend it's a new one to me. Indeed, they say that the Villa Malberti harboured some Englishmen—escaped prisoners of war, some said. The Germans searched the villa more than once, but nothing incriminating was ever found."

"Did you ever know an English family who stayed here before the war?"

"Well, yes—and I imagine that's what gave credibility to the rumours: the fact that the Malberti family had known this family. There was a young boy I remember—Fredo, he was called. Spoke marvellous Italian, with a Veronese accent."

Not so prestigious as his son's Tuscan, I thought. "And he was friends with the two boys?" I asked.

"Ye-es," he said. "But he was of the studious sort. Closer to Federico, I'd have said. I can't remember his age, mind you."

I said, "You know those tiles you showed me in the church . . ."

"Tiles?" This subject change threw him: it took him a full second to catch on. "Oh, yes, what about them?"

"You said they were a speciality of the area?"

"Yes. You have a curiously random mind." He looked across the square. Probably my way of thinking reminded him of the young people's way of working; a group of them were at that moment apparently trying to make a wigwam with scaffolding poles.

"Yes, sorry. I was just, em, reminded of them by—by the thought of the English people. You sometimes find something similar in English churches," I lied shamelessly. "But are they common in the churches here?"

"In this valley, yes."

"And they usually represent local sights? That sort of thing?"

"Yes."

"And you say they're eighteenth century?"

"I believe so. Does this line of questioning have anything to do with your research?"

"No." Another shameless lie. "But who knows: I might follow it up one day." Well, that toned the lie down a little.

"I see. Well, thank you so much for the drink." He stood up. "I really must get back and see what those young people think they're doing with that scaffolding." He scuttled back across the square.

I sat and pondered. Was it worth going and having another look at the museum? No, I could remember it all quite clearly; why disturb the old chap yet again?

It was all coming together: the tiles, that thing in the museum—and the sword, I suddenly thought. Yes, the sword. That clinched it.

Well, there was little I could do for the moment. I just had to wait for darkness to fall.

TWENTY

· · · · · · ·

AND IT FELL—WITH QUITE A CRASH. The local second-rank rock singer had been backed up by several other third- and fourth-rank performers, both local and not so local, all noisy. Coaches and cars had continued to spill people into the piazza throughout the afternoon, and by evening there wasn't room for another acoustic guitar or Snoopy toy or Garfield T-shirt.

Don Luigi had begun the proceedings with a prayer for tolerance and love, and then announced the list of speakers. One felt he'd been wise to get the prayer in first; the list included several local politicians, whose names were greeted with the gloomy resignation natural to Italians, who know that no public event can ever be considered complete without at least six different politicians from as many parties getting a few thousand words in. One of the names, I heard with surprise, was Giorgio Malberti, local councillor for the Liberal party. There were definitely a few local groans, and I saw Giorgio Malberti standing behind Don Luigi doing his not very convincing best to look tolerant and loving. The singers were welcomed more warmly, and Don Luigi announced that the evening would conclude at around midnight with a candlelit vigil in silence. The politicians all looked a bit puzzled by this last word.

The second-rank singer then started things off with a little aria entitled "Don't Be Mean with Love," which was not exactly over-generous with melodic invention, consisting as it did of three chords and a yowl, repeated several hundred times. The audience swayed and yowled back, and the politicians, sitting on one side of the platform, did their best to look as if they too were yowling. Even Giorgio Malberti nodded his balding head to the far from complex beat of the music.

Then it was the turn of the Christian-Democrat mayor of San Giorgio Veronese. This struck me as a good moment to slip away.

I made my way round the side of the square and then up the hill out of the village. The mayor's platitudes boomed hollowly behind me, interrupted only occasionally by a catcall from the amplification system. The road ahead of me was empty and dark. Once I was sure I was out of sight of the village's last house, I put my beret on and switched on my torch.

The mayor's voice became hollower and less distinct and was soon no more than a distant surly throb, with nothing Christian-Democrat about it but its tedium. I enjoyed the darkness and silence around me.

I entered the wood itself, taking the path that cut straight up the hill, avoiding the sweeps and curves of the road. The wood felt fresh and washed after the previous day's rain, and the ground was mushy under my espadrilles. The torchlight prodded forwards, with the shadows shifting around me. I told myself yet again how much I was enjoying the darkness and silence.

Of course it wasn't *totally* silent—and I told myself how quaint the occasional scuttering and leaf-thrashing noises were. Frolicsome rabbits enjoying midnight romps, little birdies stirring in their nests, squirrels startled by old clumsy Twolegs. . . .

At a certain point I stopped and switched the torch off: instant blackness, total silence (apart from the mayor's rhetorical throb). The wood seemed to hold its breath and I could imagine the trees with their twiggy claws poised, their great gnarled mouths yawning . . . But nothing happened. I stood there for a minute, while spiders clambered aboard, gambolling up and down my legs in joyous recognition. I think one even began to spin a web from my ear to the nearest tree. There was no further noise from behind me, and when I suddenly switched the torch back on the trees all had their hands in their pockets and wore innocent leafy smiles. I continued up the path.

A quarter of an hour later I came out onto the road again and tramped up it until I reached the point where the Villa Malberti fencing sagged drunkenly down. I scrambled over it and pulled myself up the little hill until I reached the old garden shed.

The shed where Linda and I had hidden from Luca: the crumbling, ivy-grown shed, with its bulging half-circle back.

Or was it a shed? I studied that half-circle back by torchlight and smiled: that was no back, that was an apse.

And that was no shed but a chapel: the same chapel I'd seen in the museum's eighteenth-century painting of the Villa Malberti and its grounds. It had lost most of its classical dignity, along with its marble, but its position and its overall basic shape showed it to be the same building. Presumably, indeed, it was the building that had housed the family's holy relics in more pious days, and the building where family Mass would have been celebrated.

Almost certainly Don Luigi would have been able to tell me if the Malberti family chapel still stood, but then he would have remembered that I'd asked—and I still had an instinctive urge to be discreet.

As I thought this I switched off the torch. I couldn't see the house myself, but there was no knowing that the house might not see the torch-glow through or above the trees—and the gardener might still be on the loose. I groped along the side of the chapel, my hands sliding over the ivy, which was refreshingly cool to the touch. I just had to hope it didn't harbour too many scorpions.

I reached the front, with its high arched doorway, and peered into the blackness. Gradually the shapes of the tottering bric-a-brac became visible to me, like a massed army of crook-backed Hulks. I could feel my heart beating, and I found myself saying quietly, "Now, now"—though whether I was addressing myself or the Hulks I really didn't know. Somewhere far below a politician's voice pulsed faintly.

I stepped into the chapel and turned the torch on. The shapes became explicable though scarcely less menacing; I would have to be very careful in shifting the stuff not to snap the vital sustaining cobweb.

I played the torch on the floor: at the edges I could see the ancient blue tiles. I stooped and pulled up the nearest piece of sacking; a little conference of woodlice broke up and the members scuttled for their lives, finding refuge in the cracks. The tiles thus revealed had the same blue, white, and grey designs I'd seen in the church: they showed highly simplified pictures of the village church and the town hall.

I pulled up all the sacking I could: I uncovered a further few local churches, a miniature St. George, and another resentful party of woodlice.

I put the torch on an old rocking chair and looked at the great mass of junk. I thought again of that mysterious note: "Come to the chapel. After midnight—the usual place, you remember? Above the castle, the stone with the ring?" Somewhere under that mountain of cracked memories there had to be a tile depicting the local castle, and nearby a stone with a ring. So all I had to do now was shift the stuff—and quickly. The stuff seemed to be growing as I watched it. I took one step back and set the chair with the torch rocking: the shadows swirled and the whole heap seemed about to jump at me.

I found I'd grabbed at something to steady myself. It was the wooden sword Linda had picked up the other day—the one she'd peeled chewing gum from. The gum must be somewhere on the floor. I wasn't going to look for it, but I was going to bear it in mind; I was sure the count and his son did nothing so vulgar as chew gum, and the gardener had no teeth. . . . Zeno, on the other hand, had apparently chewed the stuff incessantly.

It didn't constitute proof, but it was undeniably suggestive: Zeno could very well have come up here on the same mission as me. I just had to make sure my mission didn't end as his seemed to have done. As I thought this I glanced out of the door: the torchlight didn't really extend far into the night, and the windows were so ivy-covered as to be impenetrable. And I knew that one member of the household was safely away, demonstrating his love and tolerance. Nonetheless I found I was gripping that sword very tightly.

I put it down and set to work. I started gingerly removing the most removable-looking objects—a broken-legged garden bench, crippled chairs, stools, dolls—and I started to place them outside. I wondered whether Zeno had spent his last hours doing this, or whether the junk pile had been put there afterwards. Perhaps, I thought, it had simply been added to, by way of precaution.

In and out I went; each removal sent panic into another peaceful family of junk-dwellers: woodlice, spiders, ants (I hoped nothing worse). Each time I stepped outside I found myself tensely listening to the noises of the wood—and each time I just heard the tail end of a highly suspicious rustle or crackle that stopped at once as I listened.

I began to sweat freely. I had no need for earth-daubing tonight; just one wipe with my dust-and-dirt-grimed hands over my slimy face did the trick, I was sure. But on the other hand, it was impossible to keep my beret on, so my fair hair flashed my presence in the darkness.

After I'd cleared a good junk shop's worth, I discovered a bicycle leaning against one of the chapel's walls. It looked fairly ancient—it might have played a bit part in De Sica's *Bicycle Thief*—but appeared to work: the wheels went round, that is, and the handles turned to left and right, more or less in conjunction with the wheels. I had a sudden idea and carefully wheeled it to the edge of the slope and then scrambled down, half carrying it and half being carried by it. I lifted it over the fencing and laid it down gently onto the grass. Who knew but that I might have to make a speedy getaway later tonight? Okay, it was no racing champion, but the only direction I'd be going on it was downhill.

Eventually I felt I'd removed enough stuff from the building to make it feasible to reorder the stuff within. I started to create a new pile by the door. After ten minutes or so of hard work I had cleared the far end of the chapel and uncovered the altar itself: a much battered stone slab with the usual carving of St. George. At the other end of the chapel I had created something quite remarkable: a ten-foot high tower of bric-a-brac, with a quality of extravagant unexpectedness which I felt recalled the work of Gaudi. . . . Then I realised I was staring too hard: the rocking horse at the top began to slither forwards, its painted face grinning maniacally like one leading a suicide charge. Something at the bottom of the pile cracked and the whole thing started to totter: there was going to be a crash to rival anything the rock singers in the piazza could produce. I rushed forwards, blocking the avalanche with my body. I stood there, just me and my feeble strength pitted against Armageddon. Chair legs and rolling pins bulged out at me, and salacious dolls prodded, seeking my point of least resistance. Then I managed to stretch one arm out and grab a loose chair. I jammed this under the main supporting bedstead and heaved: the pile juddered backwards and then sank in on itself with a sulky crack. I wiped my neck again and stepped away.

I stood still for a few seconds, just breathing hard, sweating and listening to the pile's last baleful creaks. The chair and bedstead held firm. I cocked my ears doorwards as well: I could hear nothing from that direction.

I turned my attention to the floor that I'd cleared: more sacking. I kicked it aside and played the torch up and down. And there it was: the castle of San Giorgio Veronese. True, it looked more like a symbol in a simple video game than a picturesquely mouldering piece of medieval architecture—but there was no doubt that that was what it was. I scrutinised the floor nearby: there, a yard or so from the altar, was a flat blank stone with a metal ring in the middle of one side: it obviously lifted to reveal a crypt of some kind—which was perhaps where the saints' relics had been preserved—and was perhaps where Giorgio Malberti had hidden in games of hide-and-seek sixty years or so before, to the despair of his parents—and was perhaps where the village's greatest treasure now lay.

Next to the ring was a bolt. I slid this back and then put my hands to the ring. The stone was the size of a large newspaper and about two inches thick; all my strength was needed. It rose to an upright position and rested there. There was a rusty iron bar along a ledge underneath that lifted and slotted into a notch on one side of the stone, securing it. And below the stone was utter blackness.

My heart was beating hard as I thought of all the horror films of which I'd never dared see more than the trailers. Well, nothing had sprung out so far, so I went to get the torch. I couldn't bring myself to turn my back on the black square for even an instant, so found myself shuffling backwards to the rocking chair. I knocked it again and sent the shadows swirling. I grabbed the torch from the chair and restored order. Then I approached the hole, almost reluctantly swivelling the beam, prodding down into its depths.

A pitted face grinned up at me.

I tried to keep the beam steady, but shadows stirred in the eye cavities and the earth-stained grin seemed to crook at the corners. I trailed the torchlight down the rest of the body: earth-grimed, cobwebbed, twisted, lolling. Colourless clothes hung in tatters and the hands were blackened sticks. A pair of still solid boots covered the feet.

There was nothing else in the hole, which was brick-lined with an earthen floor. There were little alcoves in one wall, which I guessed had contained the saints' relics, but they were empty now.

I played the beam on the grey stump-toothed face again and tried to read its secrets. Something black and many-legged scuttled out of one eye.

Then a voice spoke behind me: "Yes, it's Giorgio."

TWENTY-ONE

. . . .

I ALMOST JOINED GIORGIO—not only through surprise, but for comfort.

Then I spun round and my torchlight revealed Linda in the doorway: she had that shy apologetic look which I was beginning to get used to. Well, this time she had good reason for it. If I were a fraction more flappable, she'd have been apologising to two corpses.

I told her so: in a few well-chosen words.

"Sorry," she said when I'd finished. She was wearing her black trousers, pullover and head-scarf again, and had her shoulder bag swinging by her side. Her face was smeared over with dark paste.

"And I might have screamed," I said, "which would have woken them all up at the house."

She shrugged at this.

"Look," I said, "someone killed Zeno Menegallo because he stumbled on this—or was about to."

"Yes," she said, "but Zeno was the sort of person who would get killed."

"And what are we? Immortals from the planet Krypton?"

"Don't be silly," she said. She came into the chapel.

"Don't touch that!" I said, as I saw her about to lay her hand on the bedstead-buttress. She flickered a glance at it and smiled, then came to my side to stare down at the body. "Poor chap," she said.

"You knew he was there?" I said.

"Yes."

"Don't tell me. There *was* a suicide note when we entered that room."

"Yes."

"My God. At least you could hang your head or lower your eyes as you say it."

"I had to do it," she said.

"Oh, it was addressed to you, was it?"

"No, of course not. It was for his son and wife. But it concerned his work—which meant I had to see it."

"Have you still got it?"

"Of course."

"I see. It'll go in the files. Maybe Piers will be able to see it, if he applies in triplicate."

"No, I'm afraid not. It'll have to remain confidential."

I stared at her for a few seconds. Then I said, "Come again?"

"You heard me. Do stop playing so innocent. It's rather irritating."

"How are you going to stop me telling Piers all about it? That it exists, at least?"

"Ye-es. That is a bit of a problem. But I'm sure we'll find a way. How much is Piers paying you?"

"Piss off."

She frowned. She'd never liked this kind of talk. Then she said, "I suppose you're going to play the Philip Marlowe incorruptible, aren't you? Well, I must say I admire you." She could have been complimenting me on an amateur theatrical performance. "But there are other strings we have. Like what we know about that Naples affair—which could be embarrassing for your brother at least, if not you."

I thought hard about this and then said, "Piss off." The Luca school of repartee. Then I added: "Did you follow me up here?"

"Yes."

"But you already knew what was in there."

"Yes."

"You could have saved me a lot of bother then."

"Well, one likes to be sure."

"Tell me," I said, "what's all this"—I waved my hand to the slumped horror below us—"got to do with your mysterious Masons or secret societies?"

"Ah," she said—and it was the kind of "ah" that announces a confession.

"Go on."

"Well, I have to admit I was a teeny little—well, let's say I simplified things just the teeniest bit."

"Simplified."

"Yes."

"You mean you told me a pack of lies."

"Well," she said—and once again she was strangely *un*embarrassed—"I couldn't at that point reveal the full story. You see, I *am* from MI6."

"Yes, that's the one thing I never doubted."

"But I'm from a relatively new department within it. As you know, our priorities have all changed rather in recent years—"

"You realised Hitler was dead and that."

"Oh, do stop being silly."

I found myself mumbling "sorry" before I knew what I was doing.

She went on, "Recent events in the east of course meant that certain departments could be reduced in size, if not actually disbanded, and it was decided that a new section was vital; I suppose you could even say we modelled it on the KGB. They've been awfully clever in the rehandling of their image and it was felt that we could take a leaf out of their book. Goodness knows the service needed some kind of boost in that line—as your own silly jokes suggest."

"Sorry again," I said. "Sore point, I gather."

"So the public relations department was set up. Of course we realised straightaway that the biggest problem the Secret Service has to face is the fact that it's secret; what I mean is that if anything comes to notice it's because it's gone wrong. So the public only ever hears of our failures, never of our successes. And hence my job."

"Oh." I stared down at Giorgio Malberti. You couldn't look more failed than he did. "What's that?"

"To make sure that our mistakes don't come out quite so often. I'm what is known in the business as a 'smoother.' Awful word, isn't it?"

"A smoother. Like a whitewasher, you mean?"

"Yes, I suppose so. But you do see our point. How would you like it as a private detective if only your dissatisfied clients spoke to the newspapers?"

I wondered why she bothered to go on pretending that I was a professional private detective. Maybe—as ever—it was intended as a sop to my ego. But right now my ego wasn't a big issue with me. I pointed down at Giorgio Malberti. "But this is going back a bit far, isn't it?"

"SOE business—strictly speaking, nothing to do with MI6, but in this case the op responsible then joined MI6, so we have to take it into account. At any rate, my assignment is to check that there are no scandals in Alfred Ainsley's files—or at least none that might come out."

"No skeletons," I said. I knew that one of us would have to use the metaphor sooner or later.

She didn't smile, so I went on: "So we're just going to close the cupboard door and forget all about it?"

"More or less," she said.

"Just what did that suicide note say?"

"You can read it if you like," she said.

"You've brought it with you?"

"A photocopy." She delved into her shoulder bag and brought out two folded sheets of paper. "I'm going to have to show it down at the house."

"Down at the—you're crazy."

"No, no. I need guarantees from them that the lid will remain on this case, and they'll want guarantees from me—and proof that I know what I'm talking about."

I accepted the sheets from her and opened them out with my

free hand, the other holding the torch on them. I had been about to protest that maybe we should continue this discussion somewhere safer, but now rather dazedly took the lead from her. I was, after all, intrigued to know what the note said.

In fact this was no suicide note but a suicide document—not to say file: two sheets of A4-size paper covered in small, neat, precise handwriting; there were no crossings-out as far as I could see, no awkward additions. It only lacked a reference number at the top left-hand corner. It was easy to associate it with Sir Alfred, but harder to associate it with his swollen-tongued corpse.

I read:

Dear Piers,

I address you because I know you will be the first to find this letter. It is a letter I never once dreamed that I might write, but now it seems simply the logical thing to do—the best course of action.

I am, you could say, taking the easy way out: at the moment it strikes me as being the neatest way—and I have always, as you know, valued tidiness.

I seem to be able to talk to you on paper in a way I never could in life. By now I expect you will have found out what I have spent nearly fifty years hoping would never come to light—the murder of a Communist partisan, which I connived at, even though I did not actually commit. (And what is more, of course, the murder of a childhood acquaintance.) I do not want to try and excuse myself, but perhaps I might try and put it in some kind of perspective. Then you can judge me as you think fit. My own action now will indicate to you how I judge myself.

I suppose there has never been much secrecy about the fact that during the war I was involved in SOE: my task was to establish contact with partisan forces in the north of Italy—in the area I knew from childhood days. This much is fairly common knowledge: perhaps rather less well-known is the more specific nature of my mission. I was to ensure that aid got through to non-Communist partisans. Of course the allied forces knew that the important thing was to defeat the Nazis, but we would have been failing in our duties if we had not looked beyond the end of the war. The partisans were, of course, nominally under the command of an all-party alliance—the Comitato di Liberazione Nazionale—but it was well-known that in many areas the forces in the field were Communist-dominated. Churchill was quite rightly worried by this trend, and thus agents were sent to areas where it was felt the balance could be redressed. One such area was the Veneto, and I was one of the agents sent there.

I was fully aware of what a charismatic figure Giorgio Malberti was, and had thus decided that my first task was to ensure that our aid went to some more reliable figure who might restore the odds in favour of democracy. I knew that I could count on Giorgio Malberti's own brother, Federico, in this endeavour.

As fate would have it, I arrived at the Villa Malberti to find Federico crippled, and the Nazis out to avenge a typically foolhardy assault that had been led against them by Giorgio Malberti. It then seems that the Nazis attacked a house in the hills in which the small band of partisans had taken refuge, and burnt it to the ground. Only Giorgio was saved, owing to the fact that he had been outside the building at the time of the attack. News of his safety was brought to the villa by a small boy, who told us that Giorgio was now hiding in the woods; unfortunately he had twisted his ankle in an ignominious scramble down the hillside, and thus knew he could not take to the mountains.

Federico decided not to inform his mother of this development since he felt she could not be trusted to conceal her emotions suitably from the Nazis. Federico sent a message to Giorgio—and this of course is the *message that you found in my desk. That night Giorgio came to the house and hid in the chapel crypt as he had done often as a child, raising the stone trapdoor beneath the matting occasionally for air. As we had suspected, the villa was searched by the Nazis (I myself had retired temporarily to the hills), but nothing of course was found. It was then that Federico revealed to me the fact that he had bolted the trapdoor and had no intention of reopening it. Federico was a bitter man, who owed his own injury to his brother's political choices, and who had always resented his brother's greater popularity.*

I am fully aware that my acquiescence makes me as responsible for this crime as Federico himself was: I had no personal rancour towards Giorgio, though I cannot pretend that I ever liked him. I did, however, find his political ideology deeply repugnant—as repugnant as the one we were then officially fighting. It struck me at once that this was a singularly convenient opportunity to further the cause for which I had been sent to the area. The Veneto has no real Communist tradition, as have Tuscany or Emilia-Romagna; the removal of such a charismatic figure as Giorgio Malberti would probably prove fatal to the movement in that area. I thus simply told Federico to do as he thought fit.

The only person who knew that Giorgio Malberti was still alive then was the young boy, and he was obviously emotionally unstable: his attitude to his hero had undergone a violent swing after the sight of his ignominious scramble to escape. Of course we did not inform him of our plans, but we had no trouble in persuading him immediately to leave the area, where he apparently had no other friends or relatives.

That is the whole story. We opened the crypt the next morning and he was of course dead. I saw many horrors in the course of the war but that sight is one which has never been far from my mind to this day.

I glanced down at this point at Giorgio Malberti and tried to imagine what sort of expression he would have had. I decided it was probably better to remember him as I now saw him.

We decided to leave him in the crypt, though I first took the incriminating documents from his pockets. It seems quite likely that he is still there, since Federico, crippled as he is, could never remove him. I expect he has found some way to ensure that the secret never comes to light—or at least had found till now.

Why did I keep the documents, you may ask. I cannot give you any clear answer—other than that I suppose I am a civil servant and have a civil servant's way of thinking. But I think too that somewhere in my mind there was the idea that as long as I had them, I could always one day confess to the crime. They were, if you like, an ever-present possibility of redemption.

I have of course never confessed—until now. And now only because pushed to it. I do not want you to blame yourself in any way for what I am now going to do: I say, quite sincerely, that I am in fact grateful to you. I do not deserve a quiet comfortable death, with a respectful Times obituary. I am, you might say, glad that it has happened like this.

True, until today I was still desperately hoping that I might manage to cover things up. Then I received a phone call at the hotel from Federico: my first—and last—contact with him since that fatal day. He sounded more bitter than ever, and his only concern was to make me leave the area. It was only then that I realised, from his somewhat incoherent remarks, how foul had been the consequences of our act. I had tried all these years to think of it as one swift act—ugly, brutal, but one whose consequences had at least been positive. Only now do I realise the truth of the old saying that good can never come from evil.

I am quite settled and serene in my decision now. You

*can tell your mother I have even tried a prayer. I do not
ask you to forgive me; all I can really ask is that perhaps
you too will offer a prayer. I trust you will be happy with
Rita. Do not forget me—but do not think too much of
me either.*

*All practical arrangements for the funeral you can
leave, I am sure, in the capable hands of your mother.*

With all love,

The only crossing-out in the whole letter came here: he had
automatically signed himself "Alfred Ainsley"; this was neatly
struck through and below it he had written "Daddy."

I didn't say anything for a moment or two. I handed the sheets
to Linda and she folded them and put them back in her bag.
Then she said, "So you do see how awful it would be if these
things got out."

I was still staring down at Giorgio Malberti. "It's a standard
MI6 tactic, is it?"

"What?"

"Pocketing people's last words."

"Now, come on. You're surely not feeling sorry for Sir Alfred."

"What about the addressees?" I couldn't answer her last
question.

"It would hardly be very cheering for Piers to read this, now
would it?"

"No. But cheering isn't necessarily what it's about. And if he
were to hear about it any other way."

"That's what we have to ensure doesn't happen." She looked
at me curiously. "This whole thing doesn't seem to come as too
much of a surprise to you."

I looked down at Giorgio Malberti again. "I'd had an inkling. It didn't make the first sight of him any less of a shock."

"So you'd suspected Sir Alfred—and the count?"

"Particularly the count," I said. I remembered that phrase in
Giorgio Malberti's letter, attributed to Federico: "You can

only push people so far"—who knew what resentment, what rancour had lain behind these words? Everyone had casually assumed that Federico didn't mind about his brother's continual success—he after all was the "scholarly type," "the quiet one." But this portrait did not square with the bitter man I'd seen seething at his own son's achievements. And then, to put things bluntly, there had been the inheritance: the villa and the grounds and the family's other treasures. Just the sort of goodies to come in useful if you're a dilettante, "above" the sordid world of commerce.

I said, "But to revert a second: all the secret society stuff about him was nonsense, right?"

"Oh, yes," she said. "I mean, I needed a good story, and of course in Italy it's always easy to make a convincing one. As you know, there are all sorts of rumours about this area—the missing arms store, Gladio, the Knights of St. George and all that nonsense—so I borrowed what I needed."

"Well," I said, "I wouldn't need too much pushing to believe the count's a bastard and a traitor."

"Now," she said, "I do hope you're not going to start getting all upright and legalistic about a fifty-year-old murder."

"There's a five-day-old one as well," I said. "Have you forgotten that?"

"Well, this Zeno chap doesn't really seem the sort of person worth making a lot of fuss about."

"Have you explained that to his father? And anyway, who did do it? The count's a cripple, remember, and the body was found over by the castle."

"Well, I daresay we'll sort that out when I go and talk things over with him."

"Will you be taking his big brother with you? Or are you going to post him off to MI6 to be filed?"

"No, I think we'd better close this crypt up again—and put all this junk back."

I made a decision: not a very strong one, not a definitive one, but one that would have to do for the moment. "I don't want anything more to do with it. Do as you see fit." Then I remembered in what context I'd just read these words and winced. Still, I couldn't think of another, more convincing line, so I said, "If you want me, I'll be back at the Las Vegas hotel."

"Fine. There'll be a few bureaucratic things to clear up—we'll need some guarantees as regards your discretion." She looked at the crypt and obviously decided she could rely on his unguaranteed discretion, and then looked at all the junk. "I think I'll go and see the count before I do anything about all this."

I said, "Before you go, just think for a moment: what did Sir Alfred mean by the ugly consequences of the act?"

"Oh, I expect that's just melodramatic exaggeration. He could hardly have been at his most rational at that point."

"Well, that's a comforting way of thinking of it," I said. "Give the count my best wishes. And watch your jugular."

"Silly," she said, with a last little giggle. Then she slipped out of the chapel, and I saw her torchlight weaving through the trees and out of sight. I looked down at Giorgio Malberti again. Somehow he was no longer so horrific—not when I compared him with his living brother. I thought of his last letter. He'd obviously never had any suspicion of Federico: trusted him to the last. Well, they'd never have wanted him in MI6—nor as a private detective, come to that.

"The best die young," I said to myself. I'd obviously live forever. Then I thought that if he'd lived he might have turned into one of those contorted grey men, defending Stalin, then the crushing of Hungary, of Czechoslovakia . . .

But I couldn't believe it: not from the tone of his letter—and not from such memories as Don Luigi had had of him. I looked around for something suitable to throw down to him and spotted the wooden sword. I dropped it by his side. There: he could be Sandokan—or St. George—for eternity.

While the loathly worms lorded it above ground: slithering, smarming . . . smoothing.

I left the chapel. I could no longer see Linda's torchlight. I stood still for a second or two and listened to the throb-throb-throbbing from the village. One of the singers must have started up his plea for love and tolerance in front of the statue of Giorgio Malberti. I slipped round the side of the chapel, scrambled down the steep hill to the road. As I walked down the road my mind was as blank and dull as the torchlight, with just as many dark shapes looming menacingly at its dim fringes. The only phrase that came at all distinctly to mind was Oliver Hardy's: "Here's another fine mess you've gotten me into," addressed in my case to Gigi.

Brothers: who needs them? Certainly not me and Giorgio Malberti.

What was I going to tell Piers? The truth, a half-truth, or nothing like the truth?

After I'd been walking for a few minutes—still tramping unthinkingly down the road—I heard a car coming up the hill. I retreated to the woods and switched off my torch. I didn't even bother to shudder as the spiders moved in: Giorgio hadn't seemed to mind, after all.

I saw the headlights through the trees, and the beams swirling as the car turned the corner, momentarily illuminating the quick flick and twist of a bat. I moved closer to my tree and watched the car sweep past, its driver leaning forwards as if shortsighted. I recognized him and wondered.

Had he been summoned? by phone?

Phone! And a phone buzzed in my mind: the long single buzz of an Italian phone. Someone else had received one—a fatal one. Sir Alfred. . . . From the count! And how had the count known where Sir Alfred Ainsley was?

He must have spelt the name out to several hotels: Ainsley . . . Aheenslayeeh!

Each exclamation mark was like a little pop in my brain. I'd been so stupid—but so-so-stupid. I thought back to my whole conversation with the man, and the exclamation marks detonated in my mind like a whole cellarful of ginger-beer bottles.

I was now running back up the hill. I might have been stupid, but Linda had committed a far graver crime: she'd been silly.

TWENTY-TWO

I SCRAMBLED BACK UP THE HILL, past the chapel and then weaved down through the wood, trying to confine the torch-light to my feet and their immediate surroundings. I reached the open lawn, where I switched the torch off; the moonlight gave the grass a silvery grey sheen and the statues a ghostly glimmer. I guessed it must be having a similarly picturesque effect on me so I moved to the edge, in among the statues, and kept running. I reached the balustraded end of the lawn and made my way down the winding paths to the next level lawn. I was now in full view of the house: I could see it and it could see me. On the whole I no doubt had the better view, moonlight suiting the building's classical elegance more than it did my dark-clad shiftiness. The marble and stone shimmered with ec-toplasmic magnificence—though that may just have been the wind-induced tears in my eyes.

The windows were all shuttered, but I could see light around the edge of the drawing room ones. I approached them cau-tiously and put my eye to the nearest crack.

I could see an illuminated slice of the room, containing the front half of an armchair, with the count's hand and leg pro-truding, and a big blurred wall mirror. His voice said, "You do see our point, my dear." It was quite distinct, since the win-dows were open inside the shutters. He was speaking in Italian, and the feminine *"Mia cara"* made it clear he was addressing Linda.

"Neither of you seems to have understood." Her voice came from somewhere to my right. The tone was one of intense weariness, but I could guess that that was a cover for her real emotion—which was fear. "We're prepared to turn a blind eye on all this business—forget it ever happened. We just need your guarantee that you will make no further contact with the Ainsley family."

"*You* don't seem to have understood," came a new voice from the left. "You see, you have stumbled onto something rather larger than just a dead Communist. So you can see why we are rather sceptical about your assurances." The voice was Pigozzi's, and he sounded as petulant with this century as ever, but the petulance had an edge to it.

From the quiver in Linda's voice I guessed he was holding something else that had an edge to it—or perhaps a barrel. "Look," she said, "this really is a lot of fuss about nothing. At MI6 we're just not interested in your organisations. That's the SISDE's business after all." The SISDE, I knew, was the Italian Secret Service.

"You may not be interested, but now you know. That is the point. But we don't know just how much you know. That is the next point. Nor what your blond friend knows."

"He's no friend," she said. "He's just a blundering idiot. Calls himself a private detective, but I don't think he's understood the first thing about this whole business. You really needn't worry about him." It was good of her to be so protective towards me; she acted so well, one might almost have thought she believed what she was saying.

"Well, I think we'll need to be a little more certain on that point," Pigozzi said. I noticed that the initiative always seemed to come from him, rather than from the count, whose voice seemed a shade embarrassed by the vulgarity of these proceedings. His hand gave an occasional nervous tap on the arm of the chair. Pigozzi went on: "Where can we find him?"

"I really don't know. I think he's gone back to England."

"You're lying," Pigozzi said.

"Really, my dear," murmured the count, "you'll save us all a lot of time and unpleasantness if you just tell us straightaway what you know."

"Let me make myself clear," said Pigozzi. His voice had the same sharp contempt it had had when talking about greenhouse effects. "If you do not tell us what we want to know, I will tap your teeth out one by one with this gun. And remember there is no one to hear your screams: they're all down in the village playing the guitar and smoking marijuana."

"You are both completely mad," Linda said, and the fear was quite open now.

The count made a demurring noise. "Please just do as the professor says. It will save so much trouble." He probably didn't want blood all over his marble.

As usual I'd come along without arming myself—I'd even thrown away a perfectly good wooden sword. I looked at the shutters: they were shut—definitely shut. I ran to the next window. Shut. And the next . . . Paranoid bastards.

I looked up to the first floor: there was a window with a pillared balcony, and the shutters seemed to be open. I had a mad idea: well, sane ideas were obviously going to be of no use in this situation.

I went running back across the lawn, praying that Linda would keep them talking—tell them a joke or something. Up the winding path, across the next lawn, through the woods, my torchlight unabashedly challenging the moonlight. I was back at the chapel and I grabbed what I'd come for: the broken-legged garden bench.

I staggered back through the woods, the bench clasped upright in front of me, somewhat taller than myself. My torch was in my pocket, of course, and I just relied on the bench to smash through any obstacles that I couldn't see. The Mad Gardener was going to have quite a gum-gnashing session the following morning. . . . Back over the lawn, down the path, and over the next lawn.

By the time I reached the house, my shirt was clammy and I was gasping. I had heard no screams as yet, and for one confused second I thought, pity, they would cover me at least . . .

but then I thought a little more clearly and winced. I leant the bench up against the wall and its top end rested a couple of feet below and to the right of the balcony.

Well, there was no point in standing and reasoning over it, because I knew perfectly well that reason would tell me to tiptoe quietly away. So I just gave the bench a preliminary shake to check that it was firm—and immediately told myself against all visual and sensory evidence that it was—and then ran up its rotten boards. I'm quite sure that what I did was a geometrical and physical impossibility, but the fact remains that two seconds later I was clutching the balcony with both arms, while the bench gave a skidding lurch beneath my feet. Then it dropped and the crash shook the whole house while I hung there with my legs kicking over the void.

I heaved myself over the balustrade with a sluglike squirm and a walrus-flop and then slipped in through the open window. I could hear vague noises of puzzlement from below; they would presumably investigate outside first, so my best bet was to ensconce myself firmly inside.

I ran through the room, which appeared to be an unused bedroom, and then found myself in another large marble hall, which glistened with the moonlight from big end-windows. I slid across its frosty marble to the staircase opposite me. There I paused to look for a weapon: why don't Italian squires go in for crossed battleaxes and ceremonial swords? All this Tintoretto and Veronese and Canova rubbish. I rushed on down the stairs empty-handed.

I could now hear their voices below and the scrape of shutters being opened. I was at the bottom of the stairs, peering over the banisters and under the arm of a statue of Diana surprised while bathing, when the door to the drawing room opened and Pigozzi stared up at me. Pigozzi had a gun.

For one split second Diana was the least surprised person in the hall, but then I redressed things by giving her a quick shove. She found herself rolling next to a winded Dark-Age historian on the floor.

I leapt down and grabbed the gun. Pigozzi had been

slammed in the shoulder and sent sprawling; he was still gasping as he stared first into Diana's affronted eyes, and then the barrel of the gun.

"Up you get, Pig," I said—then remembered he didn't speak English. I repeated it in Italian.

He managed to pull himself to his feet. Diana had obviously not caused him any lasting damage: she unfortunately had lost her head.

"Get back in there—but keep your hands up." It was a large pistol, and as usual I took care to keep my finger off the trigger for the moment.

He backed into the room, which was brilliantly lit by the central chandelier: a festive cascade of Murano glass. The count was sitting in the same chair by the window, and Linda was perched on a straight-backed chair in the middle of the room with her arms pulled round the back. She had her head twisted to stare in our direction: her face was still smeared with dark paste, but there was an attempt at a smile on it. "Thanks," she said. The smile couldn't quite make it to the upper part of her face, but at least there seemed to be no absentees among the teeth.

"Don't mention," I said. "What happened?"

"I was a bit silly," she said. "He said he needed to talk to a friend and I let him phone. Then when the friend came I was expecting him at the front door but he had a key to the back and—well, he clobbered me." She nodded down to her right arm. "Then they started questioning me."

I prodded Pigozzi towards a chair. He sat down. "Hands on your head," I said. I went over to Linda and examined the knots that tied her hands together. It looked like ten-fingers work to undo, if not ten fingers and teeth: so who was going to hold the gun?

"I've got a knife in my bag there," she said, nodding to the table.

Well, of course. I went over to the small shoulder bag, still keeping the gun trained on Pigozzi. The count, I decided, didn't look as if he were about to hurl his crutches or press a trapdoor button. He was merely glowering at me as if I were one of his son's successful hotels.

In usual circumstances the bag was no doubt a marvel of MI6 efficiency, functioning as a miniature office-cum-armoury, its separate little pockets and compartments all opened by pass codes and laser-beam keys: however, Linda's interrogators had ripped it open and spilt its contents onto the table. I saw the clasp-knife at once lying amidst the classified secrets of her soul.

Seconds later she was standing up and rubbing her wrists. "The count," she told me, "has arthritic fingers. Otherwise, he'd have greeted you with my gun." She picked it up from the table. I think this was one teeny final reminder of my amateur status: no pro would have sauntered into the room with quite my insouciance.

I ignored it and said, "So you were right about him first time, were you?"

"How do you mean?"

"When you told me your little story about secret societies."

"Please," interrupted the count in English, "I am suitably humiliated and prepared to grovel with apologies. But do not associate me with Professor Pigozzi and his braincracked fantasies."

"You've never seen him before, have you?" I said. "Just barged his way into your house tonight . . ."

"What I am saying is that I do not share his absurd ambitions of purging Western civilisation. I leave that to AIDS and civil war."

"And he . . ." I began, gesturing.

"Do not wave that gun in that careless fashion," snapped Pigozzi in Italian.

"He's right," said Linda, "you really must be—"

"Oh, sorry. Shall I give it to him?"

"Don't be silly."

"Just out of curiosity," I said in Italian, "is this the gun that killed Zeno Menegallo?" I looked at both the count and Pigozzi.

Linda came in, speaking in English. "Look, we don't want to spend our time talking about that little murder, do we?" "How do you measure murders at MI6?" I asked. "According to nationality, income bracket, or political affiliations?" "Yes, of course, it's horrible, but making a big fuss isn't going to bring him back to life. What we need to do now is find a way of persuading the professor to close up his little organisation and just—well, retire peacefully into private life." "Oh, my God," I said. "What does he have to do before you decide he should be locked up? Blow up an orphanage? No, little murders—assassinate the queen?" "Yes, yes, it's all horrible, I agree," she said again, "but this is Italy." "Yes, the land of St. Francis." "No, I just mean there's no point in getting involved. You never get to the bottom of anything here. Better just to keep a lid on things." "I hope you never get a job with the gas board," I said. "Look, I need to make some kind of sense of all this stuff—for my own sanity." She shook her head. "You never will, you know: not in Italy. We have a rule in the service: never liaise with the SISDE, because we just don't know who they are from one day to the next." "Whereas MI6 is as transparent a bunch of chaps as ever hung the queen's pictures. . . ." "Don't be silly," she said automatically. "You remember the P2 business? A secret society, out to subvert the state and the rest of it? Well, the whole of the Italian secret service were members, it seems. And now they say they've purged these people, but at the same time you get people in the government saying that the P2 weren't such bad chappies after all." "Look," I said, "just look." I waved the gun again and Pigozzi muttered something that didn't sound too learned. "Look at these two: do they look like an international conspiracy?"

"No," she said, "but then what good would an international conspiracy be that did—"

"Okay, okay, don't say it. I get the point. Nonetheless, my bet is that Professor Pigozzi is as nasty an antiquarian researcher as you're likely to find, but doesn't actually have his finger on the Armageddon button." I addressed him in Italian. "You were the boy who brought the message from Giorgio Malberti in the war, weren't you? The mysterious messenger we've all heard so much about."

"What if I was?" For the very first time, as he sat there with his hands on his head, looking and sounding sulky, I could actually imagine him as a boy and not a musty, fusty historian from birth.

Linda's mouth dropped. "Oh!" She at once tried to add an unflapped "Yes, of course," but not very convincingly.

One up to the amateur. I went on, "The professor did something really odd when I first spoke to him: I mentioned the name Ainsley and he repeated Aheensley—exactly as if he were reading it. But then he said he'd never heard the name. It didn't click at the time, I admit. But then we read in Sir Alfred's letter that Federico phoned him in the hotel; well, I had only told one person in the whole village that I was working for Sir Alfred, and that he was in Verona, and that one person was Pigozzi here. Come to think of it, I didn't exactly *tell* him: he got the information out of me." I reran the conversation in my mind, with Pigozzi's question-answers: *"He mentioned a foreign friend who was curious about the statue but who was staying in Verona—would that be right?"* And I'd told him it would be. Well, come to J. Esposito for discretion.

"I see," said Linda, obviously deciding to dispense with omniscience for once. "But how did that make him the little boy?"

"Well, it contributed," I said. "This boy was really mysterious: some said he had relatives here or nearby, others said he was alone. His origins ranged from Naples to Tuscany, Emilia Romagna and the Marche. All central Italy, except for that one offer of Naples—from our friend here." I indicated Federico Malberti. "But nobody knew or had seen his relatives in this area, it seemed, so I wondered whether he might not have come just out of admiration for Giorgio Malberti—Giorgio Malberti, who could become a leader of a gang wherever he went—as for example when he went to stay with his mother's relatives near Urbino, in the Marche. So maybe this little boy—obviously of an independent nature—had met and admired Giorgio there in the Marche, and then in wartime came over to be with him here. And Professor Pigozzi told me himself that he was from the Marche." Pigozzi remained obstinately silent; he was clearly not going to provide any information on his own family or background. "Even the name wasn't very clear: some said it was Gianni, and others Johnny, or something foreign anyway. My bet's that it was Yanez, Sandokan's lieutenant in the Salgari stories. Giorgio would have been Sandokan, of course." I turned to him. "Right?" He gave a little shrug. Maybe Salgari was too sacred to discuss with me. I said, "So why did you do it? Keep quiet about the murder, that is?"

"Giorgio Malberti proved totally unworthy of the admiration that I'd had for him," he said, and there was utter contempt in his voice. "I'd respected him as a natural leader, a man born to forge the new Italy, and then, at the moment of crisis I saw him become a frightened rabbit."

"What happened?" Linda and I asked together.

"He had left the hideout with me to put the statue in a cave nearby when the Germans attacked. Suddenly all he could think about was his own safety—running so fast away from the action that he twisted his ankle."

"You mean he should have taken on the whole lot single-handed?" I said.

"It would have been a grander gesture," he said. "But I delivered his note nonetheless, and then took the answer back from Federico. When Federico and the Englishman, Ainsley, then planned his end—a highly fitting one—I don't think they knew I was still there."

Linda and I were silent, as was Federico. There was something appalling in the man's certainties: he made the count, with all his twisted rancour, seem charmingly human. Then I said, "And ten years later you popped by again. Was Federico pleased to see you?"

He gave a frosty smile. "I made it clear it was in his interests to make me welcome."

"So it all comes down to blackmail," I said. "You told him you knew what was hidden in his family chapel—something that he had no way of getting rid of by himself. . . ." I remembered another little fact: Pigozzi, when talking to me, had listed some of the Malberti family's barbaric crimes against their own heritage—*pulling down their chapel,* for example. Yet another attempt to throw me off the scent. I went on: "What did you want from him? Better conditions at the museum?"

"You know nothing about me if you think I have such materialistic ambitions," he said. "It cannot be called blackmail. Count Malberti had proved that his political principles were correct—he had shown it in the clearest way possible, helping to strike at communism at its roots. I merely put pressure on him to convince him that that moment of decisiveness he'd shown in the war, in which he'd put aside all family pieties for the sake of a greater good, should not remain an isolated act, but become part of a committed strategy. The network I was setting up had need of a man of wealth and position in the area."

The count came in here. "I played a purely passive role, let me point out." Then a second or two later: "Not that I wish to repudiate the aims of the organisation—or at least what were its aims as they were first represented to me." He obviously hadn't fully decided which role he should be playing now: cringing blackmail victim, public-spirited defender of the nation, aloof aristocrat. He now lapsed into this last role, gazing into the nearest mirror as if it were the only thing worth looking at in the room.

I scratched my head for a second or two, until Linda's "Careful!" reminded me what I was scratching with. I said to Pigozzi, "But just what is this network?"

"Part of the international effort that the Free World had fortunately formed to defend—"

"International . . ." I stared at him. "Are you joking?"

He stared back at me, as if trying to decide whether it was worth explaining things to such an obviously decadent pinko as myself. Then he shrugged and said, "I was entrusted by my country with a task of supreme importance—and I may say supreme nobility—"

I kept staring at this man in his dog-eared jacket and shabby trousers. "You? An ex-commie groupie?"

He brought his hands down from his head and made a gesture of distaste. We didn't insist that he raise them again. "As a child I was simply attracted by Giorgio Malberti because I thought he showed signs of greatness as a leader. I was wrong, of course. But we all know how this country is in dire need of true leadership."

"*Viva il Duce,*" I murmured.

"Mussolini as a phenomenon merely revealed the extent to which Italians longed for leadership, to the point that they were even prepared to accept a completely fraudulent version of it."

"But are you saying that NATO or the CIA entrusted *you . . .*"

"People of importance in this country recognised my ideological soundness. I was teaching at the University of Verona at the time and was given the task of forming an anti-Communist nucleus in this area of the Veneto."

I stared at Linda. "Help me. Can it be true?"

She gave a half-smile. "I told you. We're in Italy. You must remember that when they uncovered Gladio, they found all sorts of harmless local people were involved—bus drivers, teachers, doctors. . . ."

"Yes, but, he says he was *in charge!*" I turned to him again. "Were you part of Gladio?"

"Let's say they were the military branch, and I was in charge of the ideological and theoretical branch in the area. We worked alongside one another. Part of my task was to advise on Gladio recruitment."

"Ideological . . . You mean pushing pamphlets through people's doors?"

"That may have been in the minds of the organisers, but

fortunately each nucleus was given a fairly free hand by the central committee. In fact," he said with a smile, "this hand became freer when the secret service was shaken up in one of its periodic so-called 'reforms'—all undertaken cravenly on account of left-wing pressure. But anyway one of these shake-ups resulted in the central committee losing contact with us."

"Losing . . ."

"Italy," Linda reminded me.

Professor Pigozzi seemed to be rather enjoying the effect of his story. He continued: "At this point I realised just how much foresight I had shown in ensuring the support of a local man of wealth. Despite losing our funds from central government, we had no financial problems. At the same time Gladio was ordered all over the country to bury its arms stores, and with a little local manouevring—in which again the count's wealth and influence proved most valuable—we managed to secure them for ourselves."

"Oh, my God," I said, suddenly holding the gun tighter. I think I even put my finger somewhere within reach of the trigger. "Where are they?" I felt a prickling sensation, as if we were sitting on a pile of hand-grenades. Perhaps we were. I looked at Linda. "And you say you just want him to close up his little organisation. . . ."

"Look," she said, "I told you that everything is extremely complicated here: that has two sides to it. On the one hand, you never get to the bottom of anything, because everything is connected, from the Pope to Cicciolina: if you pull one string, you don't undo the knot, you just make the spaghetti more entangled. On the other hand, nobody here understands it all either; and this means that someone smart like the prof here can practically run his own local network, even though it's supposed to be under central control; it also means he can close it down without anyone asking why—or perhaps even noticing."

"Yes, but he's got bombs," I said with infinite patience. "Machine guns, hand-grenades . . . nuclear warheads, quite likely." I turned to him. "Where are they? What have you been doing with them?"

"This is something I'm not prepared to answer," he said, and gave a little smile. A scholar refusing to reveal his sources.

"Look," I said, "I don't know if you ever read the papers, but things have been happening to the Communists recently. . . ."

"I am fully aware that they no longer constitute the greatest threat to our civilisation."

"Oh," I said. "You've discovered a substitute."

"You know perfectly well what it is that now threatens our cultural identity, what it is that is weakening our nation, once the cradle of civilisation, what it is that is destroying the very roots—"

"Oh, my God," I said again. I knew somehow he wasn't referring to guitar-playing in church. I turned to Linda. "Meet one of the Knights of St. George."

The count spoke up. He'd opted for Role Number 1 again. "Let me make it clear that I have nothing to do with this latest sick twist in his thinking. I dissociate myself from it completely."

I said to the count: "Is he the one behind these bombs and fire attacks?"

The count shrugged. "Indirectly. His latest policy has been to encourage little local formations of thugs: finance them, try and give them a smattering of rhetoric and cant. Mere local thugs, as I say."

He sounded as if his chief objection to them was their parochialism. I said, "You didn't dissociate yourself to the point of going to the police?"

He looked more aristocratically aloof than ever: any moment now and he was going to fade into the frescoes. "These people are such obvious petty hooligans . . ."

"Uneducated perhaps," Pigozzi cut in, "but why should we sneer at them for that? True warrior types: simple men who can however see when things are going wrong in society, who can recognise a cancer in their midst, and who under true leadership can be relied upon to carry out the necessary surgery."

"Oh, my God," murmured the count.

I looked at Linda. "You still think you can get this bloke to give it all up and take up gardening?"

Even she looked a little shaken. "If we explain to him it's in his best interests—that he can't hope to get away with it any longer. . . ."

"Linda, he is what psychiatrists term a raving fruit-cake, an utter nutter. He's had forty years of fantasizing—playing Sandokan with his own little private army, no one ever saying no or hang on a second squire." I made another of my lightning decisions. "I'm going to call the police right now."

Before anyone could say a word, I'd laid my gun down on the table and picked up the old-fashioned black receiver.

"Jan, don't be silly—"

"It's dead," I said in slow puzzlement. After the lightning the long, too long pause.

"Drop that gun," came a voice in Italian from the door. The thunder.

I spun round, still clutching the receiver; the phone stand was dragged through the various ornaments on the table and something went crash, in synchrony with my heart and my lower jaw.

There at the door stood two huge men with balaclava helmets, with just eye- and mouth-slits: they were both holding rifles. There was another dull crash from my right as Linda dropped her gun.

"Oh, shit," she said.

For once I didn't even look to see if she blushed.

TWENTY-THREE

· · · · · · · · · · · ·

PROFESSOR PIGOZZI WAS OUT OF HIS CHAIR at once. "Marvellous, marvellous. You are to be congratulated. I knew I could rely on you."

The bigger man said, "The boys and I were hoping for a bit of action tonight."

"Ciao Mauro," I said, my hands above my head. I looked at the other man beside him. "And that must be your friend, Carlo."

Mauro and Carlo moved forwards and I saw there were two other men behind them, also balaclava-clad and holding rifles. Mauro put a hand to his head and tore the floppy hood off: "Okay, *terrone*," he said, using the pejorative term for a southern Italian. "So you've recognised us."

"Jan," Linda said in English from my right, "please don't do anything silly."

"Like what?" I said. Was she expecting me to try a flying kick?

"Just don't antagonise them any more than necessary."

I wondered if Linda still thought we had a chance of talking our way out of this situation. It must be great to be an optimist.

Mauro said to his companions: "Take them off, *ragazzi*."

All three men pulled their hoods off. I'd been right about Carlo: his blubbery features now peered meanly at me over his gun, and I had to fight hard not to ask him to put the thing back on. I had never seen the other two before: one had a long thin moustache and thinning black hair, and the other could only have been about seventeen or eighteen and he seemed to be shaking slightly as he pointed his gun. I wondered if he'd been dragged into this by big brother, or was just high on something. Neither hypothesis seemed reassuring and I decided not to look at the state of his trigger finger.

Professor Pigozzi moved towards the four men and rubbed his hands together; I remembered when I'd found this enthusiastic gesture of his quaint. *"Bravi, bravi,"* he said. "Well, yes, I think you're right. We can't let this night go by without some action of some sort, now can we?"

"Not here, please," said the count from his chair.

"What do you hope to achieve?" said Linda in her most earnest schoolgirl fashion. "Just what do you hope to achieve?"

"Simply to let the world know that the sick message being propagated down in the village square will not go unchallenged," said Pigozzi.

The four *bravi* all said "yeah" or grunts to that effect.

I said, "Love and tolerance, you mean?"

"Tolerance is probably the quality our sick society most needs to repudiate."

There was clearly no point in trying to argue with him. The only hope, it seemed to me, lay in trying to nibble at the bond tying him and the thugs. I said to Mauro: "So you're the glamorous Knights of St. George, are you?"

"Shut up."

"You know he's crazy, don't you? He might end up in some comfy madhouse, but it'll be chokey for you."

"Shut up."

"Did you murder Zeno, or was that him?"

"We had nothing to do with that," Mauro said at once.

So it wasn't quite one for all, all for one. And this defensive instinct also suggested that Mauro and his men hadn't yet taken the final step into homicidal fury. Homicide, perhaps— but not fury.

Well, it was a point worth knowing, though I don't suppose

Lloyds would have lowered my premium appreciably on account of it.

"That was a purely, em, administrative matter," Pigozzi said dismissively. "Hardly work for warriors."

"So you did it?" I said.

"I came to the aid of my friend here," he said, indicating the count. "From the house he'd seen a light by the chapel and summoned me. It came as no surprise to me to find that young man there. He had previously called on me and aroused my suspicion by his questions, so I knew there was nothing for it but to dispatch him."

It struck me that the only reason he could be explaining things in this fashion was to impress on us his ruthlessness—on Mauro and his men, as much as on Linda and me.

He went on: "It was only a pity that he hadn't actually got so far as clearing the rubbish from above the grave. But fortunately he was the sort whose violent death would scarcely be remarked. And in case he had let fall any word of his intention to visit the count's grounds, I transported the body myself to the other side of the village."

Yes, there was definitely a kind of fierce pride as he recounted this: he was telling us that he was no mere dessicated scholar. And to my surprise I found that it wasn't difficult to imagine him doing it: hailing Zeno, shooting him, and then yanking the corpse to his car with his great spidery arms. . . .

"Our violent deaths won't be accepted quite so calmly," I said, trying to make the point calmly.

"No," he said, "so how convenient it is that you have already opened up the grave."

"Oh, my God," murmured the count again. It was probably just distaste at this violation of family property.

"Ah," I said.

"Oh dear, oh dear," said Linda. For the first time she sounded really upset.

I turned to Mauro and his men again. "So you're ready for the big one? Double murder? This little man here says do it, and you do it? Does he pay well?"

"Shut up," said Mauro again.

I noticed the other three all waited for Mauro to take the lead. The youngest one's mouth was now twitching and he had a sheen of sweat over his face. So now his finger would be slippery as well as shaking.

"Or is it the toys he gives you?" I went on, trying not to think of it. "Lovely big toys with hair-spring trigg—" Oh, God. "What do you have to do to get them? Read his books? Tell him he's Charlemagne?"

"You'll soon see what sort of toys they are," Mauro said with a big grin.

I could see from the way he held it that he loved that gun.

"And remember," said Pigozzi, "we've got bigger and better toys than that." The toy joke seemed to have tickled everyone. Well, so long as the tickling didn't reach the fingers.

"Yes," said Mauro, "I haven't forgotten. The Kalashnikovs."

This magic word seemed to send a thrill through all of them: they all obviously saw themselves with that magic shape of power pointed to the sky, as in all the best revolutions, all the best wars, all the best massacres. . . .

The ascendancy the little man had over these thugs was as simple as that: the Rambo syndrome. Mauro was the sort of thug who in usual circumstances would never have aspired much beyond a bit of football hooliganism or phone-box bashing, but he'd met someone who'd dangled a Kalashnikov before his eyes. He'd do anything for it. Anything. I could see it in his gun-drunk eyes.

And once he'd actually *got* the Kalashnikov. . . .

Well, the rifle was enough to worry about for the moment.

The count was obviously thinking along similar lines because I heard him say again, "Oh, my God."

"All in good time," Pigozzi said. "Let's first see you prove your loyalty to the cause."

"Has it ever struck you," I said to Mauro, "that at this moment *you* are the ones with the really big guns in this room. If you really want those Kalashnikovs, surely all you need—"

The youngest one spoke for the first time—and his words

were thick and ill-formed as if even his tongue were shaking and sweating, like a dog's: "He's got a point, you know. . . ."

"Shut up," Mauro said.

The young man refused to shut up now that he'd found his voice: "Look, you're always making out you're so big and in charge so why don't you prove—"

There was a *bang* and the top of the youth's head spattered open and he dropped to the floor.

The chandelier tinkled with the reverberations, but that was the only noise as we stared at the body and then at Pigozzi calmly lowering his gun: his small but smoking gun.

The count didn't even say, "Oh, my God."

Mauro started to say "But" and Pigozzi came in crushingly, "We have no room for waverers," and after a second's pause Mauro said, "No."

I suddenly realised Pigozzi had won: I wouldn't dare say another word and neither would the three thugs. He could have shot me, but that would have been too easy and would have had nothing like the same sudden stunning effect. It had been a risk: it could have turned the three men against him, but had been a risk worth taking. The three men had now committed themselves to brutality, heart and soul. They were undoubtedly already thinking that the young man had always been a worm and congratulating themselves on their ruthlessness.

"Now for these two," said Pigozzi, waving his gun at us. I felt Linda move closer to me.

The count spoke up at last: "Not here—no more blood in here, please."

"No blood at all is required," Pigozzi said. "They can die in the same way as their beloved hero, your brother." He turned to the three men. "Take them to the chapel at the top end of the garden—you know it? There you'll find an open crypt with a body. Put them in there and close and bolt it. And then—well, then we'll get some new toys—and we'll wake the village up with them."

"And him?" Mauro indicated the no-longer trembling youth.

"Ah, yes. Perhaps he had better go in first. Take him now."

He turned to us and said apologetically, "Dear me, it'll be quite a crush."

Carlo and the other men put down their rifles and took the body between them.

"Shit, what a mess," grumbled Carlo, who had the head and shoulders.

Pigozzi opened the shutters fully so they could step straight out into the garden. We watched them make their way across the moonlit lawn. They disappeared up the winding paths at the far end of the lawn.

Linda said, "My arms are aching," and I realised mine were too. They'd been raised now for some minutes; it seemed an absurd thing to be worrying about, but I suddenly found I couldn't stop thinking about them. Pigozzi's only answer was, "Shut up." I decided it wasn't worth while pointing out that we'd let him lower his arms. We waited in silence for another couple of minutes, and then saw the two men striding back across the lawn. As he entered the room Carlo said with a grin, "That other bloke didn't look at all well."

I'd had the faintest of hopes that the sight of Giorgio Malberti's body might finally waken some feeling of moral revulsion within them.

Mauro prodded me with his rifle and I moved towards the window. I said to the count, "Any last messages for big brother?" but he didn't answer. Well, to tell the truth I don't think the words got much beyond a croak. He was still staring into that blurred wall mirror.

I heard Linda say something like, "Please please," to the room in general and then she was following me out into the garden.

We crossed the lawn side by side, our arms raised to the stars, and the rifles occasionally nudging our backs. All three men were following us.

Linda said in English, "Shall we run for it when we get to the woods?"

Mauro said, "Shut up. One word, one move and we fire."

Well, maybe a bullet would be nicer than slow suffocation.

But we didn't run; I suppose we wanted that extra minute of life. We made our way in single file: first me, then Mauro, then Linda, then the other two. At the back someone was holding a torch, which helped me at the front very little, once we were in the woods. We could hear the throb-throbbing of music from the village.

We reached the chapel, with its mound of broken furniture outside.

"Get in," Mauro said as I halted at the entrance. Linda was pushed to join me. We both shuffled in together. As I entered, I kicked my foot sideways and gave the chair at the foot of the junk heap one quick shove. To Mauro behind me it must have simply seemed that I'd stumbled. He prodded me again in the back.

I glanced at the Babel-tower of junk: the chair had slid a few inches but the bedstead it was holding up showed no signs of giving. Well, I could really feel proud of my workmanship there.

Linda said in English, "Jan, I can't do it. I can't get down in there." She was gazing at the open hole a couple of feet in front of us.

No words of encouragement came to my mind.

I halted and turned slowly to face the men. "You'll grant us one last request," I said, lowering one hand to shade my eyes against the torch in the hands of Carlo by the door. Mauro and the moustachioed man were just big black shapes in front of us.

"What?"

I glanced at Linda, who'd also turned. "You don't smoke, do you?" I said in Italian.

"No."

"Ah." There was a pause and I said, "Strawberries?"

"Turn round and jump or we shoot," Mauro said.

I heard a slight creak and scrape as the chair slid another inch. No one else seemed to notice it. I said, "Could we pray . . ." My eyes were adjusting to the glare and beyond Mauro I saw the bedstead give a tiny convulsive judder. "Just a quick prayer before . . ."

The bedstead lurched forwards and suddenly the west end of the chapel was an avalanche of clattering bric-a-brac. Mauro and the moustachioed man swivelled defensively and Mauro fired a shot, but this was a situation where not even a Kalashnikov would have helped. Linda and I had leaped forwards at their first twitch—myself towards Mauro and Linda towards the moustachioed man. I added my fist to the other objects crashing down around Mauro's head—chamberpots, chair legs, drain pipes and baby baths, and he lost his cool and his balance—and then the rifle, which I jerked from his floundering hands.

Carlo had dropped the torch to pull his rifle from under his arm, but he was still fumbling with it when Linda fired the gun she'd torn from the other man. Carlo screamed and dropped his weapon. For just a second he stood there, his blubbery features managing to form a big surprised or frightened O in the dim light—and then suddenly he dived out of the doorway. Linda fired again, but we heard him thrashing his way through the trees. I made a move to follow, but Linda restrained me. "Let's disable these two first," and she'd swung her gun back to Mauro and his mate who were wriggling amid the rubbish.

"Stay where you are," Linda snapped.

They stayed. "Not down there, not down there, please not down there," the moustachioed man said, his head raised and staring towards the hole behind us.

"What do you think?" I said, glancing at Linda.

"Well, they jolly well deserve it, but . . ."

"But," I agreed. I was still wondering what she'd meant by disabling them: breaking their legs?

"We'll just have to tie them up," she said.

"Ah, yes," I said, trying not to sound too relieved. I really wouldn't have known how to set about breaking a leg. Then I said, "Er, what with?"

"The rope around my waist," and she lifted her sweater slightly with her crooked elbow.

I stared.

"Well," she said, "I thought I might have to do a spot of breaking-in tonight. You never know, after all."

"No, I suppose not."

"You keep them covered and I'll tie them."

A minute later she'd trussed them hands and feet—as ever without borrowing my thumb.

"That's better," she said, standing back up.

"Much better," I said. We went towards the doorway and stood there for a moment or two. The music throbbed up at us from the village. I said, "For a moment back there I thought we were going to go out to 'Blowin' in the Wind.' That really depressed me."

She gave my arm a friendly squeeze and said, "Come on, now for the others." She started down the pathway.

"And their Kalashnikovs," I said as I followed.

"An AK-47 is one of those things you really have to know how to use," she said reassuringly.

"Otherwise?"

"Well, otherwise you just spray the bullets all over the place."

I decided not to ask any more technical questions. We made our way back through the gardens. When we reached the balustrade at the end of the upper lawn we crouched down and looked towards the house. We could see the drawing room still lit up, and the count still in his armchair staring out. There seemed to be no one else there.

"Perhaps they've decided to take your advice after all," I said to Linda. "Just wrap the whole thing up and go off home."

She turned and smiled at me. With my usual capacity for staggering irrelevance I suddenly thought how attractive she was: mud stains, moonlight and a rifle really suited her. Then it struck me that for the first time I was really at ease with her; I felt no awkward need to make sarcastic banter.

"We ought to do this more often," I said.

She leant forwards and kissed me full on the lips. Well, I wasn't the only one who could be staggeringly irrelevant then. She knelt back on her haunches and said, "Sorry, action often gets me like that." Her eyes were glowing just as they had done when I first met her and she'd told me the story of Giorgio.

"Please don't apologise," I said.

"Well, if you could see what I've done to your face . . ." Then she looked back towards the house. "I've a feeling we're being silly again." She leapt up and ran down the nearest path, her rifle held firmly at the ready.

This was presumably her idea of being sensible, I thought as I followed her.

We reached the open window of the drawing room and the count continued to stare out at us blankly. Only his tapping fingers told me he hadn't joined his frescoed relatives.

"Aren't you going to say welcome back?" I said, as I stepped in through the windows.

"Where are they?" Linda said, displaying her more usual capacity for going straight to the point.

He opened his mouth at last and said: "On their way down to the village with a carload of hand-grenades."

He too, it seemed, could go to to the point when circumstances called for it.

TWENTY-FOUR

. . . .

"OH, MY GOD." This time it was Linda. "Oh, my God," she repeated. Well, it would take some hushing up, I suppose.

"They've already gone?" I said. And as I said it I realised I could hear a car driving down the hill.

The count looked at me and said, "What?"

"They've already gone?" I repeated.

"Listen," Linda said to me, "can't you hear the car—"

I ignored her and said it again: "They've already gone?"

"They've gone to get the grenades," he said eventually.

"Where?"

"In the—the arms store."

"And where's that?" I was asking these questions as carefully and patiently as possible; the moment he got flustered he might decide simply to opt out of this situation and join the less discommoding society of the mirror.

"It's underneath the tower," he said.

"Which tower?" Linda said, and she raised her gun menacingly.

He merely stared blankly at her and the gun.

I pushed her gun barrel downwards with one restraining hand; I don't know where I was getting all this tact and gentleness from, but there was no doubt they were needed. I spoke quietly but firmly to the count: "You said 'They've gone': Pigozzi and the thug, Carlo, right?"

"Yes."

"So who's in the car and who's at the tower?"

He concentrated hard on this, then said, "The young man went to get the car and the professor the weapons."

"And you mean the tower at the far end of the garden?"

"Yes."

"So where's the car gone?"

"The weapons are all in a cave under the tower. . . ." Then he halted, his brows furrowed.

"Yes?" I prompted.

After a second or two he resumed, "And the cave comes out on the road below the house."

"Right," I said. Well, maybe not right, but it was clear at least. Carlo was driving down the road to where Pigozzi would be waiting with as many Kalashnikovs and grenades as he could carry. (And probably he'd taken a stout shopping bag.) It struck me that we must have passed one another, the professor haring up one side of the garden as we'd dashed down the other. I looked at Linda. "So how about if I go up to the tower and you—"

"I take the low road. Okay." She had already turned to the window.

I grabbed her bag from the table, and called out: "You've got a transmitter or something here, haven't you?"

"Oh—oh, yes," she said, and turned back. She took it from my hands.

"So get on to the police, if we're too late."

She nodded and dived back out again. I followed, without another glance at the count. Linda ran along the side of the house to the bushes at the edge of the garden. I set off across the lawn—yet again.

As I ran, the gun held awkwardly across my body, I squinted up the hill to the stumpy black shape of the tower, which crowned the Malberti grounds. If it had been an English garden it would probably have been an eighteenth- or nineteenth-century folly; here it was the genuine medieval item, genuinely mouldering. I could see no sign of life there, no mysterious light. So probably he was already down in the cave, stacking Kalashnikovs.

Across the first lawn, up the winding paths with the aid of the torch, then the next lawn, and the next winding paths: I'd never been this far up the garden, I realised, as I thrashed my way through the trees. Maybe there were man-traps or cobras. I played the torch with extra care around my feet. Then suddenly I was out of the trees and the tower stood there in front of me: about thirty feet high, round, jagged-topped, and completely dark and silent. I turned the torch off and slipped it into my pocket again.

I moved slowly forwards and then stopped and listened. The wind had changed and I could no longer hear the throb of music or drone of platitudes from the village. I couldn't hear the car either, nor Linda shooting at the driver. Nor vice-versa. There was just the high-pitched electric squitter of bats and the rustle of wind in the leaves. My gun had levitated into the alert position and my finger was tickling the trigger.

I took slow steps across the grass towards the tower: there was a wooden door with a dangling padlock. I put one hand to the door and it scraped open. I stared into blackness and listened again. I took the torch out of my pocket, the gun hanging but ready to swing and fire at the slightest noise or movement. The light revealed a stone staircase winding both up and down. It was no more comforting than the skeleton had been.

Down was the direction the count had indicated, so down I went, the shadows retreating before me. The air got cooler, the stones craggier. Then the stairs stopped winding, and the torch shone straight down a descending tunnel which was closed at the far end—about twenty steps below—by a metal door riveted into the rock. There was another dangling padlock.

When I reached the door I stood still again and listened. I could hear footsteps beyond it. Well, there was no point in delaying. I turned my torch off once again and slipped it into my pocket. I lifted the gun and pushed the door.

Beyond was a huge cavern, lit by an electric torch in one corner: there Pigozzi was standing, a Kalashnikov in his arms and a smile on his face. Sylvester Stallone he wasn't, but a Kalashnikov it was unfortunately. He had clearly turned in that instant—and the next instant I dived behind a huge pile of wooden crates. Then the gun roared and the metal door pinged and clanged and clattered with bullets behind me.

I crouched on the cold crags, pressed up close against the crates. On the nearest one I read the words: "MATERIALE ESPLOSIVO" followed by several exclamation marks. I've never liked exclamation marks and these ones seemed particularly unnecessary.

"Okay," I called out, "so we both go up in smoke and what'll be the point of that?"

There was silence. It lasted long enough for me to get nostalgic for gunfire. I did my best to gauge the extent of the cavern from what little visual evidence I had: it was probably about half the size of the count's living room, and seemed to be stacked to the roof with wooden crates. I guessed it was a natural cave that had been adapted as a storeroom.

Suddenly the shadows swirled and there was a quick scutter of footsteps. Then there came another great clang of metal and I was in darkness again. A door had slammed shut—but not the door I'd entered by.

It could well be a trick, but that was a risk I'd just have to take. I took my torch from my pocket and, without switching it on, groped my way to the end of the stack of crates. I held the torch out at arm's length, put my head round the edge and then pressed the switch: St. George glared across the cave at me.

There was nobody else to be seen. Another grey metal door was firmly shut in the wall opposite me, and I could hear running footsteps beyond it. My eyes returned to the statue.

It was perched on a natural crag a few feet above the floor so as to watch over the cavern and its sinister treasures. I held the torch directly into the face and the silver eyes glittered at me. There were two candlesticks on either side of him, and I could imagine Pigozzi reverently lighting them—ready to initiate new knights into the secret rites. Did he take it seriously himself—or was it all designed just to impress louts like Mauro?

Well, now wasn't the time for pondering over such things—nor for wondering whether Pigozzi had first picked out Mauro because of his resemblance to the statue. (If anything, the original was more like him than the copy.) I turned my attention to the door: it couldn't be opened from this side without a key, and I could no longer hear those footsteps. Unless Linda had done something smart, Pigozzi was right now jumping into the car with his hoard.

Could I put a grenade—a little one—under the door and let it go pop? Well, I could, but I had no guarantee that the rest of the things in the cavern wouldn't then go *bang,* not to mention *boom.* I looked around the crates: everywhere a pop-art riot of exclamation marks and asterisks and skulls. Just looking at them was deafening.

Then I saw a Kalashnikov, lying next to the door. Pigozzi had apparently dropped it after firing it. Well, maybe he'd decided to stick to bombs. I tucked the torch under my arm, put my rifle on the ground (namby-pamby stuff) and picked up the Kalashnikov. It felt good in my arms, I had to admit. It was all too easy to understand how Mauro felt about it.

And all the other massacring madmen of the world. Fortunately there wasn't time to start fantasising about joining their ranks. I pointed it at the door and fired.

The noise, kickback and the results were all equally surprising and satisfying. Once I'd regained my balance I saw the door swinging free, the lock a jagged black gap. I pushed it open and pulled my torch out from my armpit. Another long descending tunnel was revealed.

I swung the gun's sling over my shoulders. This permitted me to hold the torch in my hand as I ran. The only thing missing, I realised, was the belt of extra ammunition. Well, I wasn't intending to kill that many people.

There was another grey door ahead of me and I fired again as I ran. It swung open—perhaps it hadn't even been locked. (Would I ever be able to go back to opening doors by their handles?) Beyond the door was a tangle of undergrowth, and I realised I was coming out into the open again. The vegetation obviously served to conceal the entrance to the tunnel, but now it showed signs of Pigozzi's hasty passage. I guessed, however, that this path hadn't been used for some time, which meant that Pigozzi might have had trouble pushing through it—which gave me hope of catching him up.

The bushes clutched and tore at me in the most impudent fashion—clearly they had no idea what I was carrying. Then the ground dropped suddenly and I saw the grey surface of the road. I could hear a car driving downhill to the left, but could see nothing.

"Jan—Jan," came a voice from my right.

I turned the torch and gun in that direction, and just managed to stop myself from giving a little burst of peevish fire. Linda was limping down the road, her face screwed with pain under the mud and dirt.

"What's up?" I said. "Where are they?"

"They've just driven off. Carlo heard me coming and there was a gun in the car—"

"You're shot?" I realised there was blood on her leg;

"It's nothing vital. Listen, I saw Pigozzi get in with a crate of bombs, I suppose it was, and then he just pushed Carlo out and drove off."

"Pushed him—"

"Yes. He ran off into the woods." Carlo's whereabouts were obviously of no importance. "You know what he's going to do, don't you?"

I knew she meant Pigozzi. "What?"

"A Beirut-style suicide charge: him and the bombs right into the square."

I stared at her. I knew at once she was right: he was going to make that "grand gesture" that his childhood hero hadn't dared to: go out in a glorious blaze of destruction.

I turned and ran back up the hill.

"What the hell—Jan—" she called out from behind me.

I didn't turn or try and shout anything explanatory. I kept running and reached the tangle of wire where I'd placed the bike half an hour or so earlier. I lifted it, straddled it, and started pedalling, the torch held in my left hand, the handlebars in the right, and the Kalashnikov jerking at my knees.

"Jan—you're crazy, you haven't got a chance," Linda shouted as I swept by her.

Once again I didn't bother answering. I swerved onto the path through the woods: Pigozzi was in a car, it was true, but the car had to follow the road with all its long twists and turns; the bike could go straight down.

Or at least I hoped it could.

I had forgotten quite how rough a path it was: the bike juddered and crashed over the roots and rocks and holes; and the torch jumped in my hand, giving the impression that the wood's massed shades were having a midnight reel. Some of the more frenzied trees did their best to rape me as I passed, and my face burnt with twig-lashes and bush-stings. The gun threatened to catch on branches and tug me from my seat on several occasions, but the brute force of my pedalling freed me each time. I was going crazily fast—much too fast for safety. But then the brakes didn't seem to work, so I had little choice in the matter.

I could hear the distant slow strains of "Give Peace a Chance" from the village and I found myself muttering: "Just give *me* a chance: St. George, please, just give me a chance."

And then I realised I could hear the car to my left and actually see its probing headlights through the trees. I had overtaken it.

The path was heading straight down onto the road; seconds later I was pulling on the brakes hard, and aiding them with my feet. The bike overturned and I spilled onto the ground, a tangle of limbs, handlebars, spokes and a Kalashnikov. I pulled myself free, together with the gun, just in time to see the headlights turn the corner and come straight towards me.

Just where I wanted them. I did my best to recall all the paintings I'd ever seen of St. George as he faced the fire-breathing monster. Head on was the only way to tackle such things. I raised the gun and waited: suddenly it didn't feel good or macho—just necessary.

The two lights increased in size and brilliance and I fired, aiming above the right-hand dazzle: I stood steady, still firing, and then at the very last moment hurled myself across the road, diving down the hill and rolling. Behind me I heard the car tearing into the trees and then there was a a terrific explosion of noise and light and I found myself flying.

Before blackness swallowed me I knew I'd killed the dragon. Pity there was no princess.

TWENTY-FIVE

. . . .

THERE WERE DISTANT VOICES, there was cool whiteness, there was a scent of flowers—and there was god-awful pain. So I knew it wasn't heaven.

I let my half-open eyes roam beyond the bed to the pale-coloured walls, the white cupboards, the clinical sink. My mind murmured the word "hospital" and then it got down to studying the pain. I worked out that it ran all down my right-hand side: a generalised ache. I wriggled a few toes and braced the leg: all seemed operational. I made a move to touch my side with my right arm and a thousand devils heaped coals, pushed forks, and sank teeth into me. Definitely something nonoperational there: I opened my eyes a little further and saw my arm was suspended in a sling. Confused recollections now came to me of people pushing and prodding me—particularly the arm—as I lay amidst the trees with bits of scrap metal adorning my person: silly questions like "Does that hurt?" had been asked and answered as they'd deserved.

And one of the voices, I realised now with a puzzlement I hadn't been up to feeling then, had belonged to Gigi.

That same voice was now murmuring in the corridor outside this room—and the voice it was murmuring to was Linda's.

This needed thinking over. But first I looked around the room a little more attentively. My first assessment had been correct: I now added to that word "hospital" the word "private." Everything here was too quiet, too comfortable, too—well, too private—for this to be any part of an Italian state hospital. I saw my jeans neatly hung over a nearby chair: protruding from one pocket I could just see the corner of a folded piece of paper. I couldn't reach it, but I could reach the telephone by my bed, I realised. I listened to those voices in the corridor again: I couldn't hear a word they were saying, but there was something impatient about them. My mind was not functioning to the fullest yet, but I still realised that I had better make this call quickly.

I lifted the receiver and pressed the button 9. This often worked. Seconds later a female voice replied: "Reception."

I said, "Esposito here." I had to repeat the words, since my throat was parched. "I'd like to make a call."

"Just press the O, sir, and then dial the number you want."

"Yes, but what's the name of this place please?"

"San Giacometto Nursing Home, sir."

"Verona?"

"Yes, sir, Borgo Trento." She didn't seem at all puzzled by my questions. Well, I suppose hospitals must be used to amnesiacs.

Luckily I could remember the number I needed. I made the call, speaking in as low a voice as possible. I had only just finished when I heard Gigi say, "Here, isn't that his voice—" and footsteps approached the door. I recomposed myself in the bed to look as if I'd just woken up in a state of minor delirium and then the door opened and Gigi and Linda came in.

"Hi," I croaked.

"Hello," Linda said, smiling.

"All right?" Gigi said. "How you doing?"

"Where am I?" seemed like a good beginning.

Linda told me the name of the nursing home again and I said, "Why?"

"Well, you're in a pretty bad state," she said.

"What's the matter?"

"Nothing irreparable. Broken arm, bad bruising, and some cuts and minor burns. But a few days and you should be out, they say."

"But why here?"

"Don't worry about that. The service is paying. Glad to."

"Really. Why?"

"Well, it's the least we could do. You saved our bacon—and a lot of other people's as well and—"

At that point a nurse came bustling in and gave Linda and Gigi the kind of dressing-down that only nurses seem capable of, telling them they shouldn't have presumed to enter without calling her first, and did they know what a delicate state I was in, and they could have set my recovery back months. I began to feel ten times worse at once. She bundled them out of the room, then set to work on me, apparently just as cross at my having presumed to wake up without asking her permission. My temperature was taken, I was allowed a glass of water, given a quick run-down on my condition ("Nothing to worry about, nothing at all"), told the time (three P.M. the day after the accident), given a wash and asked what I wanted for lunch and dinner. I asked her to hand me the piece of paper from my jeans pocket, and I slipped it under my pillow.

Twenty minutes later Linda and Gigi were allowed to shuffle sheepishly back in. I said: "So Pigozzi landed all over me, right?"

"That's about it," said Linda. "It was quite an explosion. But nobody else was hurt."

"Okay," I said. "Now tell me what on earth has brought you two together. I mean, you don't look the likeliest of couples."

"Trouble with you, mate," said Gigi, "is you're full of prejudices and social insecurities. Me and Linda have got a good working relation going."

"Working re—"

"That's right," said Linda. "I could see at once that your brother was the right material, you know, even if we didn't hit it off straight away. But I got onto him again, after the suicide."

"My God," I said. "My God." I looked at Gigi. "You always win, don't you?"

"Well," he said, "had a lot of experience, you know. I know me way around fings, and that's what counts."

I remembered Gigi's distracted air when I'd left him in

Verona and his vague attempts to put me off further investigation. He had presumably already been enrolled in MI6. I said, "Experience in what exactly?"

"Smooving fings over. That's what most private detective stuff's about."

"Well, I think even MI6's going to have trouble smoothing this lot."

"You'd be surprised, mate," Gigi said.

"Look, there must be a bomb crater twelve feet deep in the woods up there."

Linda gave a little laugh. "Oh, nobody's dreaming of pretending that that didn't happen. Nor Count Malberti's suicide—"

"What?"

"Oh, yes," she said. "Shot himself—in that same armchair."

I stared hard at her and decided I'd never know whether that was the truth or not. She was a different person from the girl who'd kissed me the previous evening—and I had to accept this was the real Linda. The other—glowing eyes, cheeks and all—had been a momentary combination of moonlight, adrenalin and—well, my own fantasies. I gave no more than an inner sigh and said, "So what's the story?"

"Well, let's say that MI6 and SISDE have made a little agreement." She gave another little laugh. It was *so* nice when people got on together.

"Oh, yeah?" I said.

"Yes. If they'll keep Ainsley's name out of it, we'll do nothing to disturb their story that the count and Pigozzi were just a couple of crazed loners. After all, it's more or less true."

"All very cosy," I said.

"And the son is prepared to play along. He's already got plans for a grand foundation-laying ceremony for his new hotel to coincide with the reinstallation of St. George in the museum."

"Nice for the saint," I said.

"Oh, well, no point in getting all upset about such things," she said briskly. "I'm sure the hotel won't be that bad."

I grunted. I felt a personal tie to St. George now, but de-cided—after a glance at Gigi's face—that I wouldn't bother try-ing to explain this.

"So that's why you're here," Gigi said. "We got you away from the scene—bundled you off quietly before questions could be asked."

"But how were you there?"

"Well, I was down in the village, just toodling around in the car, waiting for a call from Linda, and then it came, telling me to expect a bloody great bang: dunno what she fought I could do—clear five fousand people in twenty seconds perhaps—and then the bang came, but halfway up the hill. Biggest fireworks display I seen in years. So I came on up and got you out the way. You were a mess, mate."

"Thanks—and sorry if I spoilt the upholstery," I said. "But anyway, I'm not to expect any questions from the police here then?"

"No. This is a SISDE setup." He looked around at the fur-nishings. "They do themselves all right, don't they?"

"It's great," I said. "I'll have to come here more often." I wondered whether I should be protesting against this shameful flouting of the rules of democracy—but then decided I could do without a full-scale police interrogation just at that moment. Even if it did mean I never got a medal or thank-you from the mayor of San Giorgio Veronese.

I said, "But look, just tell me: how could anyone have ever trusted anything important to Pigozzi? Even the Italian Secret Service?"

Another light little Linda laugh. "Oh come on now, Jan. You know how crazy and mixed up things are here."

"Yes, the spaghetti-tangle, like you said. But even so: Pigozzi. I mean the guy was obviously a nutter. Not to keep *any* kind of control over him—"

"Have you never thought that that might be what someone wanted?"

"What?"

"There are two schools of thought about the whole crazy

scene of Italian secret politics: there's the balls-up theory, that everything is just total chaos, due to overall incompetence, and there's the conspiracy theory, that there's one big answer to all these mysteries—Moro's kidnapping, Gladio, Ustica, the P2, Calvi, Sindona, the periodic bomb attacks. . . . If one could just find the right line to follow, one could clear up the whole lot and discover the fiendish hand behind it all."

"I'm not saying that. . . ." I said.

"No. And what's wrong with that is that the deeper one goes, the more confusing things get: and so most people come round to the balls-up theory—it's all just typical Italian confusion, and why bother trying to understand? Every time anybody seems on the brink of clearing anything up, along comes another bomb or somebody else commits suicide and it's all total chaos again."

"So?" I said.

"So the third theory is that there are people whose main concern is just to keep things confused: and thus people like Pigozzi are highly effective screens. Even if they might occasionally overstep the boundaries of, um—"

"Good taste?" I suggested.

"Yes, even if they might go a bit too far sometimes, they keep the magistrates and the journalists busy—keep their attention off the people who really count."

"Oh, yes?" I said. "And who are they?"

"Not even we know that," she said with a candid smile. "And we're almost certainly better off not knowing."

I settled back in the pillows. "Well, I'm not going to contradict you," I said. "Pigozzi was quite enough for me. Just one little point . . ."

"Yes?"

"What about Piers?"

"Ah, yes," she said. "We've given him a rough version of the war incident, just to keep him from pestering us. I think he'll eventually decide it's not worth fretting too much about it."

"Oh, really?"

At that moment there was a knock at the door and Rita

walked in. Linda's jaw dropped. So did Gigi's—but that might have been due to the shortness of Rita's skirt.

"Hi," I said.

"How did you know—" Linda eventually managed to say.

"He phoned me," she said, gesturing in my direction. Then she addressed me. "Well, I came as fast as I could, like you said."

"Great." I turned to Linda and Gigi and said apologetically, "Would you mind just leaving us for a moment. . . ."

"Look here," Linda began.

"Do you want me to call the nurse?" I said.

That worked. They backed out, Gigi saying, "Look, mate, don't do anyfing really silly. . . ."

"Don't worry," I said. "No state secrets." As soon as they were outside the door, I put my free hand under the pillow and pulled out the sheets of paper.

Rita said, "I heard about that guy getting blown up. So you were mixed up in that?"

"Yes—all too literally," I said. "But look, we'd better be quick. I can't go into too much detail. Take this."

She took the two sheets. "What's this?"

"It's Sir Alfred's suicide note—or at least a photocopy."

"What?"

I gave a brief explanation of how I'd come into possession of it (I'd pinched it out of Linda's bag, back in the villa)—and how Linda had done so earlier. Her face grew furious, and I said: "Look, there's really no point in making a fuss about that. When you read it, you'll realise that Piers won't want to. What makes me mad is that they decided he shouldn't be allowed the chance to do so."

"You mean they weren't going to give it to him?"

"Afraid not. Don't read it now. Wait till you're outside. It'll tell you all you need to know. And then—well, then you judge a good moment to give it to Piers."

"Okay." She put it into her jacket pocket. "Thanks."

"My job, after all." I wasn't getting any big kick out of handing it over—it wasn't like pulling the Naval Treaty out of the breakfast dish—but at least I knew I could trust her to make things as easy as possible for Piers.

"About payment . . . ," she began.

Well, I couldn't wave my right hand in careless dismissal, and my left was busy scratching my nose. So I said, "Ah, yes, well . . ."

"I'll have to speak to Piers, of course."

"Of course. Well, choose a good moment for that too. I can wait."

"Thanks. And you're not going to tell me what all these bandages and things are about?" she said.

"Not just now. Listen, leave straightaway, and don't get into conversation with Linda or Gigi. And I'll put you right with them."

"You'll . . . ?"

"I'll smooth things—make sure there's no trouble."

She frowned, but obviously decided not to say anything more. Then she bent over and kissed me. I'd had to wait till I was half-crippled for that, I thought sardonically. I watched her leave and wondered if I'd get invited to the wedding. Probably not: they wouldn't want a smoother.

Linda and Gigi made no attempt to stop her. They just came in and stared reproachfully at me. I said, "I'll call the nurse again."

"Don't worry," Gigi said. "No harm done, I guess."

"Thank you."

"But next time, consult us," Linda said.

"Next time?"

"A manner of speaking," she said.

"Right," I said.

"Though, mind you, your brother's been giving you most impressive references."

"Thanks, Gigi," I said.

"Don't be put off by the bolshie attitude, he says. You're A-1 material underneath."

"Thanks again. But, as you know, I'm an English teacher."

"Course, Jan," Gigi said.

"And I'm going back to it," I said. "A nice steady job."

"Course, Jan."

"Maybe I'll try somewhere really peaceful next. Like Medellin or the Bronx."

"Yeah, well, we'll get in touch if we've anyfing for you, won't we, Lin?"

She didn't even wince at the "Lin," "Of course we will."

"Thanks, I'll bear it in mind."

"But now we'll let you rest."

They tiptoed out of the room, and I lay there trying to think of English verb tenses. As usual, I had trouble with the future ones.